So far, luck was with her. The corridor was empty. And so was the ladies room. . . .

She parted the curtains, hoping that a guard had not chosen to position himself in front of the doorway while she was gone. The way was clear. She took the .38 out of her handbag, aimed and fired.

There was no sound—at least, none that could be heard over the movement of expensively cased bodies and the discreet clank of coffee cups. And, of course, the amplified sound of the ambassador's voice . . . before it came to a sudden stop. A neat little hole appeared in his forehead an instant before he fell backward, toppling his chair. With any luck, she thought, it would take a minute or two before they discovered that he had been shot. . . .

✿ ✿ ✿

"Smith concocts a frothy, funny, action-packed adventure-espionage novel that should leave readers weak with laughter and full of admiration for the twists and turns of plot involving the plucky Miss Melville."

Booklist

MISS MELVILLE REGRETS

A Novel by
Evelyn E. Smith

FAWCETT CREST • NEW YORK

A Fawcett Crest Book
Published by Ballantine Books
Copyright © 1986 by Evelyn E. Smith

Library of Congress Catalog Card Number: 85-80884

ISBN 0-449-21259-9

This edition published by arrangement with Donald I. Fine, Inc.

Manufactured in the United States of America

First Ballantine Books Edition: August 1987
Fifth Printing: February 1991

To Edgar I. Gotthold

For years Miss Melville had never taken a taxi except in cases of dire necessity. Even though she was no longer living at the poverty level, the habit had become entrenched. Although tonight's necessity was not dire, at least not for her, she was late—not in absolute terms, because there was, in fact, plenty of time—but because she was behind the schedule she had set for herself. If you are not inherently well organized, she had learned, it is important to be as inflexible as you can.

And she could charge the taxi to expenses. It still bemused her that she had not only become a working professional but had achieved the expense-account level. The popular magazine articles that she had always regarded as so much pap had turned out to be true after all. A middle-aged woman could get a second shot (she smiled to herself) at life if she reached out and grasped the opportunities available to her.

Positioning herself on the corner of the street, she tried to attract the attention of a driver, but cab after cab passed as though she were not there. She walked over to the bus stop, hoping that she would not have to wait too long—the posted schedules being, as all New Yorkers knew, exercises in fantasy as well as futility—and that, once a bus did appear, it would not pass her without stopping.

Luckily someone happened to get off at that same corner, so the bus was forced to stop—a good eight feet away from the curb to assert the driver's independence. "Hurry up, lady!'' he yelled, as she scaled the steps. ''We don't have all night, you know!''

She dropped coins into the fare box. ''Could I have a transfer, please?'' She had no need for a transfer but, since they were free, she always asked for one on general principles. You never knew when you might want to go off at an angle. Besides, it annoyed the bus driver. New York bus drivers hated giving out transfers even more than they hated stopping to pick up passengers.

A seat was vacant, the single one right in front of the rear door. As usual, whenever something looked like a stroke of good fortune, however small, there was a catch. The Metropolitan Transportation Authority kept replacing their buses, hoping that someday they'd find a model that worked. That year's model had been cunningly designed so that you couldn't reach a stop indicator from the seats just in front of and behind the rear seats themselves, unless you had long apelike arms. A black marking pen had edited the legend above the indicator into reality by crossing out ''Press,'' ''ow,'' and ''Tape'' from the legend ''Press Yellow Tape for Next Stop.'' By the time she was able to put her finger on the tape, the driver, ignoring her protests, had carried her three blocks past her stop.

She walked back along the avenue conscious, as always, on the rare occasions when she came this way, of how much the once elegant area that surrounded the Grand Hotel had deteriorated. On the same side of the avenue as the Grand, the street was respectably sterile, most of the original buildings having been replaced by graceless high-rise, high-priced office towers, with restaurants, stationers and boutiques on their ground floors. However, across the way, a motley collection of elderly buildings of varying heights housed discount stores, head shops and fast-food restaurants, with the garish neon gables of a Chomp House taking the palm for sheer vulgarity.

Yet that side of the street was far more vital than the other, save for the Grand Hotel itself, which did not seem to have changed since her salad days. It had, of course, been redecorated many times since then, but always with an eye to preserving its world-famed ambiance. To outward appearances, it remained the same bastion of elegance it had been for the past sixty-odd years. She passed the picket line that had formed outside and entered what seemed to be another world, a world of the past—gracious and serene and affluent.

She knew, however, that it was largely façade. The service was not the same; the people were not the same; the feeling was not the same. Only the affluence remained.

Many of the people in the lobby were, like herself, not in evening dress. She preferred not to wear a long gown when she was working, because the type of handbag most practical on such occasions was inappropriate for dress wear. The one she was carrying this evening was, in fact, somewhat too large and leathery for even a non-dress evening occasion. But the world paid little attention to such niceties these days. Several of the gentlemen present, although correctly garbed (more or less) otherwise, were wearing sneakers. There was even one gentleman who had on no shoes at all. He was being escorted out of the hotel. The Grand might have relaxed its standards, but there was a point beyond which it could not be pushed.

Luckily the evening was warm enough so a stole was all the wrap she needed. She didn't want to get involved with checkrooms. In her youth ladies never checked their wraps, but female liberation had taken many a strange turn.

The notice board on the easel outside the elevators said: "Spanglers' Club Dinner Meeting" and "Mental Aid Society Spring Gala." She frowned. Not that she disapproved of the Spanglers, or even the Mental Aid Society. The former provided excellent buffet meals and the latter was a worthy organization, even if prone to excesses of what was, essentially, despite the trendy trappings, the same old creamed chicken.

"Isn't the East-West Association Dinner here tonight?"
she asked the elderly elevator starter.

He smiled at her. He was old enough to recognize class
when he saw it. This was the kind of guest the hotel should
be getting all the time. "They're on the fourth floor, in the
Pinckney Room."

The East-West Association was trying to keep a low profile, probably for the same reason she herself was there
tonight and, probably, why the picket line was there as
well.

"Are you definitely going to the East-West dinner?" a
voice behind Miss Melville demanded.

She turned. The woman who had spoken wore a low-cut
evening gown. She was tall, broad-shouldered, and the only
reason she didn't look like a man in drag was the incon-
trovertible evidence of her décolletage. With her was a
balding youngish man in a dinner jacket which had seen
too many dinners; it fitted his portly little person like a
mitt. Both looked slightly out of place, but they were the
kind who would look slightly out of place anywhere.

"Are you going to East-West, too, Rhonda?" Miss Melville's smile concealed dismay. In spite of what she had
been told, she had refused to believe that Rhonda could be
back so soon. Her untimely return could spoil Miss Melville's entire program for the evening. Other people would
have other preoccupations, but she knew that if she and
Rhonda were in the same room Rhonda would be watching
her.

"I understand security's very tight," Miss Melville said,
"but that makes it even more of a challenge, doesn't it?"

"No, we're going to the Spanglers' dinner," Rhonda
said. She avoided the other woman's eye.

It's working, Miss Melville thought. She is afraid of me.
But how long will that last? "Oh, what a shame!" she said.

"But I put on my tux especially for the East-West dinner, Rhonda," her companion whined. "They get a very
classy group there. Besides, I want to go with Susan."

"No, Felix, you want to go to the Spanglers'. They have much better food. Anyway—" she took a firm grip on his arm "—you're my date. A gentleman always goes to the same party as the lady he's escorting."

Miss Melville hoped the other regulars would also be attracted by the superior cuisine and inferior security at the Spanglers' affair. She preferred not to have any acquaintances around when she was working, although it was a contingency she always had to factor into her plans; she had such a large and diversified acquaintance.

"But isn't it dangerous with them there?" Mr. Tabor had asked at the beginning, when she had told him about Rhonda and Felix and the rest, trying to explain her own place in this strange social set. "What if they should see you at work?"

"What if *anyone* should see me? The whole point, as I understand it, is that I shouldn't be seen. Or, at least, noticed."

So far she'd gotten away with it, except for that one time. How long she would keep on getting away with it she didn't know. Some members of their profession, Mr. Tabor had told her when he was first making his pitch, had been able to continue in the job until age and diminished skills had enforced their retirement—a comfortable and protected retirement, he said.

She tried to believe him, but it wasn't easy. Well, she told herself, it was only by chance that she was alive, anyway. So everything that had happened to her since that day at the Regency-Ritz had been pure gravy.

A group of opulent-looking foreigners in full evening regalia was entering an elevator, followed by several others in somewhat less expensive but equally festive street clothes, who seemed to be attendant upon them.

Miss Melville followed.

Her choice had been right on target. They got off at the

fourth floor and headed for the Pinckney Room. As the ladies at the receiving table by the door rose to greet the new arrivals with the little cries of joy and kisses in the air that seemed to be the same in all languages, Miss Melville swept by, deftly palming a ticket from the table as she passed.

A bar had been set up in the anteroom. She asked for a glass of Perrier and stood there, sipping it, surveying the crowd. As far as she could see, nobody she knew was present, but that didn't mean that there weren't some lurking about or that others might not arrive later. She must be prepared, like a Girl Scout. Or was it a Boy Scout? Although in their heyday the Melvilles had contributed generously to both organizations, none of their scions would ever have been members of either group. In any case, the Scouts probably wouldn't have given her the kind of preparation she needed.

The guests at the East-West dinner were an unusually posh lot. Even though it was a "dress optional" affair, over half were in full evening dress, bedecked with gems that glittered like a dime store jewelry counter, although their provenance was more likely to be Cartier's than Woolworth's. No wonder the regular uniformed security people had been supplemented by burly men in tuxedos who didn't look like guests, who didn't even try to look like guests.

The identity of the personage in whose honor the dinner was given might have something to do with this, she thought. She had studied her subject—she always did before an assignment—not only from information supplied by her employers, which, although superficially thorough, was likely to be biased, but through her own research as well. It was clear that, even allowing for media prejudice, he was a thoroughly despicable character, known to have participated personally in many of the atrocities for which his country was notorious, as well as other evil acts too unspeakable to mention. Otherwise, she would never have accepted the assignment. She had very rigid standards.

Music began to play as people started straggling into the dining room. From the entrance there would be an occasional "ping" sound from the metal detector and a slight disturbance of the even flow of guests; once in a while, a discreet huddle among the security personnel. She wanted to sit down, but she would have to wait until the tables were nearly filled. On the other hand, she couldn't linger in the anteroom so long that she would become conspicuous. It was all a matter of timing.

When the moment came that she adjudged to be right, she drifted over to a door that, to the untrained eye, would seem to lead away from the dining room but did, in fact, bring her back here . . . by a rather more circuitous route than the other guests were using. Once inside, she headed for the table she had already chosen, one not only far from the table whose number corresponded to the number on her ticket, but one toward the side and in the back, a location generally deemed undesirable and usually among the last to be allotted.

She had hoped the table would be empty. Many latecomers sat alone on these occasions, as well as antisocial altruists and people who'd been stood up. Unfortunately, a youngish man and woman were already established there.

"Forgive me for intruding," Miss Melville said, sitting down as she spoke, "but the people at my table were so obnoxious I simply had to change my seat."

"Quite all right," the man said in a tone that contradicted his words. The woman grunted. Miss Melville was glad to note that they were Americans. Foreigners, unfamiliar with native stereotypes, might be perceptive enough to realize that she was not altogether a nonentity. If she were really lucky, they would turn out to be members of the press; in her experience, they never noticed anything.

The two ignored Miss Melville all through an exceedingly bad dinner. Since the Grand's kitchens were usually adequate, even if not up to glory-day standards, she deduced that the menu had been chosen to suit the ambassador's preferences or those of his compatriots. Even Chomp House food would have been better—a sad commentary indeed on another country's cuisine.

Shortly after each guest had been provided with a plate of some glutinous substance that she supposed was dessert—she refused to so much as set fork to it—along with coffee, a rustle at the table of honor indicated that introductions were imminent. As a large lady wearing—heaven help us, Miss Melville thought—a tiara got up on the dais, Miss Melville rose too. "I think I'd better go powder my nose now," she whispered to her table companions. "I wouldn't want to interrupt the ambassador's speech. That would be so rude!"

The man gave a murmur that could be construed as polite only by a leap of the imagination. As Miss Melville headed for the nearest archway, the woman's voice said, "Let's hope the old bitch flushes herself down the toilet."

How crude the young were nowadays. Miss Melville could not deny that when she was young she had entertained similar thoughts about obtrusive elders, but she had expressed them far more gracefully—and certainly never in the hearing.

The burly man who was standing to one side of the heavy velvet curtains that covered the archway didn't even seem to notice her as she glided through. The ladies' room was halfway down the corridor, with the gentlemen's room next door. More danger from that direction, because gentlemen's bladders were notoriously less predictable than ladies'.

So far, luck was with her. The corridor was empty. And so was the ladies' room. In the ambassador's own country, she supposed, anyone rash enough to get up to answer a call of nature when someone of exalted rank was about to speak would probably have some vital portion of his anatomy excised.

Nonetheless she took no chances. She locked herself inside a booth, where she opened her purse and made her final preparations.

She waited an additional minute to give the lady in the tiara enough time to finish her introductions and get the ambassador well launched; then went back the way she had come, pausing just outside the curtains of the doorway she had chosen, one closer to the table of honor than the one she had just left. Unfortunate if the lady in the tiara should be more long-winded than usual or if another speaker had been scheduled to precede the ambassador. Should someone come into the corridor while she waited for the interloper to finish speaking, she would have to return to her table and then go out again—which would increase her chances of being noticed.

But the voice she heard, muffled only a little by the velvet, was the ambassador's. She had listened to tapes and both seen and heard him on television the night before, when he had arrived in the city. He spoke with a plummy, semi-British accent, and his eyes were too close together.

She parted the curtains, hoping that a guard had not chosen to position himself in front of the doorway while she was gone. The way was clear. She took the .38 out of her handbag, aimed and fired.

There was no sound—at least, none that could be heard over the movement of expensively cased bodies and the discreet clank of coffee cups. And, of course, the amplified sound of the ambassador's voice . . . before it came to a sudden stop. A neat little hole appeared in his forehead an instant before he fell backward, toppling his chair. With any luck, she thought, it would take a minute or two before they discovered that he had been shot.

Miss Melville let the curtains close and pushed the gun
into her handbag. She dropped her handkerchief, bent down
and picked up the spent shell along with it, then stuffed
both in on top of the gun. She walked over to the carpeted
stairs at the end of the corridor and descended one flight.

The third-floor corridor was full of people milling about;
the Spanglers were an active bunch. The ladies' room here,
directly beneath the one above, was thick with women putting on make-up, combing their hair, straightening their
panty hose, chattering. Their glances slid off her as she
passed.

She went into an empty booth and wiped off the gun
with toilet paper, less as a precaution—she knew it was
probably useless—than out of fastidiousness, unscrewed the
silencer, rewrapped gun, silencer and shell in the scarf she
had bought at Bloomingdale's for the occasion, and pushed
the bundle into her handbag.

The cordite stink was still strong. She sprayed the interior of the bag with a vial of musky scent she'd brought
with her.

She left the booth and washed her hands very thoroughly
at one of the sinks. She touched up her lipstick, gave a pat
to her carefully coiffed light brown hair, and dabbed a drop
of the musky perfume behind each ear, thus getting it on
her hands as well, which was her real objective. Then she
went on into the dining room, where she joined the Spanglers' revelry.

10

A woman with tightly curled yellow hair, her plump body stuffed into a dress with a wavering hemline, was busy at the dessert table piling pastries onto a plate. Half turning to reach for an elusive eclair, she saw Miss Melville. "Oh, Sue, I didn't expect to see you. Rhonda said you were going to East-West."

Miss Melville had accepted perforce the contemporary custom of promiscuous first-naming—in fact, she found it sometimes an advantage here—but she did wish they would at least call her Susan. "Rhonda must have misunderstood, Shirley. She's a dear girl, but she does have a tendency not to listen to anything except her inner voices. Remember where she's been since June."

"Well, we all have our ups and downs," Shirley said. "Which reminds me, did you hear about Freddy Makepeace? He got busted at the Wine Society Reception last week."

"Actually arrested? I am surprised." Miss Melville took a cookie and nibbled at it. "Usually they just throw him out."

"I guess they probably would have just requested him to leave if he hadn't gotten up during the dessert course and started preaching on the evils of alcohol." Shirley caught a custard tart as it started to slip off her pile. "They always have such small plates here. Guess I'll take this over to the table and come back for thirds. Won't you join us?" she added hospitably.

"I'm with some people over there," Miss Melville said, waving a vague hand in all directions. "And I've really finished, anyway. I'm just going to say goodbye and go."

"Is that all you're having for dessert?"

"I just can't get any more in," Miss Melville apologized. "I'm afraid I made a pig of myself at dinner."

"You can't fool me," Shirley said archly.

Miss Melville tensed.

"You're on a diet. All you skinny people say you can eat all you want without putting on weight, but that's a crock." She sniffed. "Gee, I really like your perfume. What kind is it, if I may ask?"

Miss Melville controlled a desire to laugh. "It was a gift—something I'd never heard of before. I don't really remember what it's called."

"It's really nice. Sexy. Who knows, maybe with it on you'll get lucky tonight."

Shirley really meant well, Miss Melville told herself. She simply couldn't help being uncouth.

She waited until Shirley had settled herself at a table that also held, she noted obliquely, Felix, Rhonda and a couple of the other regulars, all shoveling food into their mouths as if they hadn't eaten for days. Enough guests were beginning to leave now so that she could depart unobtrusively. She added herself to a merry, middle-aged group that seemed to have spent most of the evening at the bar and were en route, she gathered, to further festivities.

"Seems to be some sort of commotion upstairs," a stout Spangler observed, stabbing at the elevator button with his finger; it took several tries before he succeeded in connecting.

"Wild party, maybe," a rat-faced Spangler suggested.

There was laughter. You did not hold wild parties in the Grand Hotel, except perhaps in the private suites.

Although they could see the gleam of elevators flashing past in both directions, none stopped at the third floor. "What the aitch is going on?" the stout Spangler asked rhetorically.

He asked the same question literally of the attendant when it finally stopped, but it might as well have been rhetorical. "I really don't know, sir. Perhaps they'll be able to tell you down in the lobby."

Obviously the Spanglers had failed to notice that the Grand no longer had attended elevators, or they might have realized that something serious was afoot before they reached ground level. However, when the elevator took them down without stopping at any of the other floors, and the lobby proved to be full of TV cameras, reporters, policemen, milling crowds, all the concomitants of catastrophe, it became obvious that something of a grave nature must have happened.

Miss Melville repressed a desire to preen herself.

A hotel functionary was waiting by the elevator, along with a policeman. "If you would just leave by the side entrance," the functionary said, gesturing in the direction toward which Miss Melville had intended to go all along.

She felt a touch of unease. Was this the same individual who had stood by the elevator at the Nuclear Freeze Ball? No, that had been at the Waldorf. And the reception for refugee writers had been at the Plaza.

The last job she had done at the Grand, a different hotel employee and a different policeman had been on hand; she was almost sure of it now. Even if they had been the same, she told herself, it wasn't likely that they would have recognized her. She had always made sure to be, or appear to be, part of a crowd.

"Is something wrong?" the rat-faced Spangler asked.

"Just a little accident, that's all," the functionary said. "We're trying to clear the lobby, so we'd appreciate your leaving as fast as possible."

They were herded to a small door where another policeman stood guard, and the Spanglers and Miss Melville trooped out into the side street.

By now there were crowds surging around all the entrances to the Grand. "Did you see anything of what happened?" a small, eager man asked.

"What I'd like to know is just what did happen," the stout Spangler said. "We were rushed out. Nobody told us anything."

"The word is that some foreign bigwig's been assassinated, but—"

"Move along now," still another policeman ordered.

The Spanglers held back, asking questions, but Miss

Melville moved along, changing her seemingly reluctant step to a brisk pace as soon as she crossed the street.

The Chomp House was fairly empty. Noon was its busy time, with a second surge at six. At nearly eleven in the evening, there were few people around, just the usual drug dealers, derelicts, people who had been working overtime, ladies of the evening, unemployed actors and, of course, Mr. Tabor. He sat in one of the banquettes against the wall, beneath an insufficiently abstract painting, eating and drinking with apparent relish while listening to music from the headset perched on his thick, glossy black hair.

Or so it would seem. Miss Melville knew he was not listening to music. He was listening to the news—the news she had just made.

She sat down next to him, took the gun and its appurtenances out of her handbag and slid it into the open briefcase beside him. He reached out with his free hand and closed the briefcase without looking at it. A slight wrinkling of his nose indicated he had caught a whiff of her perfume.

"I hate having to use a different one each time," she complained, as he removed the headset. "And the silencer spoiled my aim."

Mr. Tabor swallowed the food in his mouth. "You know perfectly well why it must be a different gun each time."

She did know. It would look odd if ballistics tests showed that, say, the Palestine Liberation Organization and the Jewish Defense League had used the same weapon. Not, of course, that she would consider working for either group. She disapproved of terrorists and terrorism.

"And your aim, according to the radio, was perfect. My congratulations."

He always said the same thing each time except, of course, on those unfortunate occasions when congratulations would not have been in order. "Did you know Rhon-

da Pinkerton was out?'' she demanded. ''Yes, of course
you must; you have her psychiatrist in your pocket.''

''Come now, Miss Melville, that's going too far. Let us
just say that our influence extends in many directions.''

''Why didn't you tell me she'd been set loose?''

''There was no reason to bring the matter up. I told you
some time ago that she'd been given to understand that if
she ever made 'false allegations' again, she'd be put back
under restraint with no hope of release.''

''And when she hears about the ambassador?''

''All the more reason for her to keep her mouth shut.''

That would be all very well if Rhonda were sane, but,
since she really was mad, in the long run it was doubtful
that she would be able to keep herself under control. Although that didn't mean truth would prevail, there was
bound to be unpleasantness.

Miss Melville had always detested unpleasantness.

She looked at Mr. Tabor's plate with disfavor. ''I can
understand why we have to meet in a Chomp House. What
I can't understand is how you can bear to eat in a Chomp
House.''

He smiled. There was something excessive about Mr.
Tabor. His teeth were too white, his mustache too black,
his suit too well-fitting, his manners too good. In the movies of Miss Melville's youth he would invariably have been
cast as the villain. Today he was a refreshing contrast to
local youth.

''Dear lady, when one has been forced to live off the
land in the jungles of the Amazon and the sands of the
Sahara, even Chomp House food would look good. Besides, in New York the fast-food restaurants are the only
places where it is possible to find truly American food.''

''You say that because it fits your preconceived notion
of what American food is.'' To so many people from other
countries, like her cousin Sophie, for example, the adjec-
tive ''American'' was synonymous with ''vulgar.'' But So-

phie was a von Eulenburg and she had married a Brownleaf. She had an inborn right to sneer.

Apparently Mr. Tabor felt he did, too, for he merely smiled and continued to eat.

Miss Melville was beginning to feel hungry herself, but nothing would persuade her to eat in this place. If Chomp House food wasn't enough to turn the stomach, the Chomp House radio and television commercials were. Even here, hidden speakers were blaring the Chomp, Chomp song: "Chomp your way to success; chomp for health and happiness . . ." At least a professional trio was singing; the general himself did not lift his voice in song, as sometimes happened on the radio commercials. Maybe next time they could meet at a Burger King. Their commercials were almost as obnoxious as the General's, but at least they didn't play them inside where people were eating. And the Burger King himself never sang.

"Another reason a silencer is awkward," she said, "is that it means I have to carry a big bag. Supposing that next time it's a full-dress affair? A bag like this would look ridiculous with an evening gown."

He sighed. "Are you back in that groove again? In that case, we will lay on fireworks, the way we did at the Striped Bass Ball, remember?"

Both of them smiled reminiscently.

He dabbed at his lips with a napkin; then rose to his feet in one lithe movement, like a dancer. "Allow me to get you a cup of coffee. You do not have to drink it, but, you understand, it will make you look more—more plausible."

Although his English was excellent, much better than that of a native speaker in his age group, clearly he was not a native. She had often wondered where he had come from, and although she had asked him on more than one occasion, he never answered. If he had, she knew, it wouldn't have been the truth. He was the kind of man who would have many passports and many names.

He put a plastic cup full of dark brown ink before her

and, after resettling himself in his seat, handed her an envelope, which she put into her bag without opening.

"I see you have become blasé. Do you remember with what eagerness you tore open that first envelope?"

She remembered. It seemed such a long time ago, instead of . . . two years ago, was it? At the time she had never dreamed that some day she would reach a point where assassination would become so routine it would be almost boring.

"I wish you wouldn't insist on being paid by check. It isn't professional. Or practical."

They had been through all that before. She supposed they would go through it again. In almost the same words, he would say as he said now: "There would be many advantages to your taking your fee in cash. For one, you would not have to pay income tax on it. Surely by this time you must have figured out some way . . ."

And she would answer, as she was answering now: "As I've told you before, I have always paid taxes on every penny I earned. Besides, I don't move in circles where people deal in large sums of cash. If I paid the maintenance on my apartment in cash, if I deposited a large sum of cash in my bank account, questions would be asked, even if they weren't asked of me directly."

Whereas other children's fathers had frightened their offspring with stories about ogres and werewolves, her father used to terrify her with tales of the IRS. After he had gone, representatives of that bureaucracy had audited her mother over and over, unable to believe that such an abundant fount of gold had been reduced to a trickle; and, despite the support of a team of high-priced accountants, reduced her mother to quivering jelly. She had never forgotten them. More to the point, she had never gotten over her fear of them.

Mr. Tabor nodded, forced to admit her logic. Still, he couldn't let it pass. "Our employer had to go to a lot of trouble to set up a dummy corporation just for you," he reminded her, probably in case she was thinking of asking for another raise.

"I'm sure that he has established dummy corporations before. And he's getting a bargain—not only my services, but a painting that will be worth far more than ten thousand dollars one day."

Of course he probably was paying out a lot more than ten thousand per assignment. She wondered how much of a cut Mr. Tabor got. Or was he on salary?

"I am certain the painting will be worth millions one day," he said politely. "However, in our line of work, we live for the moment."

"Did he like the last painting?"

"He found it . . . interesting."

Sometimes Miss Melville wondered whether their mutual employer had ever so much as set eyes on the paintings for which his checks ostensibly paid. He must know of the paintings' existence; otherwise, he would never have agreed to her being paid by check. And he wouldn't have agreed to accept one as a peace offering after that unfortunate incident.

Perhaps he didn't know or care anything about art. Perhaps it didn't mean anything to him that her paintings were represented in the collections of the Whitney, the Museum of Modern Art and the Museum of American Art, even though they hadn't been on view for many years and might even have been deaccessioned. Except . . . who would have bought them? Now that the Melville millions were gone, the Melville name meant little.

"I'll have my expense account ready for you when you collect the painting."

He reached for his wallet. "If you'll just tell me that amount now . . . Surely you don't object to taking cash for so small a sum? Unless you have given in this time and paid for the dinner instead of, er, crashing?"

"If I had, I wouldn't be here with you now. There was a metal detector at the dining room entrance."

"Was there, indeed? Where should we have been with-out your special expertise?"

She knew he had never been able to understand why she had begun crashing parties in the first place, long before it had become a vital part of her professional duties. It seemed to him, he had told her when they first met, a lot like stealing. "Not," he had added, "that I have anything against stealing, but, forgive me, I should have thought you would."

When Miss Melville had first started party-crashing seri-ously, it had seemed rather like stealing to her as well. But, she had told herself, the people who ran these events were thieves, too, in a way—morally if not legally. How much of the money they took in actually did go to the causes they represented and how much was drained off by "expenses"? As for the guests, how many of them went out of genuine altruism and how many out of a desire to be lavishly wined and dined largely at someone else's (sometimes their employers' and always the government's) expense? She was merely compensating for her reduced income by taking her tax deductions directly at the source.

Her entry into the world of party crashers had been for-tuitous. It had come about a week or so after Sophie von Eulenburg announced, without warning, that she had de-cided to close her European-American Academy, where Miss Melville taught. "For the past few years it has been a constant struggle to keep the doors open. Enrollment has been slipping and expenses rising. Perhaps, if I were younger, I would fight, but I am almost sixty-five. Time to retire.'' Even after fifty years in the United States, Sophie (who was, Miss Melville happened to know, in point of fact almost seventy) still had a trace of German left in her otherwise impeccable English.

Miss Melville would have thought Sophie was joking, except that Sophie never joked. ''But everyone sends their children to private schools nowadays,'' Miss Melville said, ''even people who would once have sent them to public schools.''

''But the European-American Academy does not admit everyone. We may be on the verge of bankruptcy, but we are still exclusive. Oh, I know it is the popular belief that private schools are booming. But even the 'trendy' ones are having trouble making ends meet, and heaven knows we are not 'trendy.' '' She made the word sound like an obscenity.

''But you've never aspired to be trendy. That's your big talking point, isn't it—that you teach the old-fashioned values?''

''True, but the generation that still appreciated the old-fashioned values even if it didn't espouse them personally is gone. Oh, I still get pupils, especially from the European and sometimes—'' she made a little moué ''—the Asian communities. The parents may like the old-fashioned moral values, but they expect up-to-date educational ones. At this stage in my life, I am not about to include courses in computer technology and sports dynamics. Let us face it, Susan. The time has come, both for the school and for me.''

When Sophie had come to the United States in the late thirties as a young, titled divorcée she could, Susan's mother (a distant cousin of the von Eulenburgs) was wont to say, have married ''anyone.'' She chose Bennett Brownleaf, ancient enough to be her grandfather and, although it was hard to tell, since he came of an old inbred money she was after, but not for the usual reasons. Sophie was ferociously well educated and what she wanted was a school of her own. He bought her the century-old Miss Ogilvie's Academy for Young Ladies, which was long on prestige but short on endowment. When he died a few years later, she ruthlessly ousted the headmistress, changed the school's name, and reorganized it with Prussian thoroughness.

It had been flourishing for nearly twenty years by the time Susan embarked on her career as an artist and Sophie asked her if she would like to come give art lessons part-time to the girls. Susan found the idea appealing. As she grew up, she had begun to feel a little guilty about her own privileged position. Teaching and getting paid for it would give her a sense of moral worth. And, of course, she told everyone, she would stay for only a few years, until she had made a real name for herself.

That had been over twenty years before. After that first flurry of interest—sparked, she knew, as much by her connections and talent as by the scandal—she had never made any kind of name for herself. After a while, without realizing it, she had stopped trying. Little by little, as her financial situation grew shakier, she had taken on administrative duties at the school, until she found herself working there full-time. And now the school was closing . . .

"What will you do, Sophie?"

"I suppose I will go back to Germany. I have family there. And in Europe, a woman of a certain age is still considered a person. Here, once you pass forty you no longer exist. Unless, of course, you are Leona Helmsley."

It had never occurred to Susan that Sophie would go out of her life completely. It wasn't that she was close to Sophie—nobody got close to Sophie—but that, so far as she knew, Sophie was her last living relative.

"You always said you would never go back."

Sophie gave a tight smile. "My governess back in Bad Eulenburg used to say: 'Always be sure that the words you speak are sweet, because someday you may have to eat them.' Once I thought I would die rather than go back to Germany, but it's getting to be so much like the last days of the Weimar Republic here—the inflation, the decadence, the crime—it alarms me. Everything seems to be falling apart.''

"Surely you don't think you're beginning to hear the tramp of jackboots here?''

"I don't know. I really don't know. The worst of it is that I find myself beginning to think that maybe a little more authoritativeness, a little less permissiveness could be the salvation of this country.''

It could happen, Miss Melville thought. Perhaps it wasn't only her world that was collapsing around her—even though, at the moment, it seemed that way.

If only Peter had been around to help weather the shock, if at least she could call him up, talk to him, hear his voice. But he was down in the jungle somewhere, hundreds of miles away from a phone, thousands of miles away from her. All he could do, of course, would be to lend moral support. He was as impecunious as she; however, since he'd never had any money to begin with it didn't seem to bother him, and he didn't see why it should bother her.

"You know,'' Sophie said, "the other day I asked Pamela Digby's parents to come see me. Pamela has problems, you know.''

Miss Melville knew. She also felt that Pamela's problems fell more within a psychiatrist's, or the vice squad's, province than within Sophie's.

"Two women came into my office. They introduced themselves as Mrs. and—ugh—*Ms.* Digby. 'Oh,' I said, 'I'm sorry Mr. Digby couldn't come, too. I like to talk to both the father and the mother.' And *Ms.* Digby said, 'I'm Pamela's father. I used to be Mr. Digby before I had a sex change at Johns Hopkins.' When I said Pamela had problems, I didn't know the half of it.''

"Things like that are happening all over the world, Sophie, not just here."

"Not in Bad Eulenburg. They have never learned to face reality there. Even during the Hitler years, they just closed their eyes and waited for it all to go away."

"Maybe I've never learned to face reality either," Miss Melville said. "I never even thought about the possibility that one day the school would close. I don't know what I'm going to do without it."

Sophie looked disturbed. "I was worried about how some of the other teachers were going to manage, but I never realized the school meant that much to you, Susan. Emotionally, of course. I'm sure the pittance you've been getting doesn't mean anything."

"It means a lot." Susan's stipend had, indeed, been a mere pittance—Sophie was not generous—but, added to the small income she was still getting from her trust, she was just able to get by on it. "In fact, I've come to depend on it."

"You can't mean that. I know things haven't been the way they once were for you, as for the rest of us. Still, I thought there must have been plenty left, even after your father went away. There were the marriage settlements, and I know Caroline had money of her own."

When Buckley Melville had absconded to Brazil in the late fifties, what was left of the Melville millions had gone with him, as well as a much larger number of millions belonging to other people. Her mother had divorced him, of course. Throughout their married life he had shocked her prim, Puritan soul with his wild ways, and this was one shock too many. There were rumors that he'd remarried in Rio. How odd, Miss Melville thought, that I might have half brothers and sisters who speak only Portuguese.

No, impossible. Her father had always steadfastly refused to acknowledge that there was any language outside of English. If his presumptive South American offspring wanted to communicate with their parent, they would either have to speak English or use sign language.

After his disappearance, her father had never made any attempt to communicate with Susan, which had hurt. She'd thought he felt genuine affection for her. In fact, from early adolescence on, she had been closer to him than to her mother. He had taught her to do all the things he enjoyed in which it was possible for her to participate—ride and shoot and play tennis—and had seemed to take pride in the fact that she developed into an excellent horsewoman and a crack shot, although, to his disappointment, she had never amounted to much at tennis.

To her, games had a purposelessness about them when played casually; when played to the hilt, they were little more than a socially acceptable substitute for violence, and she'd always disapproved of violence, even in such a sub-limated form. It was a primitive trait, she felt, unfit for civilized people. Years later, when she expressed these sentiments to Peter, he disagreed. Violence was a basic, healthy human trait, he'd told her. Furthermore, primitive people couldn't even begin to approach the scope and re-finement of the violence practiced by civilized societies.

Susan, however, chose to define civilization in her own terms. She had never used, or been tempted to use, her skill with a gun to join her father in hunting small game (large game, of course, was out of the question; even Buck Melville wouldn't take a teen-aged girl on a big game hunt). "I can't see the sport in it," she told him. "It isn't as if we needed to hunt in order to eat."

At first he'd been astonished and then he burst into laughter. But her mother had not been amused. Later she scolded her daughter for having talked to her father like that. "I disapprove of hunting, myself," she'd said. "I think it's a cruel sport, but there's no need to go overboard about it. You're beginning to sound like a Democrat."

Susan loved her mother and so she never told her the truth. Caroline Melville died without ever knowing that her daughter had been registered as a member of the Democratic Party ever since she reached voting age.

Susan and her mother had been by no means reduced to penury after her father's flight. Her mother's money was snugly tied up in what looked at the time like solid investments. Although they could not continue to live in their former style, they were comfortably enough off, and there still seemed no practical reason for Susan to get a college degree. She'd had two years of Vassar, to please her mother, and that had been enough. She could educate herself far better, she felt, outside academic constrictions. Of course she expected to keep on selling her pictures, but even then it never occurred to her that one day she would have to make her living with her brush . . . or in any other way.

Susan continued to live uptown in the apartment with her mother, but she had a studio in the Village where she could indulge in discreet Bohemian activities whenever she chose without offending her mother's sense of decorum. Shortly before her mother died, she had to give up the studio for financial reasons, but it wasn't until several years later that things really started to go downhill. As their financial bases eroded, the once solid investments grew shakier and shakier. Her income shrank, and inflation diminished it even more.

Yes, she needed the money she'd been getting from Sophie's school. There was little or no chance that she could get another job teaching art. The call for art teachers was small; the call for those with neither a degree nor a reputation nonexistent.

"I do wish I could help," Sophie said, "but I know no one any more for whom my recommendation would count. However, if you should ever need a home, there is plenty of room in the family *schloss* and we would be delighted to have you."

Miss Melville thanked her for the offer, but thought al-

most any fate would be preferable to spending her declin-
ing years with Sophie in a drafty castle in a country whose
language she spoke imperfectly and with a cuisine notable
for its calories.

"Fortunately I still have the apartment," she said, "so
at least I still have a home."

During the severe housing shortage of World War II and
afterward, the government had established controls to keep
landlords from raising rents so high that ordinary New
Yorkers would no longer be able to afford them and would
flee the city. The housing shortage grew worse instead of
better, and the controls continued.

Rent control hadn't been a significant factor in the life
of her family or that of anyone they knew. The fact that
their apartments also came under rent control was an amusing anomaly—and, of course, like most rich people, they
were always glad to save a dollar here, a dollar there. It
wasn't until Susan had started teaching at the Academy and
had met people who had to live on their salaries that she
realized how important rent control could be to people of
modest means.

As time went on, old buildings were torn down (or,
sometimes, abandoned) and new ones erected, which did
not come under the old rent laws. Even though a new, less
restrictive form of control was installed after rents sky-
rocketed, they still continued to go up. As the outlanders
to whom New York had always been a Mecca flocked in,
the natives fled before the colonial juggernaut.

The only tenants in the city whose rents were still reasonable were those whose families had managed to hold on
to the same apartments for years (and those squatters who
had taken over abandoned buildings and were paying no
rent at all). Luckily for Miss Melville, the apartment which
had been the family's Manhattan pied-à-terre before Mr.
Melville's departure, and their sole home (except for summer rentals in the Hamptons) afterward, was still under rent
control. Otherwise, she could never have afforded to live

in Manhattan, let alone in the handsome old building on the upper East Side where her apartment was located.

There was one way a greedy landlord—and to the average New Yorker all landlords were greedy by definition—could still extract the last drop of blood from his building. He could induce the tenants to buy him out, thus turning the building into a cooperative or a condominium. But that required the consent of a certain proportion of the tenants. Over the years, as the building in which she lived kept changing hands, there had been talk of turning it into a cooperative—and, from time to time, she had received offers to purchase which had alarmed her at first until she discovered that these were not legally binding, but were what was known in the real-estate trade as "red herrings." Apparently not enough of the tenants had been willing to purchase.

As plan after plan was proposed and rejected, her fears has been lulled. She was safe as far as the apartment was concerned, she thought, even though Peter warned her, "You're never safe. You must always be ready for disaster. That's the first rule of survival."

She had paid him no heed, still not having grasped the fact that mere survival could ever become a problem. It wouldn't have mattered if she had listened to him. Fate already had her in its sights and was getting ready to squeeze the trigger.

Most of the other teachers at the Academy had degrees, and so, except for these few who were too decrepit or deranged, they would have no difficulty in finding jobs. Teachers (except for art teachers) were in short supply. Most of them planned to leave New York, including Madeleine.

"I only stayed on here because—oh, I suppose I was used to the old place," she said. "Inertia, as much as anything else, I suppose. But when you get right down to it, job opportunities are much better elsewhere and you don't have quite that much of the class struggle. Me, I'm heading for New Mexico. That school Julia Henneker started there is a big success. She's been asking me to come for years. Now there isn't any reason not to take her up on it.''

Although Miss Melville was on amicable terms with all the teachers at the Academy, Madeleine was the only one whom she considered a real friend. The idea that Madeleine would be moving so far away was painful, but it was to be expected. Even if the Academy hadn't been closing, Madeline would have been bound to leave sooner or later. She had all sorts of advanced degrees. The only reason she had come to the Academy in the first place was because her husband had been a history professor at Columbia, and it was convenient.

As a matter of fact, it had been through the Jacksons that Susan had first met Peter, who had taught at Columbia for a while before going on to the Pansophic Institute. Twelve, no, thirteen years before she'd been invited to the Jackson's sprawling apartment on Morningside Heights. Upon arrival she'd found this strange, red-haired youngish man who talked of other cultures as if they were more familiar to him than his own culture.

''I think you'll like him,'' Madeleine had said beforehand. At first, Susan had wondered how anyone could be so wrong. Later she'd realized that Madeleine must have known her better than she knew herself.

Richard Jackson had been dead for over a year now. The Academy was closing. Columbia had given Madeleine notice that she must vacate her apartment now that she no longer had any connection with the university. There was nothing to hold her in New York. If only I'd taken a degree, Susan thought, I might have been able to go to New Mexico with Madeleine, get a job at the same school. But probably even a degree wouldn't have helped. Art teachers were a dime a dozen in New Mexico.

* * *

There must be some way she could earn money, Miss Melville thought. She was able-bodied and reasonably intelligent. Connections were the grease that made the wheels and deals of New York spin. What connections did she have that might still be of use?

She still "knew people" from the old days. Every year she sent and received over a hundred Christmas cards, most of them to and from people whom she had neither seen nor spoken to in years. People of her background made a point of keeping in touch, no matter how tenuous that touch might be. As Peter might have said: it was part of the tribal code.

A few months before, Miss Melville had received a wedding invitation from Mimi Tibbs. It was the first one of Mimi's marriages that she had missed. Since the ceremony was being held in Nairobi, she was forced reluctantly to forego it. Mimi was prone to doing things on a large scale, and she envisioned some kind of extravaganza with elephants.

Mimi Fitzhorn had been Susan Melville's best friend in boarding school. For years after that, they had remained good friends, although their closeness diminished along with Susan's income, and she could no longer afford to keep up with her affluent associates. Besides, the people in Mimi's circle hadn't gotten on too well with Peter. They did not take kindly to having their treasured customs and traditions viewed in the light of tribal practices.

The only one she had still seen a good deal of was Mimi, while Mimi became Mrs. LaFleur, Mrs. Livingston and Mrs. DelVecchio in turn. It was only after Mimi had married Bud Tibbs, a rock singer fifteen years her junior, and started "running with a younger crowd" that the two drifted apart.

Miss Melville wondered what disposition Mimi had made of Bud before marrying the new one—what was his name?—Carruthers. It didn't sound African. Maybe he was an Englishman, left over from Empire days. Were there still great white hunters around? Or had the choice of location been simply a whim? After all, Mimi had married Bud on an icebreaker in the South Atlantic. Their actual destination had been the South Pole, but the ship had gotten stuck in the ice somewhere in the Antarctic and they had never made it.

The Fitzhorns, like the Melvilles, had been patrons of the arts. But where the Melvilles had merely sponsored wings at museums and chamber groups, the Fitzhorns had founded entire museums and symphony orchestras. Unless she had changed her habits, Mimi had a way of paying her taxes in the form of contributions to cultural institutions. At least, she used to say, they showed suitable gratitude and named things after you, while the only acknowledgment the IRS ever made was to send an occasional auditor.

Fine art was the particular area Mimi had staked out for herself. She was always involved in events that were connected in some way with the art world, either on behalf of artists and artistic institutions or *in* artistic institutions. Mimi was bound to have all sorts of useful acquaintances. Perhaps she could help her friend find gainful employment.

Provided that she had returned from Kenya. There was only one way to find out.

Mimi herself answered the phone. "Susan Melville! Darling! It's so good to hear your voice after all this time. I've been pining to see you. You must come over right away. It was so sweet of you to send me one of your lovely paintings as a wedding gift; such a pity you couldn't come to the wedding. I was thrilled when I got back and found it waiting for me.''

I'll bet you were, Miss Melville thought. In spite of her interest in the arts in general, Mimi had never shown much interest in her friend's work in particular. But when the maid ushered Susan into what Mimi insisted on calling her ''boudoir,'' there it was, hanging over the fireplace, looking as though it belonged there. ''Doesn't it look wonderful? I'm going to have the chaise longue reupholstered in the predominating color. With correlated drapes, of course. Your style has changed a lot, hasn't it?''

It had, indeed. Over the years the delicate floral paintings with which Susan had enjoyed that brief popularity in her youth had grown wilder and wilder, waxing so savage—especially after she had been forced for reasons of economy to turn to plastic flowers as models—that she hadn't even tried to show them for a long time. Who would buy her paintings with those strange flowers, with the even stranger things peering out from underneath the leaves?

Mimi's style also had changed during the four, no, five years since Susan had last seen her, but then she periodically underwent transformations so drastic they amounted to virtual reincarnations. Her skin was smooth and unlined, her auburn hair thick and glossy, her eyes no longer hazel but green (thanks, she confided, to the miracle of modern contact lenses). No one, Miss Melville thought, would believe that Mimi was a year older than she was—least of all Mimi herself.

''Tell me everything that's been happening. Who got married? Who got born? How is Sophie? She must be dead by this time.''

''No, she's still alive, but the school isn't.''

Feeling like a beggar, Susan explained that the school was closing and she was looking for work.

Mimi was sympathetic. ''I understand. You feel you've got to keep busy. Why don't you volunteer for—?''

"Mimi, you don't understand: I need to work for money. I don't have anything left."

Mimi looked stricken. "You're really serious? You don't just mean things are a little tight with you, the way they are with everybody these days? In fact, Oliver thinks I ought to sell the town house. Actually, I'd been thinking about it myself. The neighborhood really is going to pot, what with all those designers and consulates and things. He says the taxes alone would be enough to support a herd of elephants for at least six months."

"Were they at the wedding?" Miss Melville couldn't help asking.

"Were who at the wedding?"

"The elephants."

"What elephants? Oh, those were purely hypothetical elephants. You've been to Nairobi. You know there are no elephants there."

"I thought perhaps it had changed."

"If it has there are fewer, rather than more. Besides, if I'd wanted elephants at my wedding, I would have gotten married at the Bronx Zoo." She paused. "What a delicious idea! Next time—well, of course there won't be a next time because this is the real thing. Oliver and I are going to stay at each other's side for ever and ever until we're both old and gray and shrivel up, disgusting thought. But, just in case something *should* happen, I'm going to have my next wedding at the Bronx Zoo. Do you suppose I'd be able to rent it for a wedding?"

"Mimi, you of all people should know that you can rent any place in New York for anything, just as long as you have the money to pay for it."

"Anyhow, I simply couldn't bear the idea of giving up my childhood home, no matter how needy the elephants. Which doesn't mean, of course, that I'm not planning to do something for the elephants."

"I thought Joe DelVecchio gave you the house as a wedding present."

"Yes, but I was a mere child when I married him. It's a pity you never got married, Susan. Then you wouldn't have anything to worry about."

"It would depend on whom I'd married," Susan said.

"Yes, supposing you had married that awful boy with the beard you used to go around with when you were in college—what was his name?"

Susan shrugged. Several of the young men she'd gone around with when she was in college had been bearded, but since almost all of them could have been characterized as "awful," there was no point trying to determine which one Mimi had in mind.

"Of course he wasn't as awful as that Sanderson boy who was so crazy about you; but if you'd married him, at least you would be rolling in gold now."

Or at least rolling in alimony, Susan thought. There was something to be said for Mimi's point of view.

"Incidentally, whatever happened to Peter Franklin?" Mimi asked. "Is he still around?"

"He's around . . . but he isn't here. He's discovered a group of natives in South America who, he says, are absolutely unique. Even their language isn't related to any of the known linguistic stocks. He's been down there off and on studying their culture for the past couple of years."

"Where in South America?"

"I don't know exactly where," Susan confessed. "He keeps the exact location a secret from everyone but the Institute, and I suspect he'd like to keep it from them, too, except that they have to send him supplies and forward his mail and so forth. Besides, they're sponsoring him."

"I don't see why he should want to keep the location a secret." Mimi's eyes sharpened. "Are there mineral rights involved, something like that?"

Susan laughed. "I don't think Peter knows a mineral from a vegetable, except that one is edible and the other isn't. No, Mimi, there are no cities of gold or lost emerald mines. It's because he doesn't want to take the least chance of the natives being 'corrupted by civilization.' Or so he says. I thing the real reason is that he's afraid another anthropologist might get the jump on him. There aren't too many unknown tribes left in the world, and he wants this one to be exclusively his for as long as possible.''

"I had no idea there were exclusives in tribes," Mimi said. She appeared to be considering the desirability of acquiring a tribe of her own and deciding against it. "But doesn't it bother you not to know where he is?"

"I do know where he is generally. I just don't know where he is specifically. And it wouldn't make any difference. Even if I could pinpoint his precise location on a map, I'd still have to write to him in care of the Institute. There's no direct mail service, no telephone, no telegraph, no roads, no anything.''

"Dear me," Mimi said, "that is carrying the primitive life a bit far. Do you suppose the natives like it that way?''

"I have no idea. I know Peter does. It keeps other anthropologists from finding out about the tribe before he can publish his book.''

"It all seems so futile. Who's going to read it anyway?''

"Mimi, in the academic world it doesn't matter whether or not anybody reads your book. The only thing that matters is getting it published.''

Mimi considered this for a moment. "Susan, dear, have you ever thought seriously about looking around for somebody else?''

"Peter is the only man in the world for me," Miss Melville said firmly.

"I used to think Henri was the only man in the world for me, and then I met Courtney, and then Joe. Joe died, of course, but them I met Bud—and now Oliver's the only man in the world for me.''

"It's Peter or nobody.''

"Oh, well, if you're going to be foolishly romantic about it, there's nothing more to be said.''

Mimi then proceeded to say a good deal more about

Peter, most of it uncomplimentary. It didn't disturb Miss Melville, because Peter had been even more uncomplimentary about Mimi, and he'd had the advantage of a larger vocabulary.

"Well, at least you can rely on me," Mimi said. "I'm going to put an end to your worries. I'll just talk to everybody I know until we find something for you. Maybe I could start some kind of a business, an art gallery or—or a magazine, and you can run it—"

"Perhaps I could sell some of my paintings," Miss Melville interrupted these grandiose plans. She still didn't have much faith in her work's ability to appeal to today's public—even though, she reminded herself, Mimi had really seemed to like her wedding present—but she had no faith at all in her ability to run an art gallery. Even a magazine, she thought, probably required some sort of expertise.

"What a good idea! I'm sure I'll be able to arrange an exhibition of your work, and it's bound to be snapped up. Everyone's collecting art wildly these days. Now, don't you worry. Everything's going to be fine, you'll see."

But Miss Melville kept on worrying. She knew Mimi meant every word of what she was saying at the moment she was saying it. However, Mimi was apt to forget the promises she scattered about so blithely unless prodded, and Miss Melville had never acquired the delicate art of prodding.

Mimi chattered on, about people, places, things that had little meaning for her friend now. She broke off and clapped her hands. "I know the very thing to cheer you up. How would you like to go to a party tonight? The Foundation is holding a dinner at the Museum of American Art in honor of something or other—"

"Could it be the opening of their new Eakins show?"

"That's it! You're so knowledgeable, Susan. Say you'll come. That way I can introduce you to a lot of useful people. Who knows, they might even find some sort of job at the museum itself. That would be perfect for you. You belong in a museum. I mean, the ambiance would suit you.''

''That's very kind of you, Mimi.''

Once Susan had gone to that kind of thing all the time. It had been unavoidable, since her mother had been on the boards of several museums. The young Susan had found such festivities dreary. The middle-aged Susan, about to refuse, found herself tempted. It would be nice to see the Eakins exhibit comfortably instead of having to buy a ticket and wait in line. The way museums put on their exhibitions these days, they might as well be circuses. And she might meet someone who could help her find a job.

''Is it a dress affair?'' she asked.

''Yes, would that be a problem? You do have an evening gown, don't you? You must. Everybody has an evening gown.''

Actually Miss Melville had a number of evening gowns. One thing she did not lack was wardrobe. Her mother had taught her never to throw away any garment that was really good, no matter how hopelessly outmoded it was. Someday the wheel of fashion would turn, and the clothes would be back in style.

She could never have anticipated that the day would come when the wheel of fashion would spin at so giddy a pace that *all* of her outmoded clothes would be in style at the same time, and that the old clothes of the forties and fifties would become not only fashionable but collectible. Miss Melville had been astonished when a dealer who had come over to inspect her remaining possessions had offered more for her mother's couturier gowns than for the Waterford glass. Of course the gowns had cost more originally, but second-hand clothes were second-hand clothes.

''I'd love to come,'' Miss Melville said finally, ''and I'm looking forward to meeting Oliver.''

''Oh, Oliver's still in Kenya. He says the instant you take your eye off an endangered species it vanishes.''

Miss Melville wondered how they were going to stay

together side by side forever with Mimi in America and Oliver in Africa; but, after all, she and Peter had been together, although never side by side, for over ten years. Maybe that was the best way to keep a relationship alive.

At eight o'clock, Miss Melville presented herself at the squat gray limestone building that housed the Museum of American Art. She was dressed in a classic black silk gown with a sable stole cunningly draped around her shoulders so that the moth holes wouldn't show. Although she hadn't worn the dress in years, she was pleased to note that it fitted her as well as it had the day she first put it on. After she finished dressing, she had regarded herself in the mirror and was reasonably satisfied with what she saw there. Her eyes were still bright and blue, her hair, although darker than it had once been, still thick and barely beginning to gray.

She was a presentable woman by any standards except those of the Oupi, who, Peter had informed her, preferred their women shorter and fatter . . . and a lot younger. "Among the Oupi, a woman is over the hill when she hits eighteen," he'd told her.

Miss Melville couldn't help wondering if he had taken any of the native women as wives during his long sojourns in the jungle. She had never asked him. Theirs was an open relationship. At the beginning, when she'd still thought occasionally about marrying and settling down (not that she had ever been unsettled), she'd had flings with several other men, though none of them had aroused in her the slightest desire for, as Peter would have put it, a permanent pair-bonding.

For the past half-dozen years she hadn't wanted any man but Peter. She accepted the fact that his work would keep him away for a great deal of the time; in fact, she wasn't sure she'd be able to take it if he were around all of the time (although she would have been willing to try). All she asked was that he be around more of the time.

It would have been nice, for example, if he could have accompanied her to the benefit tonight. He liked parties. "It's through its feasts and festivals that the basic nature of a people expresses itself most fully," he always said.

Surely there must be primitive tribes closer to home that he could study, she had suggested, but all of them were already taken, he'd told her.

She mounted the flight of shallow steps that led to the main entrance of the MAA and went into the festively decorated lobby. Masses of flowers were all around. In the distance she could hear the tinny strains of a chamber orchestra.

Through the open double doors facing the entrance she caught a glimpse of the Hall of Primitives which, as in the old days, was being used as reception area and bar. The front desk was manned by three evening-gowned ladies—one in red, one in dark blue and one in off-white. This could have been a tribute to the American nature of the museum—or simply coincidence.

Miss Melville opted for coincidence. The American Museum was not known for its subtlety; when they said something, they said it with bunting.

She addressed the lady in off-white, who seemed to be in charge. "Good evening. Mrs. Carruthers invited me to join her here this evening."

The lady in off-white beamed. "How nice of you to come. May I have your ticket?"

"I thought I was supposed to pick it up here."

"Of course. That will be one hundred dollars, please. We'll be delighted to take a check."

Miss Melville stood still for what seemed like a very long time, although it couldn't have been more than a few seconds. The smile congealed on the other woman's face. Her companions had stopped attending to newcomers and focused on Miss Melville.

She could feel the people moving past on their way to the Hall of Primitives turn to look at her. It was like a nightmare, worse than being naked. In an art museum, another nude would hardly arouse comment.

She indicated her diminutive evening bag. "I'm afraid I didn't bring my checkbook."

Another silence.

"I'd understood Mrs. Carruthers was going to leave a ticket for me."

The three ladies looked at her. So, she sensed, did the people in back of her. She didn't turn, but she could hear the stir and murmur of what sounded like a vast throng.

The lady in red pulled a small file box toward her. "Name?"

Miss Melville hated having to say her name out loud in front of all these people, but there was no help for it. The lady in red searched through the file box, while her two associates kept their beady eyes fixed on Miss Melville. Like three rats, she thought. Like three vultures. Like three witches.

"I'm sorry," the red witch said finally, not sounding at all sorry. "There must be some mistake."

"Indeed there must. If I could just speak to Mrs. Carruthers, I'm sure—"

"She isn't here, and she left no instructions." The words were minimally polite, the tone not even that.

"I'd better call her then. Where are the nearest phones?"

She knew perfectly well where the phones were, but she wanted to establish her bona fides for heading in that direction. Otherwise, the navy blue witch might tackle her; she certainly had the build for it.

The off-white witch gestured toward the alcove on the left, where a bank of phones in oaken cabinets had stood from time immemorial. "Over there."

Miss Melville walked away, keeping her back erect. She fancied she could hear whispers and a stifled laugh behind her. Tears stung her eyes. Although there was nothing she wanted less now than to attend that dinner, she forced herself to go over and call Mimi. The phone rang and rang. There was no answer.

She could not make herself turn and walk back through the group of people in the lobby, though she saw now that there weren't as many as she had imagined before. If she lingered a few minutes longer, those who had witnessed her humiliation would have gone in. The three witches would still be there, though, no getting around that. If only there could be a miracle; if God would strike them dead.

She decided to sit on a bench for a while, as if she were waiting for someone. There used to be a bench around the corner beyond the telephone booths, right under the arrow that pointed to the Melville Wing. The bench was still there—and so was the arrow—but it was, improbably, occupied by a shopping bag lady. Looking closer, she saw that is was one of these statues cast from living models and painted to look like the originals. Another bench held a derelict; in the corner was a street vendor—all people who would never in their pristine form have been allowed to pass through the museum doors.

Behind the street vendor was an oak door marked "Employees Only." From time to time, she remembered, janitors used to emerge from it with mops and brooms and buckets that they carried around the museum, listlessly dabbing at things.

She gave the door a push.

It was not locked. Beyond lay what proved to be more of a small utility room than a janitor's closet. The mops and brooms and buckets were there, along with a sink and a powerful smell of disinfectant underlaid with a subcurrent of mold. In addition, there was a row of lockers; two doors—one marked "Toilet," one with nothing to reveal what lay beyond it; a few wooden chairs folded flat; and a metal table full of glass stemware.

One of the chairs had been unfolded. She thought about sitting down on it for a few moments. The atmosphere matched her mood. But how to explain her presence if a janitor came in? Say she felt ill and had come in here to recover? Nobody would believe it. They would think she was lurking there so she could sneak out later and steal the bag lady.

Miss Melville pushed at the unmarked door. It swung open; the American had always been run in a slipshod way, even before standards had declined generally.

Beyond lay the Statuary Court. The Statuary Court had always been used for such occasions: it was the only area large enough to hold large numbers of people. A favorite museum joke had been that the intimidating nature of much of the sculpture would help maintain decorum. But it hadn't maintained decorum on the occasion of the first—and last— Artists and Models Ball held there. That must have been almost twenty-five years before, not long before her father had taken off.

As she remembered back to her adolescent years, she recalled how she and Mimi and several of the other young people in their crowd used to, in moments of utter boredom, go to parties to which they had not been invited. "Crashing," it had been called then and very likely still was.

At the time it had seemed like fun, even when they got thrown out, because they could tell everyone afterward how mad and daring they had been. Still, they were seldom thrown out. Even if the hosts didn't recognize them, someone else was bound to. And no one would dream of ejecting a Fitzhorn or a Melville.

Today, the Statuary Court had been set up as a dining room which was why, she supposed, some of the statues had been moved into the lobby. There weren't too many people sitting down yet—most of the guests would still be lapping it up in the Hall of Primitives—but there were already a goodly number helping themselves to food from the lavish spread set out on long buffet tables. The chamber orchestra was audible but still not visible. They must either be in the Hall of Primitives or in the Trustees' Room that opened off the Statuary Court (and which had been known to the irreverent youth of her day as the Hall of Fossils).

Well, she thought, now that she was here, why shouldn't she crash? It was an outrage that the museum to which her family had given so much should humiliate her in this way. She would risk a second humiliation in front of the whole group, if only to have the chance to stand up in front of everybody and denouce both Mimi and the museum. It might even make the newspapers . . . it would probably be the only interesting event of the evening, even if it was the kind of publicity that a museum didn't like to get, even in those razzle-dazzle days.

She was fantasizing, of course. The idea of figuring in the papers in any way except perhaps for a small paragraph on the society page or a larger one in the culture section was anathema. Moreover, she could never be capable of the sheer vulgarity of getting up before a public gathering and denouncing anybody.

All the tables held ashtrays and floral arrangements and were numbered. Some also bore little stands with cards that indicated for whom the seats or, sometimes, the entire tables, were reserved. Others held only the ashtrays and floral arrangements. These were the less desirable tables, pushed in among the statues, kept in reserve, she recalled, for latecomers, nonentities and the suburban press. After making a mental note that this was where she'd sit, Miss Melville crashed the party.

She put some salad on a plate, making sure it didn't

contain seafood—to which she had discovered many years before, she had some kind of idiosyncratic reaction. She buttered a crusty roll, poured herself a glass of wine and sat down at a table in front of, almost underneath, a fearsome, life-size bronze Indian warrior holding a tomahawk that cast a shadow across her face.

Although ordinarily she didn't warm up to strangers, she was glad when a chubby, fortyish woman with long lank brown hair, wearing a flowered dress that was full length in some places, ankle-length in others approached, bearing two laden plates and a bottle of wine, and asked, "Do you mind if I sit at your table? The people at my table have been so disgusting, you wouldn't believe it. I—"

She broke off and looked at Miss Melville more closely. "Oh, so you finally did get in. I didn't think you were going to make it."

The other woman must have been behind her during that ghastly moment at the reception desk. But what did she mean? Was she about to unmask Miss Melville as an intruder? It didn't sound as if that was her intention.

"I can see you haven't been at this long. That 'somebody was supposed to leave me a ticket' approach never works. It marks you as an amateur. What you've got to do is slip past while they're not looking. I got in while they were all busy with you."

"Been at what long?"

But the answer was already beginning to dawn.

"Crashing, of course. Or is this your first time?"

"No . . . I've done it before, but not for years now. I'm afraid I've grown a little rusty."

"It'll all come back to you, once you get into the swing. I'm Shirley."

"I'm Susan—er, Susan."

Shirley arose. "Forgot to get a glass. I was so busy concentrating on getting a bottle. Watch my stuff while I'm gone, won't you, sugar?"

She returned with a glass, still another laden plate, and

three nondescript individuals who could have been of any age between thirty and fifty and who didn't seem to be of any particular sex, although their clothes would seem to indicate that two were female and one male. Shirley introduced them as Dana, Hilary and Shalimar. Shalimar was the one in men's clothes several sizes too large for her. She was, Shirley explained later when Shalimar had gone off for a fresh supply of food, very trendy, which wasn't always desirable in a crasher. "You stand out too much if you're too fashionable," and, after smoothing the scarlet and green polyester over her own ample hips added, "You've got to dress in quiet good taste for these affairs."

At that moment Miss Melville realized that at least she was not alone. If she got thrown out, she would have to be thrown out en masse.

And they weren't likely to be thrown out, Shirley explained. "They never get a full house here, so what's it to them? The food's there. As long as we keep a low profile and look all right, they're not likely to bother us."

They didn't look all right from Miss Melville's point of view, but she understood what Shirley meant. They didn't look any different from many of the people who had paid for their tickets.

Mimi never did show up. Or even call. It was quite in character for her not only to have forgotten about her friend but about the dinner itself.

Still, Miss Melville enjoyed herself in a perverse sort of way. When she finally got up to go after a thoroughly bad dinner, of which she had enjoyed every morsel, even going back for seconds and thirds, she grabbed the floral arrangement from the table and took it along with her. "Way to go, Sue," Shirley said.

It was only when she reached home that Miss Melville realized she had neglected to go look at the Eakins paintings. As far as she could tell, so had everyone else.

From that time on, Miss Melville became a confirmed party crasher. Why she did it she was never sure, although from time to time, in moments of introspection, she kept wondering. She could tell herself it was for the sake of a free meal and an evening (or, in the case of a luncheon, afternoon) out. But the food, although pretentious in conception, was often mediocre in execution, and the company less than scintillating, especially since she confined herself for the most part—at least at the beginning—to the society of other crashers. She was wary about talking to any of the bona fide guests, living in perpetual apprehension of being unmasked as a free-loader.

The regulars laughed at her fears. As long as they played "by the rules," they told her, crashers could make the rounds with virtual impunity. "These days some places actually have special tables set aside for crashers," Shirley told her at one of the earliest events she crashed, a benefit dinner for the National Pernio Foundation. "Saves trouble in the long run. It kind of spoils a party when you see people being carried out kicking and screaming."

That made a degree of sense. But Miss Melville could not help feeling disbelief when they tried to convince her that there were certain affairs where crashers were not only tolerated but welcomed. "N-n-nowadays any p-party that nobody tries to c-c-crash," Hilary said, her pale eyes earnest behind her pseudo-designer spectacles, "j-just isn't a p-p-party, kn-kn-know what I m-m-mean? Also, if n-not too m-many g-g-g-guests show up, the c-c-c-crashers kind of f-fill up the p-p-place, m-make it look g-g-g-good."

Her frown indicated deep concentration. "Of c-course, if the c-c-crashers kn-kn-knew in advance that at-attendance was g-going to be so l-low, they wouldn't b-bother to c-c-crash. B-but nobody t-tells us in advance." She thought some more. "I g-g-guess m-maybe they don't kn-kn-know in advance."

Shirley moved in quickly before Hilary could get launched again, to Miss Melville's relief. "Some crashers get to be so well known they become celebrities, and people *invite* them to parties."

"But then they wouldn't be crashers any more, would they?"

"Oh, we're all very relaxed about things like that."

"It must be w-w-wonderful to be a c-celebrity," Hilary said wistfully.

In her new role, Miss Melville went to receptions and dinners, to garden parties and cocktail parties, to costume balls and come-as-you-wish-you-were-hops, to designer lunches and moonlight cruises, to restaurant openings and theater closings, to celebrity sports events and amateur fashion shows, to picnics and banquets, to galas and extravagazas, to cocktail *dansants, thé dansants* and one breakfast *dansant* (a failure). They were held indoors and outdoors and, in the grand old nineteenth-century tradition, under tents . . . in hotels and hospitals, parks and parking lots, museums and department stores, libraries and banks, concert halls and clubs, schools and skating rinks, churches and shopping malls, private homes and zoos . . . sponsored by a variety of organizations on behalf of a variety of causes, worthy and otherwise; and most with one thing in common: the price of the ticket was tax deductible.

The only kind of affairs she preferred not to attempt were private parties—those that were sponsored only by their givers, for the benefit of no cause but themselves (and pos-

sibly their corporate affiliations), and where the invitation
list was restricted to a few hundred of the host's most in-
timate friends. The reason she gave herself for this reluc-
tance to intrude was that, since there was no admission
charge, they were not tax deductible; therefore she could
not justify her intrusion to herself, but that had a feeble
ring, even in her own mind.

Finding out when and where these events were scheduled was part of the art of crashing. Many were, of course,
listed in the papers—in fact, most of them were, if you
knew where to look. Then there were periodicals, ranging
from *Town and Country* to the *New York Almanac*, which
offered up the information. Best of all, though, was the
grapevine. The crashers would exchange information with
one another; the more you gave, the more you got—a basic
barter system of which, she thought, Peter would have approved.

Miss Melville found that the benefit scene was one of
the few contemporary ambiances that did not place a pre-
mium upon youth. Although there were always plenty of
young people present, especially among those upwardly
mobile types who fancied that the mere purchase of a ticket
would entitle them to hobnob with the elite, for the most
part both sponsors and guests, even though starved and
cosmeticized into the semblance of youth, (especially those
in the upper financial brackets), were middle-aged and
more. The crashers she met were, in the main, not young.
Most seemed to be in their forties and fifties; even those
who were in their thirties were somehow elderly, as if life
had passed them by before they could quite get the hang
of it.

"There is a downtown scene," Shirley had told her,
"but it's very hard to crash. Sometimes they don't let you
in even if you have a ticket if you don't look punk
enough." After which, several of the other crashers had to
explain to Miss Melville what the current meaning of
"punk" was; in her ignorance, it had seemed to her that

Shirley looked sufficiently punk to be accepted anywhere that punkness was the criterion.

But the uptown scene was more than enough for Miss Melville. She acquired more souvenirs than she knew what to do with, as manufacturers, taking advantage of the well-known greed of the affluent, were always lavishing samples of their wares and small objects of little value on the guests. At the conclusion of such festivities, she always helped herself to the floral arrangements quite openly; many of the paying guests did the same.

Many of the crashers—and, again, some of the paying guests—also carried home food, having providently equipped themselves with bags in which to carry it. Shirley had a wrap she had devised herself, which started out as a cape at the beginning of the evening and at its conclusion converted to a giant tote bag sufficient to hold food to feed a hungry family for weeks.

Sometimes, a little to Miss Melville's dismay, Shirley, as well as a few of the other crashers, took other things also. "It's only fair," she explained to Miss Melville, as she dropped a cream pitcher and a string of cultured pearls into her bag, "since we don't get a crack at the door prizes."

As time went on, Miss Melville got to know most of the regular crashers, especially Rhonda Pinkerton, who would never have bothered with the likes of a reception at the Museum of American Art or anything else of such lowly ilk. Rhonda was, although not everyone agreed, queen of the crashers, the stuff of legend. She was said to have crashed exclusive parties and thousand-dollar-a-plate dinners. She knew secret entrances to many of the best places (secret as far as the public was concerned, though well known to maintenance workers, garbage men, and morticians). She had made her unpaid way into that holy of holies, Tavern on the Green, when taken over for a private party—not once but several times. She had attended the wedding receptions of some of the richest and most fashionable people in the city including, Miss Melville was interested to learn, those of some of her own old friends who married and divorced frequently.

Younger crashers—and these were, as she had already noted, few—sucked up to Rhonda, hoping to find out her secrets. Older crashers hinted that much of the legend was self-generated; moreover, that Rhonda was merely following trails that others (chiefly themselves) had blazed.

Sometimes the crashers worked in pairs. Other times they would arrive singly and either join or avail the others as circumstances or their own inclinations dictated. So it was easy for Miss Melville to become one of the fellowship without becoming a friend. In fact, it was wiser not to become too friendly with them because, she had observed, the friendships that sprang up among them from time to time were almost invariably followed by enmities. At any given time, there were at least a dozen regulars who were not speaking to one another.

Miss Melville couldn't help feeling a bit miffed that they accepted her so readily as one of themselves; she felt that they should have known instinctively that she didn't really belong with them. But, then, who would expect them to have the right instincts?

One of her earliest worries, the possibility that she might be embarrassed by running into someone she knew from her other life at one of these events, proved to have been without foundation. Not that the possibility was without foundation, just the embarrassment.

She did, in fact, run into old acquaintances, even old friends, from time to time. In most cases she was able to avoid them since they tended to be sponsors of the events or at least honored guests, who moved in areas far from the humbler sectors where she lurked. In several instances some failed even to recognize her, so far removed was she from the context in which they had once mingled.

As occasional meeting was unavoidable. When it did happen, they simply accepted her as a legitimate guest. It did not occur to them to wonder how someone in her circumstances—for some of them, at least, must have known how reduced they had become—could afford to attend a hundred-or-more dollar-a-plate dinner. Possibly they assumed she was someone else's guest.

Still, she could not accept the occasional invitation to join one or another of her old friends for lunch or cocktails, for much the same reason that she had originally drifted away from her old milieu. She couldn't afford to become involved in reciprocal obligations. Moreover, most of them wouldn't have been able to understand how someone could be of such limited means that she couldn't afford to have lunch at Le Cirque or a drink at the Pierre. Those who did understand would have been kind and offered to pay for her. Although she might have been able to bring herself to accept discreetly veiled charity, she was not going to lower herself for the sake of a fifty-dollar mess of pottage.

She supposed that one reason she had joined the coterie of crashers was that it filled the space in her life left by the closing of the Academy and Madeleine's departure for New Mexico—where, she wrote, she enjoyed her work and the people she worked with, adding conscientiously that of course she missed her friend and hoped she would be able to come out to Santa Fe for a visit very soon. When Susan wrote back, bright letters full of inconsequentialities, she never mentioned the crashing, since she felt Madeleine wouldn't understand. It got her out of the house and kept her from spending too much of her free time, when she wasn't painting, watching the television screen.

Which didn't mean she gave up television. On the commercial stations, she watched "Magnum, P.I.," "Simon and Simon," "The A-Team," "Remington Steele" and reruns of "Mission Impossible," all of which were to prove very useful in her subsequent career. On public television, she watched English soap operas and animal adventures and technological advances and tiny puppetlike dancers—all of which were to prove of no use at all.

But the most compelling images on TV, the ones that lingered in her mind long after the shows themselves had faded into oblivion, were the commercials: . . . "Our prices will drive you in-sane" . . . "twice as much medicine as the other leading brand" . . . "ring around the collar" . . . "chomp your way to happiness" . . . "five hundred thousand dollars by the end of pledge week or else" . . .

Once upon a time, only used-car salesmen used to extol their wares personally, roving across the screen in the wee hours of the morning, their eyes meeting the camera with determined candor while their bodies slid away furtively. Now they all seemed to be doing it, instead of hiring trained actors—for the most part ill-advisedly, she thought—especially in the case of those individuals who headed their own companies.

Even the man who represented Patterson, Pennypacker, Baldwin & Snook. Instead of sitting decorously behind a desk as befitted a respected stockbroker, he roamed restlessly around his office, chanting, "Patterson, Pennypacker, Baldwin & Snook. We take care of your money as if it were our own." The technique did not inspire trust. Even Crazy Eddie stood still.

She stopped crashing when Peter came back to New York for a couple of marvelous months that spring. She had never told him about the crashing in her letters, and she certainly didn't intend to tell him now. Not that she felt *he* wouldn't understand; he would understand all too well and tell her how the Oupi had similar practices, which he would go on to explain in detail. Worse yet, he would want to come with her; then put the lid on her career by attempting to interview the natives.

In any case, she didn't need to crash while he was there. When he was with her, she had no desire to go to parties. A movie or an Off-Broadway play, with a snack at a coffee shop afterward, was all the entertainment she wanted. Sometimes they would stay at the apartment and order up

Chinese or Italian food and watch television, which Peter enjoyed enormously. "How the Oupi would love it!"

"Don't you feel it would be one of those corrupting effects of civilization you're so worried about?"

"Oh, they'd take it as pure fantasy, like their own folk tales of ghosts and mythic warriors and—well, the word I had in mind translates as 'demons,' more or less."

Now that the Academy was closed, and she was free, he suggested, why didn't she go back to the jungle with him? "There are all sorts of interesting jungle flora down there. You could paint to your heart's content. And you'd love the Oupi. Do you know, they have no word for *stranger*? They call someone from outside the tribe, 'friend whom I have never met before.' "

"How, er—warm-hearted of them, but I really don't think I'd feel comfortable down there. Or safe."

"Nonsense, it's perfectly safe. The snakes are really active only during the rainy season, when you'd be staying in your hut—you'd have your own hut, you know—most of the time, anyway. And, as a rule, the predators keep away from the village, unless they're especially hungry. You'd be surprised how comfortable it is once you get used to doing without electricity and running water and telephones and things. Remember, man lived without them up until the last century or so."

He paused, because he was an honest man. "I do have to admit that the heat and humidity take a little getting used to, but you'd forget about them. Eventually."

She shook her head, a little regretfully. She would have liked to be with him, but this was calling for a devotion beyond the bounds of rationality. "I'm afraid I've been spoiled by civilization, Peter."

"Don't simplicity and a genuine concern for other people matter more than plumbing?"

"No," she said with equal honesty, "they don't."

So Peter went back to his jungle and continued to study

the Oupi and she went back to hers and crashed more
doggedly than ever.

ooo **VII**

Miss Melville hadn't done much painting when Peter was
around, having neither the time nor the inclination. After
he had gone back to South America, however, she found
herself painting more than ever before, perhaps because she
now had a continuous supply of reasonably fresh flowers
as the result of her party-going, filling the spaces in her
apartment where the pieces of furniture that poverty had
forced her to sell had once stood with canvases and their
appurtenances.

"The place is beginning to look like a warehouse, Miss
Susan," Nellie said. Nellie had been her mother's house-
keeper in the days before penury had set in. Now, although
officially retired, she came in to "help out" once a week
informally (off the books). "And a pretty messy one, too."

And she would throw out the most moribund of the flowers and try to stack the canvases in some kind of order,
which was hard, she said, because they were all different
sizes and shapes. Obviously she thought it would be much
neater if Miss Melville painted pictures that were all the
same size and shape.

I really should try to figure out a way to sell some of
them, Miss Melville thought, if only to get them out of the
house. But she had no idea of how to go about it now. She
could not see herself trudging from gallery to gallery with
a painting under each arm. That was for the young and the

tough. Even when she'd been young, she hadn't needed to
be tough. Things like that had always been done for her.

She still had to figure out how she was going to make
ends meet or, at least, bring them closer together. She
looked up some friends of bygone years to see if they might
prove to be more rewarding than Mimi had been. Like
Mimi, they were distressed by her plight and promised to
do everything in their power to find some post that she
could fill.

The trouble was that there didn't seem to be anything
she was qualified to do. And qualifications were important.
"Everybody's so degree-happy these days," Amy Patterson—an old and one-time close friend whom she hadn't
seen for years until she'd run into her at a benefit for Dis-
placed Academics—told her. "My maid has a B.A. in Applied Economics, and my cook has a Ph.D. in Gourmet
Arts. Maybe you could be a social secretary. Can you use
a word processor?"

"I can barely type," Miss Melville acknowledged.
Everything seemed so hopeless. It was as if you didn't
exist in today's world unless you had money or a degree
or were young.

"I don't suppose that Peter what's-his-name of yours
could be of much help. He never struck me as the supportive type."

"He's very supportive," Miss Melville said loyally. "He
just happens to be engaged in some very important research
work down in South America right now."

Amy gave a skeptical sniff. "Perhaps you could get a
grant," she suggested.

She was knowledgeable about educational matters because her family had been big in that area, giving huge
sums of money to various universities which, as far as
Susan knew, no member of the family had ever attended.
They were also fond of sponsoring chairs and scholarships
in fields with which they had only a dictionary acquaintance.

But it had all paid off handsomely. The current generation of Baldwins (Amy had been a Baldwin before she married her cousin Baldwin Patterson, right after school) and their collaterals were, as the result of their forebears' providence, attending the best schools in droves, while Amy herself, although functionally illiterate, was on the boards of a number of educational institutions.

"A grant?" Miss Melville repeated. "How do you mean, a grant?"

"A grant," Amy said impatiently. "You know what a grant is. They give them out right and left. People like your Peter what's-his-name—"

"Franklin," Miss Melville interjected. "Dr. Peter Franklin, Ph.D."

"—couldn't survive without them. But you have to know how to get a grant."

"No doubt there are schools for grant-getting."

"Not whole schools, just grantsmanship departments. But I shouldn't think you'd need to study for years just to get one grant. There's probably some kind of survey course you could take."

"Exactly what would I get a grant *for*?"

Amy looked exasperated. "Well, that would be one of the things you'd be taking the course to find out, wouldn't it?"

How middle-aged Amy was beginning to look, Miss Melville thought as she made her farewells, but then Amy Baldwin had always looked middle-aged, having staked out her role as earth mother so early in life that she actually had worn sensible shoes in her teens on all except the most gala occasions.

At first Dilys Fender, another old schoolmate, though not as close as Mimi and Susan had been—her family was new money—seemed to offer more promise. "What you've got to do, Susan, is think of some idea for a business of your own and get people to back you. Like Deirdre Pangborn."

"Dodo Pangborn? She went into business?"

"You remember how she was always interested in Oriental culture—spent all those years in the Near East?"

As Miss Melville remembered it, Dodo had been far more interested in Oriental young men than in Oriental culture. She had been the only one in their senior year to have been carried off by an Arab sheik, as she had put it, although everyone knew it had actually been she who had carried off poor Omar.

And so now Dodo was in some business, presumably of an Oriental nature, or why else had Amy brought up her Oriental interests? "You mean she became an importer—something like that?"

Surely there was some post, however humble, that she might be able to fill in such an enterprise if Dodo were disposed to be cooperative.

"No, nothing like that. She founded a new religion and set up a church."

"She founded a *what*?"

"Oh, not one of those cults like the Reverend Bliss's, where they brainwash people into giving up all their money and turn them into zombies. Just a quiet, comfortable place where people could come to relax and meditate . . . and worship, of course." Dilys frowned. "The Temple of Inanna, I think she called it."

Vague memories of early cultures through which she had passed with Peter stirred in Miss Melville's mind. "That's quite an old religion, I believe."

"That's what she claimed; only they didn't believe her—but I'm ahead of myself. She got a lot of people to invest in it as a tax shelter, but it started making money from the very beginning. The decor was so beautiful. All in quiet good taste and nothing but the best. It's a pity you never got to see it before the police closed it down. They said it was nothing but a brothel, and the priestesses nothing more than prostitutes . . ."

Miss Melville searched her memory. "I believe that in

certain of the old—well—cults, it was part of a priestess's religious duties to, er, minister to the comfort of male strangers. That was what supported the temple in the old days.''

"And what supported this one, too. Dodo was simply rolling in treasury notes before the authorities cracked down. Too bad she and her backers set the operation up as a shelter, or she probably could have gotten off on whichever amendment it is that guarantees freedom of religion, although I don't suppose the Temple would have been allowed to continue, at least not in the same way. She's up in Bedford Hills now. I think her sentence has a year or two to run yet.''

"I must remember to send her a note.''

"I know she'd love to hear from you. The reason I brought the whole thing up is that if you could think up something pratical like that, you wouldn't have any trouble getting backers. In fact, I could put you in touch with some of Dodo's old customers—that is to say, followers—who would be only too happy . . .''

"I doubt that I could manage anything like that; I'm really not spiritual enough,'' Miss Melville said, thinking she'd better not tell Peter about the suggestion, even as a joke.

"Actually,'' she coughed, "I was thinking that if only I could arrange to have my paintings exhibited somewhere . . .''

"That sounds like a good idea,'' Dilys said without enthusiasm. "I know a lot of people are buying art these days, although frankly I think the old tried and true investments are the soundest.''

Dilys, as it turned out, was able to fill Miss Melville in on what had happened to Mimi, since Dilys's current husband was on the Museum of American Art's board. Mimi had gone to Kenya. It seemed Oliver Carruthers had been gored by a rhinoceros, and Mimi had flown to his side. Since them, nobody had heard from her. "Things like that are bound to happen if you marry foreigners,'' Dilys observed.

Miss Melville wondered what Dilys would think if she knew that Rhonda had attended her last wedding reception (to a true blue American) and pronounced it "pretty chintzy for people of that class."

Miss Melville dialed Mimi's number.

An unidentified male voice said Mrs. Carruthers had returned to Kenya and couldn't be reached because she'd gone into the bush. The town house was on the market, the voice volunteered, perhaps envisioning Miss Melville as a prospective client.

Well, Miss Melville thought, no doubt the elephants are a worthier cause.

ooo **VIII**

Miss Melville looked up a few more friends from her old social circle, tracking them down through the multiple name changes caused by the serial marriages that were, as Peter might have put it, the practice of their group. Never having sought nominal liberation, they did not keep their birth names but added on each new spouse's, as a scalp rather than a token of marital submission. However, nothing came of her quest save a few luncheon (and one dinner) invitations.

As for the friends with whom she had shared interests rather than background—the artists and creative types—they had disappeared, having dispersed to strange, cheap parts of the world or gone back to the hinterlands from which they had sprung. As Madeleine Jackson had often observed, New York was no place except for the rich and the ruthless, unless you had been born there.

Miss Melville managed to get by on the small amount of money that was still coming in from her trust, delaying her rent check each month as long as she could. The new landlord was Sanderson Associates. Mark Sanderson had been an associate of her father in the old days, as well as a family friend. She had called him Uncle Mark and had been fond of him, unlike most of her other courtesy uncles. Even then, Sanderson Associates had been one of the largest real-estate firms in the city. Now they were one of the largest in the country, perhaps in the world.

Should she go talk to him? No, it would be too embarrassing. She would simply have to sell the few of her remaining possessions that could be converted into cash, no matter what their sentimental value was to her.

That meant she would have to part with her father's gun collection. She had hung on to it all this time, not because the guns meant so much to her but because they had meant so much to him. Most were antique, and antique guns were valuable. She consigned all of them to an auction house of international repute—all, that is, save for a few relatively modern hand weapons of no particular distinction that she suspected her father had had no legal right to possess.

The collection didn't realize nearly as much as the auction house had estimated. Even the pair of flintlocks that had been reputed to belong to Black Buck Melville himself went for a paltry sum—and to a collector, she was given to understand, not even a museum, so she couldn't console herself with the thought that now the public was going to be able to enjoy them.

After the auction house's share had been deducted, along with costs she had not anticipated, the check they gave her was surprisingly small. "So sorry, Miss Melville," the elegant Englishman who had handled the transaction told her, "but an estimate is—how do you put it here?—simply a ballpark figure. One never can tell in advance."

That was a disappointment, but not a blow. The blow fell several days later. By this time most of the rent-controlled tenants in her building had either died or crumbled into dust. A new kind of people had moved in—a younger, strident group of a type that, in the old days, the doorman would have been reluctant to admit; people who seemed to feel that paying high prices was a mark of social distinction. Their rents were stabilized at a much higher level than hers, and so they were far more susceptible to the siren song of cooperative conversion.

What previous owners had failed to do, Sanderson Associates had succeeded in achieving. A registered letter arrived, advising her that a cooperative plan had been "finalized" and that she was entitled to purchase her apartment at an insider's price.

She had ninety days to make up her mind.

No help for it; she would have to go see Mark Sanderson now. It could be awkward. She had no idea of what her father's relationship with Uncle Mark had been at the end, whether any of the millions with which Buck Melville had absconded had included any of the Sanderson millions. On the other hand, Uncle Mark could hardly hold her responsible for having a felonious father, any more than she could hold him responsible for having an obnoxious son.

She phoned his office. When she identified herself as a a tenant of one of the firm's prospective cooperative conversions, the woman who answered tried to foist her off with a Mr. Steinmetz, who dealt with "that sort of thing."

She was no more cordial when Miss Melville further identified herself as an old friend of the family. Apparently there were no depths to which tenants anxious to penetrate their landlord's defenses would not stoop. However, she agreed grudgingly to "go find out."

When she returned, her voice dripped so with honey that Miss Melville felt an urge to wipe the telephone receiver.

"Miss Melville, Mr. Sanderson says he'll be delighted to see you. Would you come in tomorrow, if it's convenient?"

How kind of him, Miss Melville thought. But Uncle Mark had been a kind man. She was sure now he would do something to help. Maybe he would even find a job for her. She should have gone to him long before; it had been silly to let pride stand in her way.

If Louis XIV had been a twentieth-century real-estate magnate rather than a seventeenth-century monarch, his offices would probably have been much like those of Sanderson Associates in the Sanderson Tower on a street which, although it retained its name of Fifth Avenue for the moment, was undoubtedly going to be retitled Sanderson Boulevard at the earliest possible opportunity. An attendant, patently chosen as much for her pulchritude as for her business skills, led Miss Melville into an office so vast that she had waded through approximately an acre of Aubusson before she realized that the man who rose to meet her was not Uncle Mark.

Why hadn't it occurred to her before? Uncle Mark would be in his eighties by now, if he were still alive. It was his obnoxious son, Mark Junior, who stood behind the ten-foot desk, apparently carved out of a single block of onyx. Except for a computer terminal and some silver- (or could it be platinum-?) framed pictures, it was elegantly bare. He smiled at her with white teeth designed by a prosthodontic artist who belonged to the surrealist rather than the natural school.

He must be . . . forty-five? forty-six? now. He hadn't worn well at all, Miss Melville thought. The porcine traits he had evinced in youth had flowered into full pighood. A good tailor had done his best, but he was no miracle worker.

Mark came around the desk, extending both hands to her. "Susan, my dear, it's so good to see you again. We should have gotten together long before this. Sit down, sit down.''

He led her to a couch covered in the hide of some animal so rare the species had vanished before it could be put on the endangered list, and sat down beside her. "Now, tell me, what can I do for you?''

"I got a notice that my building was going co-op.''

"Ah, yes, it's a wonderful opportunity for you, Susan. You'll be able to buy your apartment at over a third less than the going market rate, and the maintenance won't be much more than what you're paying in rent now.''

"Mark, I can't afford it.''

"Well, buy it and rent it out. Then, after a suitable period of time—whatever the current regulation is, and we can always get around that—you'll be able to sell it and make a handsome profit. Manhattan really should be reserved for front-office business and those people who need and can afford to live here. It's a shame wasting prime real estate, or what could be prime real estate, on people who—'' he caught her eye and coughed "—people who could just as well be living in the outer boroughs. And you can move some place less expensive—Queens, perhaps, or Nova Scotia. We have some very fine buildings in both areas, and I can let you have a beautiful apartment at a very special price for an old friend.''

"I don't have the money to buy my apartment.''

Even if she could break the trust in which the pitiful remnants of her capital were tied up, the resulting sum would be so small it wasn't worth the effort. "And I can't take out a loan. I have no collateral to offer.''

Would she accept it if he offered to lend her the money himself?

No need to make the decision. He didn't make the offer. "Surely you have friends from whom you can borrow the money.''

She shook her head. She might be able to shame some of her friends into lending her the money to buy the apartment. But then there would be the maintenance, which could be considerably higher than the rent she was paying now, and the ever escalating expenses of day-to-day living.

"I'm really sorry. If it were up to me, of course you could live there as long as you liked. But this is a corporation. I'm responsible to my board of directors."

Board of directors, indeed! she thought. You know as well as I do that you're the one who runs the show.

"Of course you'll be given a reasonable amount of time to find somewhere else to live. So long as you pay your rent on time. Your building will soon have its own board of directors, and I'm afraid they won't be as lenient with you as I—we—have been. But I'll try to find you a rental apartment in one of our other buildings, although of course there wouldn't be anything available at the rent you're paying now, not even in Brooklyn."

She remained silent.

"It isn't as if you had a family or anything. You never did get married, did you?"

"No, I didn't."

"Pity. You missed out on a beautiful experience."

You could have had me, you silly bitch, was what he meant. Only you thought I wasn't good enough for you. Now I'm worth millions.

And I'm still too good for you, you creep, billions or no billions, she thought.

"Are you still painting?"

"Of course."

"You must show me your work. The firm might like to buy some of your paintings. We use original art in all our offices, even the secretaries' little rooms."

He got up. Miss Melville rose also.

He took her hand in his. "I can't tell you how good it's been to see you again. We mustn't lose touch now. You've got to come over and have dinner with us some evening very soon. You've never met my wife, have you? Oh, of course not. Linda was still being finished in Switzerland when we knew each other.''

He picked up one of the framed pictures and held it out.

She stared at the woman's picture. Linda looked very finished, indeed. "She's very lovely.''

"Isn't she? We have three beautiful daughters. The oldest had just been accepted at Harvard. We're very proud of her—of all of them.''

He held out other pictures for her to inspect. It was as if he were offering them for sale: for only one million dollars, you too can have a lovely family exactly like this one. Except, she suspected, this little group would run quite a bit more than a million dollars.

"I'm sure you must be very proud of them. I—'' she tried not to gulp too palpably "—I'm looking forward to meeting them.''

"Linda will call you and you can work out a dinner date. Perhaps we could fly Dad up from Florida. You were always one of his favorite people. He's senile, you know.''

She let him kiss her on the cheek. As an artist, she had been prepared to suffer for her art. As a tenant, she was prepared to suffer for her apartment.

If Linda really called her, she thought as he ushered her out of the office with what he probably considered to be old-world ceremony, she would go through with it, even if she choked to death on the dinner.

Going down in the elevator, Miss Melville had second thoughts. What would be the use of trying to ingratiate herself with him? He might give her extra time before she was forced out of her apartment, but what good would that be in the long run? Besides, whatever he might do for her, whether find her a place to live or buy her paintings for the "secretaries' little rooms," he was going to make her crawl first. As for managing on her own, she would never be able to find a decent apartment in any of the boroughs of New York for the rent she was paying.

If only she could get in touch with Peter . . . The jungle was beginning to look better and better. At least Peter had promised her her own hut.

She called the Institute. They told her it was the rainy season now where Peter was (the time when the snakes are most active, she recalled). It would take months before a letter *might* be able to reach him. And any trip there would be especially hazardous at this time.

"If it's extremely urgent, we could send a courier out ahead of schedule, but—"

"No, no, it's not all that urgent," she said hastily.

Sophie, having taken refuge in her castle, could be of no help either. Miss Melville had gotten a querulous letter from her complaining that the castle was falling to pieces and her relatives were barbarians.

Miss Melville took the remaining pistols out of their

drawer. In the back of her mind, she had known all along the reason she'd kept them.

The problem of which was to use was solved when she could find ammunition for only one. Before she killed herself, however, it would be necessary to set her affairs in order. She would have to write a suitable notice for the *Times*, since there would be no relatives or close friends to do it after her death. All her friends would have to be informed individually as well, and since there would be no one to respond to the messages of condolence, she would have to do it herself while she was still alive. She decided to save time and combine the two by informing them that she was dead—there would be no need for them to write and say how sorry they were, because there would be no one to read the letters.

She couldn't sit down and write all the letters by hand. If she got writer's cramp, she would be in no condition to shoot herself. Even if she yielded to informality and typed them, it would still be hard on the fingers.

The hell with it, she thought. I'll have them photocopied. Let them talk about me; I'll be dead, anyway.

There still remained the formidable task of stamping and addressing the envelopes. That would take days, but *noblesse oblige*, as Sophie always used to say.

And, finally, the letter to Peter. She would have to offer some sort of explanation to him, and it was hard to put it into words. Everything just seemed to have grown to be too much. "I'm tired of living and not afraid of dying," she almost wrote. But she didn't want to leave the world on a misquotation from "Ol' Man River."

If she'd had time she would have looked up some primitive parallels to offer him comfort. She would also have made a new will in his favor, except that she didn't want what little she had left to go to further research into a tribe that she had come to hate—quite unjustly, she knew; they hadn't asked to be studied.

Now she had to choose a time (at least a week from

now) and a place. She would have preferred to kill herself in the privacy of her own apartment, but that could mean she might not be found for days. She would hate to have her death detected by an odor.

Before she went to bed that evening, she took a look at the *Times*, which she'd been too distracted to read in the morning. As she skimmed through, she noted that the following week the Realty Foundation was going to give a five-hundred-dollar-a-plate dinner at the Regency-Ritz to benefit the homeless.

Wouldn't it be simpler just to provide them with homes? she wondered, and would have skipped the rest of the article if Mark Sanderson's name hadn't caught her eye. He was to be the guest speaker.

That settled it. This would be even better than her fantasy of standing up at the MAA dinner and denouncing all and sundry. She would rise up at the Realty Foundation dinner in the middle of Mark Sanderson's speech and shoot herself right there in front of all the power brokers and philanthropists. And she would leave a letter in her handbag explaining why she had put an end to herself at that time and in that place.

It was bound to hit the newspapers. On a slow day, or if enough of the people who really mattered were there, it might even make the front page. Mark Sanderson would be embarrassed. And she would be beyond embarrassment.

At first she thought she would buy a ticket to the dinner. But, no, she wasn't going to give five hundred dollars of what remained of her money to the Realty Foundation. Where she was going, a tax deduction would be of little use. She would crash to the bitter end.

For six days she addressed and stamped envelopes. On the seventh day, she put on the classic black evening gown which, like most classics, was as suitable for a funeral as a party. She searched for a handbag that would conceal the

gun and finally chose a squashy scarlet velvet pouch big
enough to shroud it.

She cleaned and oiled the gun and loaded it. Would she
still remember how to shoot? Or had her hand lost its cunning?

She laughed. How much cunning did you need in order
to put a gun to your head and shoot yourself? She hoped
that ammunition didn't have a limited shelf life. It would
be too humiliating if her bullets turned out to have gone
bad and the gun merely went "phffft" and blackened her
face.

She had already mailed her death notice to the *Times*
along with a check, although she had not mailed the letters.
The obituary should appear before the letters arrived. That
way at least there would be some semblance of the regular
order of events. Now she placed the photocopied letters in
stamped, appropriately addressed envelopes on a table in
the foyer of her apartment. The police would find them
later, and she trusted they would have the courtesy to put
them in the nearest mailbox. Time for her to sally forth to
her doom—no, to her death. She had been doomed for a
long time now.

To her surprise, the very first taxi she hailed stopped.
They know, she thought. They know.

She bypassed the reception desk via a private route she
had learned and found a table in a quiet corner not too far
from the dais on which the guests of honor would be en-
throned. Half of the table was concealed by a column, the
rest shadowed by a swag of crimson velvet looped back
against it. She wanted Mark to notice her at the moment
of truth, but not before. It would spoil the surprise if he
saw her in advance and came up to shake hands. The affair
wasn't heavily attended; the homeless didn't seem to be
very popular, even among crashers, so she had the table
all to herself. In fact, she had the whole corner to herself.
Nobody who had paid five hundred dollars for a dinner
liked to sit in the shadows.

The food was excellent. Those real-estate people really did themselves proud. She ate with an abandon she had never permitted herself before, even indulging in lobster. No need to worry about getting sick tomorrow. And the champagne was of such superior quality and such a good year that she had already drunk far more than she should have before she remembered she would need a steady hand to accomplish her task. Still, she thought as she finished the bottle, how steady a hand did you need for such a close-range target?

Her table had been swept bare of all except her coffee cup, her liqueur glass and a beautiful floral arrangement (too bad it would have to go to waste) when Mark Sanderson got up to speak. Beneath the shelter of the tablecloth, she opened her bag and took out the loaded gun.

As his voice droned on, she released the safety catch and stood up. No one seemed to notice. The beginning of the speechmaking at these affairs so often coincided with a rush to the restrooms or the bar; and, of course, she was almost concealed by the column and its drapery.

She raised the gun.

". . . And why are so many people today without homes? Because the city has deliberately allowed its housing stock to deteriorate. We will never be able to find homes for all of those who need them until we rid ourselves of the pernicious rent-control and rent-stabilization regulations which have strangled the economy for so long by preventing landlords from getting fair market returns on their investments. . . ."

Suddenly something clicked inside her. She remembered her Irish nurse's saying that she had "Come over all queer," in explaining why she had once chased the cook around the dining room with a cleaver. At the time, Susan hadn't understood the cook's expression. She did now, because she was coming over all queer herself. Why should *she* be the one to die?

She took aim and fired.

* * *

There was a long bang. Mark Sanderson collapsed on the table in front of him. Her hand had not lost its cunning.

ooo **X**

For a moment Miss Melville stood there like a candidate for the Museum of American Art's Statuary Court. Then, putting her gun tidily back into her handbag, she turned, pulled back the swag of crimson velvet and walked out of the nearest exit, just beyond the column. She had prepared herself for public demise, but not for public arrest. She did hope they wouldn't cuff her hands behind her back the way they did on the police shows. So ignominious—and so likely to be painful for anyone suffering from a touch of bursitis.

There were probably many criminals and alleged criminals who suffered from bursitis. It had never before occurred to her how painful such a procedure must be for them. This experience is making a more understanding person out of me, she thought.

She envisioned the evening news with a film clip of herself being led off in shackles, and such of her old friends who happened to be watching saying, "Dear me, isn't that Susan Melville? I'd been wondering whatever happened to her."

Followed by a commercial. She hoped it would be something dignified, like A.T.&T. or an investment company. Much nicer to be coda'd by the mellifluous tones of the man declaiming, "Patterson, Pennypacker, Baldwin &

Snook; they take care of your money as if it were their own," than the rasp of General Chomsky: "Friends, come down to the old General's Chomp House and fill your tummies with the tastiest food in the country," segueing into a chorus of "Chomp your way to success, chomp for health and happiness," as the red-faced, white-sideburned face of the General was shown bearing down on a Slamburger with carnivorous glee.

A hand grabbed her arm. "This way," a waiter said. She let him lead her down several flights of stairs and through a twisting maze of corridors.

He was a handsome young man, the kind of waiter her boarding-school friends were apt to have crushes on after they'd graduated from the family chauffeur—except for those barbarous few who went for pop singers.

Never Susan, although she was as likely at that age as any other adolescent to fasten her affections on unsuitable objects; in her case, they had to have more meaningful roles in life, like art teachers or ski instructors.

But, of course, the young man couldn't really be a waiter. He must be a policeman—a plainclothesman, even if he was wearing fancy dress, for the costumes in which the Regency-Ritz bedecked its waiters would have been considered flashy in the court of King Ludwig of Bavaria.

Switching on a light, he pushed her into a small shelved room piled high with sheets and towels and fragrant with the aroma of clean linen, then placed himself with his back to the door in classic cinematic style. "All right," he snarled, "tell me for whom you are working."

The snarl was only figurative. In actual fact, he had a pleasant, cultivated voice with a slight foreign accent that she could not place. It was the idea that snarled. And not many people nowadays, she thought, would have known enough to use the objective case of the pronoun; but then foreigners, as Shaw had pointed out, so often speak the language better than the natives.

"I asked you whom you were working for," he said

again, repeating the inquiry in a number of languages, only a few of which she was able to identify.

She couldn't seem to find her voice. He gripped her by the arm again, more firmly this time, as if planning to shake the words out of her. Surely, she thought, they were supposed to read you your rights before they gave you the third degree.

But would there be any need for them to give her the third degree if she confessed at the outset?

"I admit everything, officer," she said. "I killed him."

"I know you killed him. I saw you kill him. And please do not call me officer. I am not a policeman."

Was he telling the truth, or was this some cunning ploy, perhaps on behalf of some other government agency, to get her to talk? Certainly he could not be simply an ordinary, law-abiding citizen or he would have called the police instead of attempting to grill her in a linen closet.

Her thinking was beginning to fuzz around the edges. Maybe she had drunk a little too much wine—a lot too much wine—but it had been such a splendid vintage, so suitable for her last supper, almost like being present at her own wake. And it obviously had not affected her aim, although right now she wouldn't have been able to hit the Great Wall of China with an elephant gun.

"Do you mind if I sit down?" she asked. "I'm afraid I am not at all well." Tiny poisoned darts were beginning to attack her abdomen from the inside.

He muttered something in one of the languages she hadn't been able to identify and looked around their retreat. He finally discovered a large carton labeled "Paper Products" upon which he disposed one of the Regency-Ritz's thick, fluffy bathmats. He waved her to it with a gesture worthy of a more elegant occasion.

"So kind of you," she murmured, torn between the equally ignominious impulses of bursting into tears or throwing up.

The young man's sang-froid was beginning to heat up.

"I insist upon knowing who paid you to kill Mark Sanderson! That was my assignment. You don't know the trouble I went through, smuggling a gun into the room. They were searching everyone at the door. Then you pull a gun out of your handbag and bang, you kill him, just like that!" He snapped his fingers.

That settled it. He couldn't be a policeman. Policemen weren't paid to kill people. Of course they had to be prepared to do it from time to time in the public interest, but there was no extra charge.

Could it be that there was an assassin's union? Was he accusing her of being a "scab"—if that was the right word when no strike was involved? The thought pained her. She had never crossed a picket line in her life.

"I'm sorry," she said. "I didn't mean to . . . to interfere. And nobody paid me to kill him. He is—was—my landlord."

He stared at her. "Do you expect me to believe that you killed this man simply because he was your landlord? That is absurd."

Obviously, my young friend, she thought, you haven't lived in New York very long.

The agonies in her abdomen could no longer be dismissed as mere twinges. She wished he would stop talking and let her die.

But he persisted. "I still cannot understand how you contrived to get into the room with a gun. They searched all the ladies' handbags."

"I didn't go in through the regular door. You see . . . I . . . crashed . . . party."

And, as he opened his mouth to speak, "Sorry to be rude . . . really can't go on chatting . . . really . . . lovely . . . but, you see . . . I'm very sick. . ."

He took a look at her and muttered something in another unidentifiable foreign tongue, or perhaps the same one. "Wait here."

The overhead light went out and he left, leaving her

alone in the dark. Not that it wasn't better to be alone in the dark than with some people.

She didn't place the young man in that category. Even though he professed to be a paid assassin—a paid would-be assassin, she thought with a melancholy chuckle, I beat him to it—he seemed curiously nonthreatening.

After a time, he came back and helped her to her feet. "I have found a room on this floor that appears to be unoccupied," he said. "You will be more comfortable there."

"So thoughtful . . ." she murmured, as he helped her to her feet and led her down the hall into the plusher environment of the guests' quarters.

"It is not likely that anyone will check in this late," he said as he unlocked the door. "Still, who can tell? It is a risk, so we must not stay longer than we can help."

At the moment her distress was too great for her to wonder how he had managed to get the key. Later, there was no need to wonder. She discovered that he could get anything he wanted.

The big double bed covered with a spread in a pleasing pastel pattern was a welcome sight. Kicking off her shoes, she threw herself upon it and waited for death—as she had, she was beginning to recall through the mists, on several occasions in her youth. But that was before Dr. Gatewood had identified the cause of her recurring ailment. She hadn't died then, and, she was beginning to fear, she wasn't going to die now.

"Is this, then, the first time you have ever killed anyone?" the young man asked, picking up her handbag from the floor where she had let it fall and taking it in the direction of the dressing table. She had heard or read somewhere that professional criminals were very neat, especially murderers.

She fought for breath. "Matter of fact . . . yes . . . but this . . . not reaction to . . . killing . . . reaction to . . . lobster."

He passed his hand across his thick, sleek dark hair and

said something in what she decided must be his native tongue, then spoke in English: "It pains me to add to your suffering, madam, but I must insist that you tell me the true reason why you came here to kill Sanderson."

"Didn't come here . . . kill . . . him. Came . . . kill . . . myself . . ."

Pain was making her babble in a way that was utterly alien to her. She heard her own voice telling him things that she never would have dreamed of telling a stranger, things she wouldn't have told a friend. She could only hope that she was so incoherent as to be incomprehensible.

After a while she became aware that she had stopped talking and he had picked up the conversational thread. "Unfortunately, under the circumstances, it will be impossible for me to fetch a doctor for you, you understand. However, if there is any medication that might help . . ."

There were, she remembered, some pills that Dr. Gatewood used to give her. Dr. Gatewood had retired years ago. The pills might not be manufactured any more. Anyway, they had been available only by prescription.

The young man didn't seem to think that was an obstacle. "I will be back with them just as soon as I can," he promised. "In the meantime, try to get some rest. I trust you will not be discovered while I am gone. However, if by some mischance someone should find you here, I would appreciate it if you made no mention of my existence. It would do you no good, you understand, and might cause me a certain . . . embarrassment."

He turned out the light. The door clicked shut. She was alone.

Now that she was no longer under any social obligations, she could relax and suffer comfortably. Although a few minutes before she would have thought the possiblity ridiculous, she fell asleep.

Dawn was beginning to glint at the edge of the blinds when the sound of the door opening awakened her. To her surprise, she was not only alive but feeling far less wretched. Still, she dutifully swallowed two of the pills that the young man handed her, hoping they weren't poison, and took water from the glass which he had filled in the bathroom. Then she sat up and attempted to tidy herself, although she knew that, after sleeping all night in her clothes, there was no way she would be able to achieve a truly *soignée* appearance.

The young many had changed his clothes, she noted. He no longer looked like a waiter; rather, in his superbly tailored Italian-cut suit, he looked like a headwaiter—possibly even a maitre d'—from one of the best restaurants on his day off, although he was a little young for a post of such dignity. Early to middle twenties, as far as she could judge, it being hard to tell with a mustache.

As she bent over to put on her shoes, she caught a glimpse of herself in the mirror. That state of her hair would have put her in the forefront of contemporary style; however, she had never aspired to be a fashion plate, particularly in view of so much of what passed for fashion these days.

She reached for her bag. It wasn't on the dressing table.

The young man handed it to her. It seemed much lighter. He must have removed the gun. Well, she should have expected that.

"No need to do anything about your appearance right now," he said, before she could open it. "We are in a hurry. You can make your toilette at leisure when we get downstairs."

"Downstairs?"

"I have taken a suite on the floor below this," he explained, drawing her to her feet with a grip that, though gentle, admitted of no resistance. "I have registered you as my aunt. I hope you do not mind."

Even if she did, there was nothing she could do about it. "Wasn't registering here dangerous?" she asked as she once again followed his lead down the corridors. If she had known there was going to be so much walking, she wouldn't have worn high-heeled shoes. "I know it's the 'Purloined Letter' principle. But I've never placed much faith in its practical application."

"There is nothing to worry about. Even if he had seen me before, the night clerk would not recognize me. To him a waiter is a uniform, not a face. And the people on the day shift will not even know that you did not arrive at the same time as I did; that is, if we make haste."

They made haste, down picture-lined corridors—pictures, pictures everywhere, she thought fuzzily—meeting no one on the way, for which she was grateful, although the young man would probably have been able to deal with such a contingency. He seemed prepared for anything.

Except me, she thought. He wasn't prepared for me.

Even the smallest suites at the Regency-Ritz were costly, and the one he had taken was far from being one of the smallest. A lot of money involved here, Miss Melville thought. Professional assassins, since that was what he seemed to be, must do quite well for themselves.

How awful, she thought; I am turning into one of those vulgar people who price everything.

They had hardly gotten inside when a knock come at the door. If she had been a jumper, she would have jumped. She was a freezer. She stood, petrified.

The young man smiled. "Only room service. Since at this hour service is not of the speediest, I called and ordered breakfast before I went to fetch you. However, I think perhaps you would feel more comfortable if you retired into your bathroom and changed into something more appropriate while I deal with the waiter. I trust you will find everything you need here. My choices were limited, so if I overlooked anything, or anything is not quite what you would have chosen for yourself, please accept my apologies."

The suitcase he handed her bore a Mark Cross label and held not only a complete set of toilet articles and make-up in all the right colors, but a full outfit of street clothes, all in her size, all expensive and in such quiet good taste that she couldn't help feeling miffed. After all, she thought, I'm not quite the queen dowager.

When she emerged, suitably garbed for an early morning review of the troops, she found a breakfast table laid for two. Twenty, even fifteen, years ago she might have been apprehensive, perhaps pleasantly so. Mimi, faced with a similar situation, would have been expectant. In view of the wardrobe he had selected for her, Miss Melville thought, there was nothing for her to worry about.

"I trust you feel well enough to have something to eat," he said. "I myself am famished."

As well you might be, running around all night organizing, you busy little beaver, you, she thought.

Actually she was feeling much better than she would have expected, but she was not morally ready for food. Under the circumstances, it would be wrong to have an appetite. "I couldn't eat a thing," she said, "but I would like some coffee."

A minute later, she was sitting across the table from him, sipping coffee as if she were indeed his out-of-town aunt and everything was quite natural and ordinary. He or perhaps the breakfast waiter had raised the blinds. Outside, the sun was rising over Queens—or possibly Brooklyn; from this distance it was difficult to tell one borough from the other.

"Looks as if it will be a beautiful day," he said.

She, too, had been brought up not to discuss business or anything else unpleasant at meals, especially breakfast; but, after all she had been through, she was not going to let herself be inveigled into a chat about the weather. She wanted to know where she stood, and she wanted to know right away.

"I know the police aren't likely to think of looking for me here in the Regency-Ritz, but I can't hole up here forever. Sooner or later, I'm going to have to face the music."

As she recalled, there was no death penalty in New York State. Probably she would be sent to the Women's Correctional Facility in Bedford Hills. It would be nice to see Dodo Pangborn again . . . not that she'd ever liked her that much, but her society would probably be superior to that of thieves and murderers.

Then she recollected that she herself could be considered a murderess and her father a thief. How circumstances did change one's viewpoint!

"But there is no music to face." He smiled. "Oh, I am familiar with the idiom. It's merely that no one is looking for you. No one saw you shoot Sanderson."

She set down her coffee cup with a bang. "That's absurd. There were hundreds of people in that room. Somebody must have seen me shoot him."

"Oh, a number of people say they saw *somebody* shoot Sanderson. But nobody saw *you.*"

She firmed her jaw, stoutly resisting its urge to drop—a temptation to which it had never been exposed before. "Would you please explain that?"

"Three people saw a beautiful young woman—with a slightly Oriental cast of features, according to one—aim the gun. Another said the killer was a man; still another said it was a priest. As for you, most people didn't even remember that there had been someone sitting at your table."

He looked as if he expected her to be grateful by the

news. From the standpoint of personal safety, she supposed she ought to be. However, in the larger sense, she was not. "It's as if I have been invisible."

"Better than invisible, my dear Miss Melville. Unnoticeable."

Why was he smirking like that? Did he think he had paid her a compliment, that she *liked* being a nonentity?

But, of course, he was a foreigner. Perhaps he thought that just because they were allowed to vote and move around freely, middle-aged women here enjoyed a status equivalent to that of middle-aged men.

"In our society," she explained, remembering what Sophie had said, "a middle-aged woman, unless she has some special claim to recognition—power, money, past glory, a notable sex life—simply doesn't exist. Even when she gets up and kills somebody, people see a man or, at most, a young woman. They refuse to as much as see someone who, by their lights, ought not to be there."

"Precisely. And your society is the worse for such an attitude, just as I hope our society will be better."

People whose native tongue was not English, she thought, should not attempt word play in that language.

"You see, we are perceptive enough to appreciate your advantages. Where this world sees a middle-aged woman as someone less fleet of foot that a young one, we see someone who does not need to flee because she can blend into the background. Where your world sees her as an individual whose eyesight may be dimming, we see her as an individual more likely to take careful aim. Where your world sees her as timid, we see her as someone unlikely to take foolish chances. Where—"

"Enough," she said. "Don't you think you're laying it on just a bit too thick?"

He looked at her with reproach. "Miss Melville—"

"How do you know my name?"

Not that she didn't know already, but it would gratify

her to be able to embarrass this preternaturally poised youth.

But of course he was not embarrassed; how foolish it was of her to have expected him to be. He merely shrugged and said, "I took your handbag with me when I left you, and while I was, ah, waiting for your prescription to be filled, I glanced through its contents. Naturally it grieved me to have to do such a thing, but considerations of privacy cannot apply in a situation like this, you understand."

"Stop telling me I understand. I don't understand anything."

"As you have no doubt noticed, I removed your gun. A safety precaution. Not a good thing to be carrying around with you at any time, but especially imprudent now."

"It was my father's gun."

"We will get you another one," he said soothingly. "A much more up-to-date gun that will shoot many more bullets."

"Stop talking to me as if I were a child."

"I would not offer a gun to a child. By the way—" he rose from his seat and bowed across the table "—I do not want to have the advantage of you. My name is Alex Tabor. Since you are my aunt, even if only my make-believe aunt, you may call me Alex."

"Mr. Tabor," she said, inclining her head.

Unsnubbed, he sat down and buttered a brioche. The Regency-Ritz's brioches used to be quite superior, she recalled, telling herself sternly that a Melville's mouth did not water.

"Now, to business. I have spoken to my employer and he agrees that you would make a valuable addition to our staff. Accordingly, he has empowered me to make an offer to you."

"That I should become a paid assassin, I suppose?"

"He would not put it in those terms, but that is the general idea. You have been looking for work, have you not? You will never get another offer as good as this one: light hours, good pay, and opportunity for advancement.''

She winced. How she must have talked last night! And of course he must have read her farewell letter. It had been in her purse. Useless to expect scruples from a man of his type, although, to be fair, the envelope was unsealed and addressed "To whom it may concern," so she really couldn't blame him.

She'd thought she'd experienced humiliation before, but never like this. No wonder it took a saint to be a saint.

She was about to snap out a refusal when discretion took over. It was neither polite not prudent to antagonize a hired killer, no matter how genteel his behavior or how high his prices.

"It's a flattering offer, and I'm honored by your confidence in me," she said. "However, I'm afraid I must decline."

"Why must you? You can scarcely say you're morally opposed. You did, after all, kill Sanderson."

"He was a terrible man," she muttered, embarrassed by the melodramatic sound of the words. "Besides, I did it on impulse. It was almost an accident, the kind of thing that might happen to anybody who happened to have a gun in her handbag."

"I understand your point of view completely," he said. "As you say, it could have happened to anyone. However, the law is not likely to accept that as an excuse."

"Are you threatening to, er, turn me in?" she asked.

He looked pained. "Turn you in! My dear Miss Melville, it would be entirely against our principles, even though we are taking care of your gun, with your fingerprints on it."

She wondered how she could ever have thought him a pleasant young man.

"What we are doing is offering you an exciting new career," he said. "You should be jumping at such an opportunity."

"I don't see why I should," she said. "It's not my type of thing at all. I wouldn't be good at it. Anyhow, it's wrong."

"Wrong?"

"Bad. Evil. Immoral."

"Illegal, yes. Immoral, no. You see, Miss Melville, we would not ask you to . . . dispose of anyone who was *not* bad. There are many individuals in this world who are even worse than Mark Sanderson, despicable creatures who do not deserve to live, whose continued existence, in fact, creates an ever-spreading tide of misery, but whom, for one reason or another, the law cannot touch."

Perhaps, in his native tongue his eloquence would not sound quite so . . . eloquent. It would have been almost funny if it hadn't been for the very real menace underlying it.

She tried to deal with his offer as she would deal with any of the other ordinary offers and choices in life. "I'm sure there are a lot of people who are not very nice. However—"

"—On the other hand," he continued, "there are a number of philanthropic organizations and individuals who are anxious to serve humanity by making sure those monsters cause no further injury to humankind. And also," he added, to cover all bases, "to the animal kingdom and the environment. However, these good people lack the expertise to get rid of the bad people. They do not know where to begin, and if they try to do the job themselves, all too often they bungle it, sometimes destroying innocent lives as well as, or instead of, the guilty ones. We would not want that to happen, now would we, Miss Melville?"

She resisted the temptation to say, "It is none of our business," afraid that would unleash another torrent of rhetoric to the effect that improving the human condition was everyone's business, so she said, "And that's where you and your boss come in?"

He made a face. "My employer, please. He does not care for the word 'boss.' "

And I suppose he is entitled to his sensitivities, the same as anyone else, she thought, although it didn't seem quite fair.

"Many philanthropic organizations, as I am sure you are aware, hire outside agencies to provide services they cannot perform effectively for themselves, like publicity or fund-raising. What we do is provide another such service."

He smiled. He smiles too much, she thought. Who was it that smiled a lot in Shakespeare? Iago. Of course. Who else?

"I don't suppose your services come cheap," she observed.

"We are not, after all, a philanthropic organization ourselves. And efficiency never comes cheap."

Suddenly Miss Melville found she was hungrier that she had ever before been in her life. She reached for a brioche and buttered it. The Regency-Ritz's ovens had not lost their touch.

"In other words," she said after she had swallowed a few delicious morsels, "people go to him and take out contracts on their enemies then he employs a hitman—or hitwoman—to do the job?"

He stared at her, then laughed. "My dear Miss Melville! I can see you are a devotee of the cinema. I suppose organizations of that kind do exist, but this is an agency of a far higher order. We deal only with public figures, not with private vendettas. Try the jam; it's excellent."

It was. Imported, of course; they didn't make *cassis* jam here, even though the Agriculture Department had legalized the growing of black currants some years back.

He gestured with a piece of brioche. "We do not accept an assignment unless we feel assured that it is in the best interest of society that this person should be removed from it. For example, if Hitler had been terminated early in his career—"

"That was tried on more than one occasion, I believe."

"By inefficient amateurs who bungled the job. If our organization had existed then and been called in, believe me, Miss Melville, we would not have failed."

He slathered jam on a brioche—his fourth, she noted; the young had such hearty appetites—and devoured it. "Let me assure you that for every bad life our organization takes, at least a hundred good lives, on the average, are saved—or allowed to be lived out in peace."

Now he sounded like a life-insurance salesman in reverse.

He dabbed at his lips with a napkin. "Look at it another way, Miss Melville. What else are you going to do? You came to the dinner to kill yourself, didn't you?"

She colored and looked at her plate.

"It is not I who am being cruel. It is reality that is cruel. I am merely forcing you to face that reality. Your financial situation remains the same, does it not? Yet do you continue in your original intention of killing yourself? Has not life suddenly become very sweet?"

But how did he know? Had he, too, been pushed to desperation before he started on this career?

"What will you do, Miss Melville?" he persisted, like an American Express commercial. "What will you do?"

She had been asking herself the same question, but she wasn't going to admit it to him. "I'm sure I'll find something. I gave up too soon. I didn't really try hard enough to find some sort of regular work."

"It is possible that you will find something," he conceded. "Perhaps your wealthy friends will create some post for you—if you hound them or shame them enough. Your kind always stick together."

Was there a trace of bitterness in his voice, or was it merely implicit in his words? My young friend, you are a snob, she thought.

"Let me see, how would you like to be a companion to some old lady with money? Or, in the literary tradition, a governess? No, that wouldn't do. Today a governess needs more qualifications that you have.''

He was trying to break her down, but she was a Melville, a descendant of Black Buck Melville, who had started out in the shipping business in the eighteenth century and had achieved fame and fortune through his own efforts. In the course of those efforts, a number of people who had gotten in his way had either come to a violent end or vanished.

As the years rolled by, the family stoutly denied that he had been in any way responsible for any of the dark deeds of which he'd been accused. Still, even if the tales *had* been true, those were just ordinary business practices in those times. She felt sure that Black Buck would never have allowed himself to be bullied into doing anything that went against his principles.

She got up. "If you don't mind, I think I'd like to go home.''

What would she do, she wondered, if he refused to let her go? Hold her prisoner in the Regency-Ritz?

But the problem did not arise. "Of course you must go home, if you wish. Although we would be pleased if you stayed here in the hotel as our guest, as long as you liked, while you considered our proposition. You'd be under no obligation.''

She shook her head. "It's out of the question. I couldn't possibly do anything like that.''

"As you wish, but you must allow me to see you home.''

Since he knew her address anyway from the contents of her handbag, she accepted with fair grace. Besides, she was a little leery about going home at such an early hour in the morning.

He left her at her front door, insisting that she keep the suitcase as a memento of the occasion. Since the clothes she had worn to the dinner were inside, she could hardly refuse. Besides, she supposed she had earned it.

"I'll be in touch very soon," he promised. Bowing, he kissed her hand, to the doorman's gratification, and left.

○○○ **XII**

When she opened her bag to get out her keys, she discovered why it still bulged even though the gun was gone. It was stuffed with fifty-dollar bills, forty of them. Two thousand dollars. "With gratitude, A. T.," a card inside read. She wondered how much he himself had been paid for the job that he could afford to be so generous. Of course, the money wouldn't have come from him but from his employer, who would probably be able to deduct it as a business expense.

For a moment she thought of giving the money to an appropriate charity. But to do that she would have to declare it on her income-tax return, which could lead to embarrassing questions about its provenance. Besides, charity began at home. I shall spend it on myself, she decided.

When she turned on the radio, voices sang, "You deserve a break today."

"You're so right," she agreed.

It turned out that Mr. Tabor had spoken the truth: although several people claimed to have seen *someone* shoot Mark Sanderson, none of the conflicting descriptions that they gave of the shooter even remotely resembled her. It was like that cheap old trick psychology teachers used to be so fond of playing on their classes, where a couple of people burst into the classroom and pretended to commit a crime, after which the students were questioned about it.

Usually no two descriptions of the perpetrator and/or victim were the same.

But this time it was even more than that. No one at the dinner seemed to have remembered that someone had been sitting at her table. Moreover, a number of the guests had apparently disappeared between the time of the shooting and the arrival of the police—and they were hardly likely to volunteer any information later, even if the police tracked them down through the guest lists. The old adage, "See no evil, hear no evil, speak no evil" was the motto by which New Yorkers lived when it came to the law. No one had the time or inclination to get involved. Even the Oupi had something like it, Peter had told her. If you bore witness to a crime, the demons inhabiting the criminal would leave him and enter you.

No one seemed sure of exactly why Mark Sanderson had been killed, although a number of organizations, several of which had never been heard of before, telephoned the newspapers and TV stations to claim credit. This was quite normal, Mr. Tabor had told her, when a newsworthy crime was committed. Even more individuals would turn themselves in to the police claiming to have been the perpetrator, he'd explained, their numbers rising with the waxing of the moon.

And so it was Sanderson's death that received the coda of commercials: ". . . Reach out and touch someone . . . No more ring around the collar . . . Chomp your way to happiness . . . Twice as much active ingredient as any other brand . . . We take care of your money as if it were our own . . ."

She wondered just who it was that had actually contracted with Mr. Tabor's employer to put an end to Mark Sanderson, but of course he wouldn't tell her if she asked. He might not even know, himself.

Later in the morning she went downstairs and bought all the papers, like an actor anxious to read his reviews, just as she herself had done years before when her paintings had been exhibited. Not even Andy Warhol had ever gotten the space she was getting now (albeit anonymously). She— or, at least, her handiwork—made the front page on every one, even *Newsday*, which took pains to point out that Sanderson Associates had extensive holdings in Queens and Nassau County. Although the *Times* played the whole thing down as something that might happen to any landlord, the *News* and the *Post* covered the full spectrum of specula- tion, while the *Voice* took it as the springboard for a ten- page article on the housing situation.

Although there were the usual pious tributes from poli- ticians and realtors, reading between the lines she sensed a certain lack of sympathy for the deceased, a certain admi- ration for the skill and daring of the assassin. She tried not to feel smug, reminded herself that her success had been mostly a matter of luck.

Since she had expected to be dead, she hadn't made any plans for that evening, but she was too restless to stay home reading or watching TV—except for the news, of course—or even painting. She had every intention of watching the five and six o'clock shows, but the eleven o'clock news was usually a repeat of the earlier offerings. There would always be the late, late news if her thirst for current events was yet unslaked.

She didn't usually crash two nights in a row, but this was a special occasion, one that called for celebration. Crashing was the only way she could think of to celebrate at such short notice. She knew that there was going to be a dinner at the Metropolitan Club which most of her crash- ing acquaintances were planning to attempt, but it didn't appeal to her. The last time she had seen Shirley, at the gala opening of a new sushi restaurant, Shirley had men- tioned that the Quagga Memorial Society was going to give a dinner dance at the Venturers Club on this very night, "in honor of something or other nonprofit."

"The *Quagga* Memorial Society?"

"Named after one of those old naturalists or philanthropists or something."

"You don't mean *equus quagga*, by any chance?"

"That's the one," Shirley said, "but he's dead and that's what the party's bound to be, too. Lots of stuffed animals and stuffed shirts."

A classic case of sour grapes. The Venturers Club was simply a tougher nut than Shirley could crack, not only because of the difficulty in successfully crashing, but because of the rather high-handed way of dealing with interlopers that it was rumored to employ.

"You'd think Venturers, of all people, would understand," Shirley had observed bitterly, "but Freddy Makepeace said they came at him with spears the last time he managed to get past the front door. Now he just preaches outside, as close to the windows as he can get, so they can maybe hear him inside. 'If only one word falls on fallow ground,' he says, 'it will be as a seed that . . .' I forget the rest."

Miss Melville had heard Freddy give that same speech. "I remember. And, of course, he's exaggerating. About the spears, I mean."

"You think so?" Shirley said darkly. "Well, if you get inside, take a look at those shrunken human heads over the fireplace in the entrance hall. The one third from the left looks a lot like Shalimar. A little over a year ago, she said she was going to crash the Carib Cotillion at the Venturers, and nobody's seen her since."

Even allowing for exaggeration, the Miss Melville of yesterday would not have dared attempt the Venturers. As a matter of fact, she hadn't been on the club premises since the days when she used to go as a legitimate guest. Her father, of course, had been a member.

Tonight—well, I am a venturer myself, she thought. She would dare anything except the cuisine; as she recalled, they used to serve such delicacies as roast lion and crocodile stew.

That afternoon she went out and bought a new dress, the first she had allowed herself in a long time. While it was far from the quality of those in her holdover wardrobe, it was brand new and of a particularly pleasing shade of blue crêpe de chine that complemented her eyes. Clothes had never meant much to her in the old days. She dressed well, as befitted her position, and that was it. Now she was surprised at the lift she got, not so much from the new dress but from the pleasure of being able to buy it.

Making a surreptitious entrance to the club premises through the little door in the brick wall that separated the Venturers' garden from the back courtyard of the Peabody Residential Hotel for Women, a door which everyone assumed had been sealed shut for years, Miss Melville encountered Rhonda in the underbrush. Rhonda was also wearing a new dress, far costlier than Miss Melville's and, like most of Rhonda's wardrobe, in execrable taste, Miss Melville thought uncharitably.

"How did you know about this way in?" Rhonda demanded in a fierce whisper as they beat their way through the bushes, alarming small creatures which variously flew, crept, and wriggled out ahead of and sometimes on them.

"Why, I thought everyone knew about it," Miss Melville said, dislodging something with feelers that was crawling along the back of her neck.

"I'm the only one who knows and I never told anyone about it, nobody at all!"

Rhonda brushed aside a sprawling shoot. Really, Miss Melville thought, you'd think the Venturers would take better care of their property. In the old days they used to hold parties out in this garden.

"Nobody except Felix," Rhonda amended her statement. "I took him in this way once, but he promised never to tell anybody about it." She glared at Miss Melville as if she were Circe and Salome rolled into one. "You *weaseled* it out of him!"

It didn't take any weaseling to get information from Felix. All you had to do was keep quiet and listen, but that was a tactic Rhonda couldn't even begin to understand.

"Oh, do be careful," Miss Melville begged as a garbage can—fortunately plastic, or their adventure would have ended then and there—swayed under the impact of Rhonda's substantial sandal.

"Don't you tell me what to do, ordering me around like—like the place belonged to you. You don't belong here and you know it!"

Rhonda swelled with the effort of keeping her voice down while her dander was up. Her face turned crimson, a notable clash, Miss Melville reflected, with the rich puce of her dress.

"Sorry if this is your private entrance. Perhaps you'd like to call the guards and have me removed."

Clinking sounds came from the kitchen, very close now. Silence was imperative. Unable to express herself in words, Rhonda emitted a hissing sound, like a boiler about to erupt. Most of the other crashers were careful not to antagonize Rhonda, not only because they hoped to learn from her, but because they were afraid of her.

"She's a very nervous girl," Shirley had explained, "and sometimes she does get a little violent," adding that Freddy Makepeace was sure he had seen her at what Shirley delicately termed "a mental retreat." But Freddy often saw things that were not of this earth.

Rhonda doesn't scare me, Miss Melville told herself. Maybe she did before, a little—but not now.

Rhonda pulled open the back door, and Miss Melville caught it before it slammed shut in her face. The two ladies crept past the dangers of the kitchen and down a side passage that led to the room marked "Memsahibs." Oh, God, Miss Melville thought, you'd think they would have changed that by now.

They brushed themselves off without speaking to each other. It was amazing how little damage their wilderness walk had done to their clothes, but Rhonda was skilled in unorthodox entries, and I, Miss Melville thought, I am learning fast.

The Venturers' dining room was colorfully decorated in a jungle motif that wasn't nearly as realistic as the club's own garden had been. It saddened her a little, reminding her of Peter off in his jungle.

Since the occasion was a benefit for endangered species, she had wondered how the Venturers would deal with the animal head trophies that had always been the focal point of the dining room's decor. She had half expected them to be removed for the evening, if not permanently, now that times had changed and big game hunting was no longer fashionable.

The Venturers' way of dealing with the shift in attitude was to place a wreath around the neck of each trophy, with a ribbon reading, "In Memoriam." Quite a nice touch, she thought, and so much less expensive than finding something to fill up the gaps their removal would otherwise have created.

The dinner was a buffet, which Miss Melville preferred since it allowed for so much more freedom of movement, as well as of choice. The food was better than average, with no exotic species being offered, as far as she could tell, although she was careful to select only those dishes that she recognized—salmon mousse, filet of venison, and a salad that consisted of vegetation untainted by either pasta or pesto.

The guests were a cut above the average, too, although there were a number of unusual-looking people, including a few individuals who were either in costume or in actual native dress. Among them was a band of musicians that could have been an authentic African group or some kind of new-wave rock combo—you certainly couldn't tell by what they were playing. From what she could see, she and Rhonda were the only crashers there.

The idea of standing shoulder to shoulder with Rhonda,

the other woman's eyes poisoning every bit of food Miss
Melville put on her plate, was not conducive to an enjoy-
able meal, so Miss Melville let Rhonda get some distance
ahead at the buffet. She took her time about selecting her
first course and was about to look for a suitably obscure
table when a voice hailed her: "Susan, Susan Melville,
how wonderful—you're alive!"

Mimi Carruthers was waving a plate at her with happy
disregard of its contents."I've been trying to call you for
months and months, but I mislaid your number and Information was terribly uncooperative."

"My number's unlisted."

"Of course it is, dear, but I told her I was one of your
very oldest and dearest friends and she still wouldn't give
it to me. The phone company just hasn't been the same
since A.T.&T. divested. And then this morning Oliver was
reading the obituaries to me, and there you were. I was so
upset I nearly didn't come tonight, but something told me
I should, and it was right."

Miss Melville kicked herself mentally. How could she
have forgotten that obituary? She was going to have a lot
of explaining to do.

"The paper listed me as dead? How strange. It must
have been some kind of mistake. Someone else with the
same name perhaps."

"And the same address?"

"Must be a practical joke, although I can't imagine who
would do such a thing."

"Well, you're alive, and that's what counts. You must
come meet Ol—dear me, why are the twins dragging out
that extraordinary-looking woman?"

A struggling and screaming Rhonda was not precisely
dragged but rather forcibly urged out of the dining room
by two large young men wearing safari suits and pith hel-
mets.

"You remember the twins, Potter and Palmer?"

Mimi seemed to take it for granted that Susan would remember whose twins they were, so Susan didn't ask.

"We use members and relatives rather than regular guards as much as possible. They have more of an eye for people who don't belong. Besides—" she wrinkled her nose "—they volunteer their services, of course, and every penny saved is a penny more for endangered species. Or whatever, as the case may be."

Rhonda managed finally to pull the two young men to a halt in the doorway. Although Miss Melville was too far away to hear her words, she knew what their import must be. Rhonda was committing the sin of sins: she was ratting on a fellow crasher.

Miss Melville turned her back to avoid Rhonda's accusing eye, but she could sense the finger that pointed at her. In another moment Potter or Palmer would start in her direction . . .

"You will join us at our table, won't you?" Mimi asked. "Or are you with a party?"

She was saved!

She wanted to throw herself on Mimi's neck and weep tears of gratitude, but even Mimi would have thought that excessive. "My friends couldn't make it, so I came alone," she said. "I'd be delighted to join you."

"How loyal of you," Mimi said obscurely as she swept Miss Melville off to a gorgeously bedecked table up front, as befitted a sponsor or co-hostess or whatever her role was on this occasion.

Out of the corner of her eye, Miss Melville could see Rhonda being carried out. Her mouth was open, but her shrieks couldn't be heard because, at that moment, the native drums hit full decibel.

Mimi, it seemed, was back in the United States permanently. "You heard what happened to poor Oliver?" she asked, gesturing toward a tall mustachioed man who was almost too British to be true. His white mess jacket and scarlet cummerbund, although slightly inappropriate to the

season, fit the occasion to a T. For this marriage, Mimi
had gone back to her own age group; Oliver appeared to
be in his mid-forties. Miss Melville hoped he'd be able to
keep up with his bride.

Miss Melville said she was glad to see that he had recovered from his accident.

"Good of you to say so," Oliver said. "Unfortunately
the rhino didn't. Recover, I mean."

"I know it was a rare specimen," Mimi said, "but Oliver is rarer still."

"Only to you, my sweet. The ESS was a bit sticky about
it."

"And don't think that because we're raising money for
endangered species tonight," Mimi said, "the affair has
any but the most *tenuous* connections with the Endangered
Species Society, because I'm not having anything more to
do with them!"

It seemed the ESS, by which Oliver had been employed
in a capacity that was never clearly defined, had proved to
be so sticky that, in the end, Oliver had been forced to
tender his resignation.

"Luckily," Mimi continued, "that awful Alfred Brad-
wyn who was the executive officer of the Foundation had
to retire because of his age. He must be nearly ninety now.
You remember him? Dreadful man; he used to give all the
jobs at the Foundation to his friends. And Oliver was in-
duced to accept the post. He didn't want to come here
because he didn't think he'd like New York, but he's grown
quite used to it, haven't you, Oliver?"

"A lot more like the jungle than I expected, har, har,"
Oliver agreed.

Peter had often said the same thing, Miss Melville recalled.

"And the reason I was trying so hard to reach you—that
was before I found out you were dead, and here you are,
alive, before I even had a chance to grieve, isn't it won-

derful?—is that there's going to be a job at the Foundation for you.''

Miss Melville said she was surprised and delighted. She was truly surprised and she should have been delighted. ''It was awfully nice of you to think of me, Mimi. What kind of job is it? I mean, what would my duties be?''

The question seemed to surprise Mimi. ''Well, it hasn't been precisely defined yet. Art acquisitioner, perhaps. It's about time the Foundation started an art collection. But, besides that, you'd be Oliver's right-hand woman. He needs somebody he can really rely on, don't you, Oliver?''

''Oh, definitely,'' Oliver agreed. ''All sorts of thing to be done—correspondence, memoranda, documents, what not.''

So Mimi had come through, after all, even if she was a year or so late. Mr. Tabor had been right: their kind did stick together. Perhaps if ''his kind,'' whatever that might be, had stuck together, he would be a dull little clerk somewhere, although somehow she doubted it.

Here was the solution, handed to her on a silver platter, and it wasn't entirely a made-up job because Oliver obviously did need a keeper. All she had to do was accept it and she would be able to live in modest comfort for the rest of her life—modest because foundations did not, as a rule, pay large salaries to any but a few top executives.

Mimi was looking at her with shining eyes.

Miss Melville chose her words carefully. ''It's very kind of you, Mimi, and I truly am grateful. But if you don't mind, I'd like to think it over. I've had another job offer, and I need a little time to make up my mind.''

Mimi reached over and patted her hand. ''Of course, dear. You take just as long as you like.'' She smiled at her husband.

Miss Melville knew, as she left for Memsahibs, that Mimi would be saying, ''So proud, like all the Melvilles. You have to honor her for it.''

And Oliver would pull at his mustache and say, "By Jove [or perhaps he wouldn't go quite that far], yes. Dashed fine woman, that." Too Kipling for words.

Miss Melville couldn't help noticing that there was another back passage through which you could get to the powder room from the garden without having to go anywhere near the kitchen. Early in the evening the rest of the place was likely to be deserted, and there still was that musty little lounge on one side that looked as if it hadn't been used since Teddy Roosevelt's day. You could hide there for hours and nobody would come near you . . .

Whatever was she thinking of? She would never be able to crash the Venturers Club again. Oliver, who had hitherto been a corresponding member, had just been elected vice-president. From now on Miss Melville would be a welcome guest at all functions.

In any case, a trusted employee of the Fitzhorn Foundation would not be able to continue a career as a crasher. It would not comport with the dignity of the position.

Dessert was being served when she returned to the table—tropical fruit bombe and iced cookies in the shape of animals, but far from the traditional animal crackers of yore. "We were talking about Mark Sanderson," Mimi said, as Miss Melville sat down. "Of course you've heard what happened to him?"

Miss Melville tried not to sound too casual. "I did read something in the paper about his getting shot."

"Hunter, was he?" Oliver asked with interest.

"Realtor. As a matter of fact, my landlord. The building I live in was set up as a corporation, the way these things usually are, but he was the majority stockholder."

Oliver looked bewildered.

"That means he actually owned it and could do pretty much what he liked," she explained.

Oliver looked even more bewildered.

"Oliver is such an innocent when it comes to business.

You see, my dearest, by incorporating, he personally couldn't be held legally accountable for—for anything. That's the way it's always done."

Oliver pulled at his mustache. "It doesn't sound quite, er, cricket to me."

"Oh, Oliver," Mimi said, "this isn't a game. It's real life!"

Oliver opened his mouth and shut it again.

"Now that Mark's dead," Miss Melville said, "I don't know who'll take over. Not that it matters. They're turning the place into a cooperative."

"Oh, bad show," Oliver said.

"No, Oliver, good show! It just means that she'll be owning her apartment instead of renting. Oliver and I have a lovely condominium in the East Sixties with a marvelous view of both rivers. So much more practical than a house, and it didn't cost much more."

Mimi took a bite out of a chocolate-covered lion. "I must remember to send a letter of condolence to the Sandersons. I suppose you've written already, Susan?"

"I'm afraid I haven't had a chance. After all, it happened only . . . yesterday, was it?"

She was a little surprised, herself. Already it seemed so remote, like a part of history. Of course she would have to send a letter; she owed it to the family.

She wondered whether she should send flowers. No, that would be pushing hypocrisy beyond the bounds of good taste.

She left the Venturers Club at the end of the evening carrying a tiger-striped tote bag full of the usual loot distributed at affairs of this nature, and especially lavish when you were an honored guest rather than a skulker at the back tables, picking up whatever you could get away with. There was a miniature gold quagga brooch; a bottle of Eau de Quagga Parfum, specially created for the occasion; a silk designer scarf decorated with endangered animals; a button saying "Friend of the Furbish Lousewort" ("We must not forget our floral friends," the lady who passed them out had said); and various other trinkets suitable to the occasion.

Out of deference to Mimi, Miss Melville had asked for one of the rather spectacular floral arrangements, rather than simply stuffing it into the bag. "To use as a model, you know . . ."

"Oh, Susan, to think they'll be immortalized by your brush! Take them all!"

But Miss Melville had no intention of returning to her apartment looking like a parade float. She assured her hostess that one bouquet would be sufficient.

As she went out, she couldn't help taking a good look at the heads in the entrance hall. The third one from the left did look a lot like Shalimar.

Descending the front steps and making for the car that Mimi had called for her, she passed Freddy Makepeace who was preaching to a small, seedy-looking group.

". . . Friends, there is no species as endangered as the human soul. The quagga may be one of God's creatures but it is man who was made in the likeness of God. Is it right that inside they should be feasting on salmon and moose, while the children of Bogota are starving?"

She thought of telling him that the quagga was extinct and that Bogota—at least, the way he pronounced it—was in New Jersey, but opted in favor of pretending not to see him.

◇◇◇ **XIII**

Three days later Mr. Tabor called (Miss Melville didn't ask how he got hold of her unlisted number) and she accepted his job offer.

She couldn't start right away; there were a lot of things that had to be worked out first, she told him. "For one, I have to make sure I'm still a good shot, that my hitting Mark Sanderson wasn't just a fluke . . ."

"Miss Melville, please, this is not a subject to be discussed on the telephone. Let us—"

"Nobody could possibly be listening in unless—do you think the phone could be *tapped*? Or rather *bugged*? I can't see why anybody would be interested in my phone. And you must be speaking from a pay phone."

In the movies the man who gave the orders to kill always used a pay phone, which seemed rather reckless these days, since there were few outside phone booths any more, just open phones where *anyone* could hear you.

"It is a matter of—of professional protocol," he said. "Matters like these are always discussed in person. Perhaps we could meet in a café or a restaurant. Somewhere anonymous. A Chomp House, perhaps?"

She pretended not to hear that last suggestion. "How about the café outside the Stanhope Hotel? Across the street from the Metropolitan Museum. It's quiet and very conveniently located."

The Stanhope was a link with the past, as was the Metropolitan, even though the latter had turned art into a branch of show business. You shouldn't, she thought, have to stand on line to see art work or file reverently past a painting or a statue as if it were Lenin's tomb.

But the approach seemed to work. Apparently the museums had tapped a variation of the basic herd instinct: the primal urge to queue up.

"Across the street from the Metropolitan Museum?" Mr. Tabor repeated. "An outdoor café on Fifth Avenue? Hardly an appropriate site for a rendezvous of this nature."

"In Paris, people in your—this line of business always meet in outdoor cafés."

His laugh was without mirth. "But this is New York, not Paris. And this is real life, not the cinema. And we have been talking for too long on the telephone. Very well, Miss Melville, we will meet at the Stanhope at—shall we say?—three o'clock tomorrow afternoon."

"Three o'clock it is."

She almost hadn't picked up the phone when he rang; she'd grown so tired of answering the calls from old friends and acquaintances inquiring when and where the funeral was to be held that she'd begun to consider taking the instrument off the hook. Most of the callers were not satisfied to discover she was alive and well. They were inclined to discuss the question of how such an error could possibly have occurred, and to recommend a good lawyer, since, of course, she was going to sue the *Times*.

Over and over she told them that it must have been a practical joke, an explanation that sounded increasingly unconvincing each time she repeated it, especially as she had to admit she had no idea who might have played such an unpleasant trick. They must think she knew some very strange people. And, of course, she did, but not that kind of strange.

Most of her old associates asked her to have lunch with them. Apparently they felt that to be the approved method of dealing with someone who had risen from the dead.

Most depressing had been a long-distance call from Germany, at six in the morning. Either Sophie had forgotten about the time differential, or she was taking advantage of Bad Eulenberg's night rates.

"I was sorry to hear of the death of my cousin, Susan Melville," she began, before Miss Melville had a chance to say anything. "Naturally, as her only remaining relative, I shall inherit the estate, and I am anxious to receive it as soon as possible. If it would facilitate matters, I would be happy to come to New York, provided that the estate will advance me the price of the fare . . ."

"Sophie, Sophie!!" Susan had been interrupting at intervals, "I'm alive! It was all a mistake!" her voice rising as Sophie plodded on with Teutonic thoroughness.

Finally, the words got through. "A mistake! You are joking. It is not seemly to joke about such things."

"Don't you recognize my voice, Sophie?"

"You are someone pretending to be my cousin Susan. It is all part of a conspiracy to deprive me of my rights."

"Aren't you glad I'm alive, Sophie?"

"You are not alive!" Sophie screamed. "It is a plot against me. Everyone is plotting against me."

Suddenly she burst into tears. Never, in all the years she had known her, had Susan heard Sophie weep before.

In the background, she could hear a voice making soothing German noises. Sophie's wild sobbing receded.

"I am so sorry," a heavily accented voice said, "but Cousin Sophie has not been well. Please accept my felicitations for still being alive, Cousin Susan, and my hopes for your continued well-being."

So, when Mr. Tabor called that same afternoon, Miss Melville was almost glad to hear his voice. He sounded so sane and normal. She found herself looking forward to meeting him again.

At first it looked as if the café had been a good choice for their meeting. Although it was late September, the day was muggy, with none of fall's characteristic crispness, and the place was virtually deserted.

"A pleasant spot," Mr. Tabor agreed, blinking in the steamy sunlight, "and it is true that we are not likely to be overheard, but I must confess I would be happier indoors, all the same."

He dismissed the question of her putative skill at the outset. "Obviously the offer is contingent upon your ability to do the job. In the event—the remote event, I am sure—that you cannot regain your old skills on a consistent basis, well, then, we shall shake hands and part friends. However, I feel certain that even if you are a little rusty we shall soon have you back in top form."

Still, she couldn't help wondering, if she failed her trials, would it be as easy as all that? Could they afford to let her go with a handshake, now that she knew about them? Not that she knew all that much. How much did she actually know that anyone would believe? It was she who had shot Mark Sanderson. And they who had the gun with which she had done it.

There was no reason for them to do away with her if she couldn't or wouldn't work for them. On the other hand, if their hearts were really set on her services, they could all too easily blackmail her. Nonsense, she told herself, there's no reason for them to force me to work for them. I'm not that good.

"Now, let us get down to business," Mr. Tabor began.

"Very well, let's do that. First of all, I want it understood that I will not, er, take on an assignment unless the—the object—" that was a good, dispassionate way of describing the intended victim "—is utterly without redeeming social value."

"But that is understood. As I have already told you, we would not dream of taking on anyone who did not fall into that category. Believe me, there are quite enough people who do to give our organization full employment for the next century or two."

Could they really be as high-minded as all that? So long as they didn't ask her to do away with someone who wasn't completely vile, it would be presumptuous to concern herself with the assignments given other employees.

"Then . . ." She hesitated. Although she had been able to overcome her inhibitions against murder, it was less easy for her to come right out and discuss money. "There is the question of, er, my fee."

What a genteel way of expressing it, she thought. How utterly bourgeois. "How much do I get paid per hit?" she demanded.

He laughed. "Miss Melville, you are going to be a priceless addition to our staff. However, since we must name a price, shall we say five thousand dollars per assignment?"

Since she had no idea of what the going rate for an assassination was, she had no idea of whether the offer was fair or not. Her only experience of direct business dealing was when she had accompanied her mother on rug-buying expeditions in the Middle Eastern bazaars. She knew that you never accepted the opening offer; you were expected to bargain.

This didn't seem too much different from buying a rug, except that here she was selling, not buying. "Well, I will have expenses, and then there's the question of my apartment . . ."

"I assure you, if you work for us on a regular basis, you will earn more than enough to pay your rent."

Of course he'd know what her rent was. He'd know everything about her that had ever been fed into a computer or recorded in a file . . . or babbled out by her in a delirium.

"Maintenance," she reminded him. "Mark Sanderson's death won't stop the building from going co-op. And the work you're offering is hardly likely to give me a good enough credit rating so I can go to a bank and take out a loan."

"Don't worry, although we can't provide the usual job benefits, we do offer some. Once you are in our employ, a bank loan will be arranged on the most favorable terms. Now, does that cover everything?"

"One more thing. It may seem like a minor point to you—"

"Yoo-hoo, Susan, Susan Melville!" a voice called.

Perhaps the Stanhope hadn't been such a wise choice after all, she thought, as Amy Patterson, accompanied by a girl who looked like an unmade bed, materialized at their table.

"Tinsley and I were on our way to see the Treasures of the Seven Cities of Cibola. She's going to the Columbia School of Business, and she has to go see it for her course in Corporate Art. I thought I'd go with her because we both think it's important for parents and children to share cultural pursuits."

Tinsley grunted.

"And when I caught sight of you, I simply had to stop and say hello and welcome you back to the land of the living. Mimi told me you were alive; otherwise I would certainly have sent my condolences."

Amy looked at Mr. Tabor, who had risen to his feet with old-world courtesy. How would she explain him? Miss Melville wondered. Business associate? Amy would want to know what kind of business, not that it was any of hers. And if she made something up, she was likely to get into deeper water, even though, in his well-cut three-piece suit and handmade shoes, Alex did look a lot more businesslike than Tinsley, with her wrinkled tunic over calf-length skirt, and her ankle socks and sneakers or—what was it they called them now?—running shoes. Hardly what Miss Melville would have expected from a budding young executive.

She could not avoid introductions. "Amy Patterson . . . Tinsley Patterson . . . Alex Tabor."

I hope Amy doesn't think I'm the type to have a young

lover, Miss Melville thought—knowing that, given no plausible alternative, this was probably what Amy would think.

A model? No, that would be even worse, particularly since Amy might remember that Susan painted flowers.

Mr. Tabor bowed and kissed both ladies' hands, to Amy's delight and Tinsley's amazement.

Miss Melville didn't bother to ask the pair to join them. No need. Both sat down without being asked. Tinsley and Mr. Tabor eyed each other with interest.

"You don't have to tell me who this is," Amy beamed. "I knew the instant I saw him. I'd always been sure you never really lost touch with your father, Susan. You and he were always so close."

This is too much, Miss Melville thought.

"Look, Amy, I haven't heard from Buck since he left the country. I have no idea whether he's alive or dead. And I don't have the least idea of what you're talking about."

"Come, Susan, don't pretend with me. This is your young brother from Brazil, isn't it. He looks so much like your father it's uncanny."

Mr. Tabor had a fit of coughing. "Old war wound," he apologized.

As a matter of fact, he didn't look a bit like Buck Melville. The only resemblance was that both were (had been?) dark and handsome and up to no good—although, of course, that didn't show.

"You're quite mistaken . . ." Miss Melville began, and looked for Mr. Tabor to help her out with his customary resourcefulness.

He grinned like an exotic Cheshire Cat. "We prefer to put it on the basis of a distant connection. For the family's sake."

"Of course, we quite understand, don't we, Tinsley?"

"Oh, absolutely," Tinsley said.

Miss Melville wished she could say the same. As soon

as Amy and Tinsley had left, which wasn't nearly as soon as she could have wished, she burst out, "Why did you let her think you were my brother?"

"It made things so much simpler. How else could you have accounted for me? You couldn't be my aunt; she probably knows you have no brothers or sisters."

He didn't say, "And it was your idea to meet at the Stanhope," or even, "I told you so."

He didn't have to. Next time they would meet at a McDonald's or a Chomp House—somewhere she couldn't possibly run into anyone she knew. Even the crashers held themselves above such places; when you've been accustomed to sneaking into hundred-dollar-a-plate dinners, you get choosy.

"You seemed to know what she was talking about. About my father, I mean."

"Believe me, Susan—as your brother, I must call you Susan, must I not?—I am sure you are aware that we had to check into your background very thoroughly before we could offer you employment."

"You aren't really my brother, are you?"

He shook his head. "That would be too much of a coincidence. No, I am not your brother."

He saw the question in her face. "Your father died some years ago—without issue, as they say. And," although she hadn't been about to ask, "without money."

She was silent, twirling the glass in her hand. She could see no reason for him to lie to her. Someday she would ask him about her father during the twenty-odd years since she had last seen him, how he had lived and how he had died—and why he had never gotten in touch with her, even after the statue of limitations ran out. But not now; there was too much of the present to think about . . .

"Before the ladies joined us, you were saying there was one more thing to be considered," he reminded her.

She had to stop and think. "Yes, yes of course. Just

how do you propose to pay me? I mean, what form would the payment take?''

He looked surprised. "Cash, of course. You must know that from the cinema. What do you want? Traveler's checks?''

"Your other employees are probably—well, they're used to accounting for large sums of cash, or, rather, to not accounting for it at all. I'm not. There would be no way I could explain how I make my living. How would I declare it on my income tax?''

He was shocked. "Your income tax? My dear Miss Melville, nobody pays taxes on hit money! It simply isn't done.''

"And nobody in my circumstances fails to pay her taxes, either. If you're rich, you might be able to get away with it, but not if you're of modest means and a law-abiding—previously law-abiding—disposition, and come from a family in which the IRS takes an abiding interest.''

He looked thoughtful. "You are right—all that does present a problem. Of course you would not have prepared a cover. We could arrange for an inheritance tied up in a trust. No, that could present even more problems.''

She already had a solution in mind; she'd just wanted to make sure he was aware there was no alternative before she broached it.

"If you've looked into my background, you must know that I'm a painter.''

"And a very good one, I understand. One day you must show me your work. However—''

"I propose that each time I carry out an assignment for your employer, he should 'buy' a painting from me. That would account for the money, and he could pay me by check.''

He raised an eyebrow.

"Oh, don't look at me like that. The check doesn't have to be in his name. He can establish a corporation to invest in art. It's done all the time, quite legitimately.''

He rubbed his smooth olive cheek. "The idea being, I suppose, that to the world you will present the appearance of a working artist who lives on the proceeds from her painting."

"The idea being that I will present the *reality* of a working artist who is living on the proceeds from her painting. Which means that, since my paintings have value over and beyond my, er, other services, I think I should get more than five thousand dollars per assignment. Shall we say ten thousand dollars?"

He smiled. "You drive a hard bargain, Miss Melville. Shall we split the difference and say seven thousand five hundred to begin with? With a rise to ten thousand after you have completed a few successful assignments?"

Since she was still new to the art of bargaining, she had to be content with this, although she realized she could have gotten ten thousand—perhaps even more than ten thousand—from the outset, if she had persisted. One step at a time, she told herself. You're doing very well for a beginner.

She started to rise and Alex Tabor rose with her.

She sat down again.

He sat down, too.

"What happens if I get caught?" she asked.

He gave her a reproachful look. "A cinema enthusiast like yourself must know the answer to that: you will be on your own. There is nothing we will be able to do to help you."

"That's for spies," she said, "not assassins."

"It applies to assassins as well. The two categories overlap. Oh, we might be able to give you some discreet assistance behind the scenes, arrange for bail, suggest a lawyer, but—" he spread his hands wide "—nothing overt, you understand."

"I understand," she said. "But—"

"Another thing. The contingency is remote, of course, but if it should come to pass that you do fall into the hands of the law, you will not mention our existence to the authorities or to the media. In the first place, there is no way you could prove it. They would not believe you."

"Some of the weekly tabloids might," she suggested.

"Yes, but nobody would believe *them*. Which brings me to my second point. My employer has an arm that is even longer than that of the law. If you even tried to talk . . ." He made a gesture that wasn't as explicit as drawing his finger across his throat. It didn't need to be.

He got up and reached out a hand to her. "But enough of dwelling on the dark side of things. You will not get caught, Miss Melville, I assure you. You are far too clever for that—and, if you should by any chance happen to attract the law's attention, all you have to do is deny everything. Nobody would believe that a woman of your birth and breeding, a Melville, could possibly have anything to do with a paid assassination. The idea would be ridiculous."

He was right. It did sound ridiculous, at that.

✧✧✧ **XIV**

One fine morning a week later, Mr. Tabor, dressed less formally than usual in a natty Brooks Brothers blazer and slacks, arrived in a silver Mercedes and took her to a wooded area somewhere in Westchester, she thought, or it might have been Rockland County. He used back roads so she could never be sure exactly where they were.

It seemed remote from human habitation, except that from time to time she heard a dog bark, and usually dogs have owners. Otherwise it was very quiet, except for the crunch of the leaves under their feet.

He set up the target in a clearing.

She was nervous. "Suppose someone sees us."

"Suppose someone does. A man takes his sister—or his aunt or a friend—to the woods for a little target practice. Nothing wrong with that."

"With a target like *that*?"

The target he had brought with him was in the shape of a human being, a man.

"No use wasting time with bull's-eyes. You are not going to be shooting bulls."

When she still demurred he added, "You will notice that it is not a custom-made affair but a commercial product. People do not practice with hand guns in order to shoot game. They are interested in defending themselves, a matter of great concern nowadays, especially to the ladies. It is a very violent world that we live in."

"Supposing the owner of the property comes along?"

"I have permission to practice here."

She had thought as much.

"And there is no need to worry about a possible accident. Nobody will come this way."

The dog barked again, closer this time. She heard no footsteps, but she had a distinct feeling that someone was watching them, and that Mr. Tabor was very well aware of it.

It made her nervous and she fumbled her first few shots. Once she had gotten over her initial self-consciousness, however, she found that she had not lost her skill.

What had worried her most was her eyes. She was beginning to need glasses to read, but her far sight did not seem to have been affected. In fact it seemed to have improved. And she had no trouble adjusting to the newer, more sophisticated weapons he had brought with him. In fact, she found them a pleasure to handle.

The only thing that troubled her was the silencer, which

he produced toward the end of the session and insisted that she try. If anyone came upon them and saw her shooting with the silencer, it could hardly be passed off as an innocent outing.

By this time she knew, though, that no one would come upon them.

She didn't like the silencer; she felt it spoiled her aim. "A few more sessions of practice," Mr. Tabor said, "and you will hardly notice it is there."

"Do you mean I am going to have to use one of these every time?"

"Not every time, especially with the noise levels in most public places. But you must become accustomed to it, in case there should be a need."

It took away from the sport—but then this wasn't sport, was it? she thought.

"You have done very well," he told her as they packed up for the day. She couldn't help feeling pleased.

On the way back to the city, they stopped at an old-fashioned ice cream parlor in Riverdale for sodas. It was a place very like it that her father had taken her to after they had driven out to the country for a day of shooting, and they also had ordered ice cream sodas. Unlike most things remembered from childhood, these tasted just as good now as they had then.

"We must do this again," Mr. Tabor said as he dropped her off at her front door.

"Thank you for a very pleasant day," she said for the benefit of the doorman, but it really was true; she had enjoyed herself in a way she hadn't done in years. It was like going back in time.

◇◇◇ **XV**

Two weeks after their shooting session, Miss Melville was given her first assignment. The chosen victim was the cult leader who called himself the Reverend Bliss. According to her research and the dossier Mr. Tabor had given her, the Reverend Bliss professed to have come from a planet that circled a star in a distant galaxy. His stated purpose was to bring the Word of the All-Powerful Omneity to the people of Earth.

In the year 2007, according to *The Book of Bliss*, the Reverend Bliss was scheduled to return to the Sacred Planet, taking with him those Accepted Ones who had passed through the various stages of Exaltation and Beatitude and were ready to become one with the Omneity, while the rest of the people of Earth were doomed to perish along with their planet in a series of disasters both natural and unnatural, including fire, flame, wind and the malignant attentions of various unspecified numina, most of which seemed to Miss Melville to be a direct swipe from the *Book of Revelation*.

In order to achieve the state of Ultimate Acceptance, the neophyte was required to give up all his worldly goods and join one of the Temples of Bliss that the Master (as the Reverend Bliss was informally called by his disciples) had established at various locales throughout the world, principally in the United States, as most other so-called unenlightened countries lacked the equivalents of the First Amendment or the Civil Liberties Union. Although names

114

of the Reverend Bliss's sanctuaries seemed to indicate some sort of affinity with Dodo Pangborn's ill-fated establishment, any resemblance between the two was mere semantic accident. Chastity, obedience and poverty were required of all the Blissful; and, far from being a tax shelter, the Temple of Bliss dedicated all of its assets to the Omneity in the person of its Surrogate, the Reverend Bliss, who, as a man of the cloth, of course paid no taxes at all.

According to Bliss's spokespeople, his followers numbered in the millions, while the media put the number in the hundreds of thousands. Both agreed that whatever the figure, it was increasing rapidly; there seemed to be a need for spiritual guidance that the Reverend Bliss was able to fill in his own extragalactic way.

The Temple was supported not only by the investments made by the Sacred Council, (which consisted of the Master himself, his wife, his brother and his two oldest children), but by the Labours of Love the Accepted Ones performed for the Cosmic Cause. Those, in addition to basic spiritual duties, included peddling herbal remedies and fruitcake, offering street entertainment of an uplifting nature, operating fleamarkets, and housecleaning.

"Although how they can work in those gauzy robes is beyond me," said an acquaintance of Miss Melville's who had once employed a Blissful cleaning lady, firing her only after she had converted her employers' three post-adolescent children to the cause. All had left home to join a Temple of Bliss in Poughkeepsie. Miss Melville wondered whether Fenella had ever succeeded in retrieving them, or whether they were off banging tambourines somewhere.

Nominally, today's dinner was in honor of Oneness Day (the big holiday on the Sacred Planet). In actual fact it was to provide the platform for a pitch to new members and to attract Semi-Accepted Ones from among those who, although reluctant to give up everything to follow the Master, might be persuaded to give something as a hedge against Doomsday.

Until the evening before, Miss Melville had felt confident that she would have no trouble in knocking off the Master without a qualm. Lying awake that night, she found herself counting qualms instead of sheep. It was one thing to kill Mark Sanderson on impulse; quite another to set out in cold blood to eliminate someone, no matter how worthy of elimination that individual was.

She tried to psych herself into an appropriate attitude, but by morning she had reached the conclusion that it was no use. She had lost her nerve. She simply could not go through with it.

She would have to call Mr. Tabor and tell him he'd have to get someone else to do the job.

The trouble was that she couldn't call Mr. Tabor. He had neglected to give her his telephone number, even though she had asked for it on more than one occasion.

"I must arrange something," he had promised, but never did. She suspected he never intended to.

The next time she spoke to him she would insist. There could be dozens of reasons why she might need to get in touch with him. She could be sick. She could be stranded. She could have cold feet. She did have cold feet.

There was no way to reach him now, and she was afraid simply not to show up. And there was an even more compelling reason why she couldn't chicken out. She had burned her bridges behind her; she had called Mimi to tell her she couldn't take the job at the Foundation; she had accepted another job offer.

When pressed, she said she'd been commissioned by a collector to do a series of paintings for him—which was the best she could do on the spur of the moment.

"But that isn't a *job*," Mimi argued. "Surely you can work for us and paint too. I assure you, the hours won't be onerous. And Oliver needs you. He's a wonderful administrator but he has no head for detail."

"I can't, Mimi. He—the collector, that is—wants me to devote all my time to the paintings."

She realized belatedly that she should have prepared herself with a plausible story before she phoned. No wonder Mimi got suspicious, especially after Miss Melville refused to divulge the collector's identity.

"You aren't doing art forgeries or anything like that, are you? Not that I think you would stoop to such a thing, but you're acting so *furtive*. Believe me, Susan, they've grown very cunning about detecting fakes these days. They use radiation and chemicals and lasers and all kinds of technological devices. Why, some of our most treasured masterpieces have turned out to be frauds, and some of our Old Masters nothing more than crooks. It's heartbreaking. Only the other day, Tom—he used to be with the Met, you remember, was telling me—"

"—Mimi, it's quite legitimate."

The painting part of it was, anyway, so it wasn't a complete fiction. "It's just that he—he doesn't want anyone to know he's collecting."

"But what's the point of collecting if you don't tell people about it?"

"You'd have to ask him. That is, if I could tell you who he is, but I'm sworn to secrecy."

"But surely you can tell *me*. After all, I'm your oldest friend. We've always told each other everything."

Which was not and never had been true. Perhaps in the old days Mimi had told Susan everything, but Susan had never reciprocated with her confidences. Not only was Mimi a blabbermouth of the first order, she tended to confuse facts, or, rather, to rearrange them to conform with her own interpretation of reality.

Mimi should have been a modern painter, Susan had often thought. She had the vision for it.

"I'm sorry, Mimi. I'd love to be able to tell you who he is, but I gave him my word."

"Oh, very well, but I'll bet he's underpaying you grossly, and that's why he wants to keep everything so secret. I would be the last person to stand in the way of your art, dear, but I think you're making a mistake in not coming to work for us.''

"I'm sorry I can't, Mimi. I really would have liked to, but—''

"I understand. Your art is your life.''

"You could put it that way . . .''

The loan for the down payment on the apartment came through as promised, from a small private bank that Miss Melville had never heard of before. On reaching the address she'd been given, however, she realized she had passed the modestly proportioned limestone building a thousand times without ever having noticed the discreet brass plate outside indicating that a financial institution was to be found within.

The interior was palatial even by private bank standards. She was received by a stately silver-haired lady in a luxurious anteroom dominated by a large-scale Poussin depicting the Israelites worshiping the golden calf. She was then ushered into an even more luxurious office that contained an oversize Tintoretto version of Christ chasing the moneylenders out of the temple (somebody here must have a curious sense of humor, she thought). A dignified gentleman with a British accent that overlaid something slightly more exotic conducted the interview, offering her terms so favorable that they would have aroused interest in anyone who became aware of them. However, as both she and Mr. Kahn implicitly agreed, there was no reason in the world why anyone outside of themselves should be aware of their arrangement.

The final papers had not been signed, though. She knew the loan would not go through until she had completed her first assignment successfully. There really was no choice but for her to go ahead.

Everybody's nervous the first day on a job, she assured herself. For all she knew, that was true.

* * *

The Blissful festivities were to take place in the main ballroom of the Grand, one of the easiest places to crash. It
was so large and had so many entrances, including several
underground passageways, that it was difficult to provide
effective security.

Tonight, however, she would not crash. Still a beginner
at this game, she had thought to avoid one source of potential trouble by paying the modest fifty dollars at which
a plate was priced—no doubt to ensure a packed house. It
was only after the attendant Accepted One offered her a
receipt (for tax purposes) that she realized her error. Fortunately the crowds were so great that her refusal passed
unnoticed.

Next time she would know better.

At first glance security seemed lighter than usual—nonexistent, in fact; for the husky-looking men in uniforms
and, sometimes, tuxedos, usually present at such events,
were not evident. However, among the pale and scrawny
flock of disciples fluttering around the ballroom like diso-
riented moths, there were several healthy-looking men of
powerful physique who seemed embarrassed by the flowing
robes of pastel gauze draped around their massive forms.

". . . The various colors of garment," the elderly man
in pince-nez who appeared to be a representative of the
Reverend Bliss in mufti said to the guests at the table to
which Miss Melville had been assigned, "represent the
various steps of Exaltation through which the Seeker
advances until he reaches the final level. The colors
range from the earthbound apricot to the transcendental tur-
quois . . ."

The undercover guards, Miss Melville noted, were all
appropriately clad in apricot. Really, she thought, they
should have either worn slips or shaved their legs.

Miss Melville didn't see any of the crashers she knew
except Freddy Makepeace, who was sitting near the front.
It was understandable why most crashers would tend to
shun this event. Why go to the trouble of crashing a fifty-

dollar-a-plate vegetarian dinner when you could just as easily crash a hundred- or two-hundred-dollar-a-plate meal with medallions of veal or, at the very least, chicken marengo?

She was glad to note Freddy's presence, as he could be counted on to make a disturbance. As usual, however, she tried to make sure that he did not catch sight of her. At the best of times, he was an embarrassing acquaintance, given to expressing noble sentiments at the top of his lungs. Right now it would be awkward to have anyone claim acquaintance with her.

Felix, she thanked the All-Powerful Omneity, was not there either; otherwise, he was bound to try to attach himself to her. Miss Melville had been the object of his attentions ever since the day Rhonda had introduced him to her at a benefit for unemployed thremmatologists. In his clumsy way he reminded her of the young and not-so-young men who had tried to attach themselves to her in the days when her family still had money.

Felix had no such motive. He liked her for herself, which only went to show how meaningless motives were.

"On this occasion," Mr. Tabor had told her, "you will have no need for a silencer."

She now understood why. A group of individuals wearing the rose and mauve draperies of disciples on the way up from Exaltation to Beatitude were assaulting the ears with flutes, cymbals, drums, tambourines and other instruments. She could not tell whether the resultant cacophony resulted from lack of skill or whether that was what it was intended to sound like. It was almost worse than rock, so she was grateful that it muted as the food was served; otherwise she feared for its potential effects upon her digestion.

The meal proved to be edible if not palatable. At least, since it was vegetarian, she could be assured that the things that looked like worms must be sprouts or something of that ilk. The mushrooms looked odd as well, but surely the Reverend Bill's followers must know their fungi.

The Reverend Bliss himself did not share the meal but sat rotund and smiling upon the dais, spreading what the literature had described as his "Ineffable Aura" over those gathered around him. The Master had reached so Exalted a State of Being, the gentleman in pince-nez explained, that he no longer required physical sustenance. He had probably pigged out in a fast-food place beforehand, Miss Melville thought. He was too shiny to be a vegetarian.

"But he's a human being," a pink-haired lady at the table protested. "I thought he came from the stars."

"He went from the Earth to the stars," their mentor explained, "and came back with a message for all humankind . . ."

A number of the guests sitting up front, near Freddy, ate little if anything, but they hardly looked as if they had reached an Exalted State of Being. They didn't look like guests at a festive occasion either. They were too determined-looking, too grim.

Not fans of the Reverend's, she deduced. Doctrinal opponents. Parents and loved ones of those who had been Accepted. Troublemakers all. Good.

The television cameras were out in full force. Television cameras were often present at the events she crashed, but coverage was usually routine, a courtesy to the organization, the names involved, and network stockholders. Beyond that, there was always the hope that the ceiling might collapse or the building catch fire to keep up the morale of the second-stringers usually assigned to cover such routine events.

At last the meal came to an end. The music grew loud again, while the disciples behind the Reverend Bliss chanted in what the gentleman in pince-nez explained was the secret language the Reverend Bliss had brought back from the stars. It sounded to Miss Melville like a cross between Esperanto and Welsh.

The chanting grew softer as the Reverend Bliss—clad in robes of palest blue, sparkling with what were, according to *People* magazine, genuine diamonds—rose to speak. The lights in the ballroom dimmed, and a spotlight hit him in such a way as to make it look as if a halo were hovering over his gleaming dome.

Freddy got up also, as did several of the other people up front. The aura surrounding them was definitely hostile. The security guards, still clinging to their cover, glided toward the dais. The television crews followed.

Since the Reverend Bliss was rather short, he was almost hidden from view. The guests at the tables started getting up in order to see him. Miss Melville followed suit. As some started to move toward the dais, she moved along with them, taking care always to take shelter in the shadows behind the glare of the television lights. It was like a great rippling movement of people and machinery, slowly converging on the dais.

A man in a tuxedo rose and, after delivering a lengthy and rather woolly speech about the joys of Blissfulness, concluded with, "And now you will have the indescribable joy of hearing the message that the Reverend Bliss has brought back from the stars."

This was true only in part. The crowd, especially those nearest to the stage, was beginning to get noisy. Only at intervals did the voice of the Master manage to penetrate the shrieks and howls.

He had a slight lisp, which the amplification accentuated. ". . . People of Earth . . . blethings . . . therve the Great Omneity . . . methenger of peath and therenity . . . thave your thouls . . . learn thelf-denial . . . thelf-control . . . thelf-thacrifith . . ."

Somebody should have advised him to avoid words with esses in them.

Vision was obscured by the television equipment and the

increasing press of bodies. As the crowd shifted and parted, Miss Melville could only occasionally catch a glimpse of her quarry. Her concern was not how she should conceal herself—there was no problem in that respect—but how she could see in order to take aim.

Suddenly, over the heads of the crowd, two pudgy hands appeared, followed by two arms swathed in pale blue mousseline and upraised, whether in benediction or malediction it was impossible to say. By that time the din of the crowd had drowned out the Master's voice completely.

At that point the music began to play loudly, augmented by a systhesized organ, and the rest of the Reverend Bliss came into view, bit by bit, floating upward.

He hung poised over the dais, apparently without support.

"By God, he's levitating!" someone cried.

For a moment the crowd was silent. The music swelled. Miss Melville, still standing in the cover of the shadows behind the television lights, took comfortable aim and fired.

The Reverend Bliss gave a squeal and disappeared like a punctured balloon. The crowd surged onto the dais and engulfed it completely. There were shouts and screams and the sound of glass breaking.

Miss Melville dropped her gun into her bag and snapped it shut. Mr. Tabor had told her to pick up the spent shell, but she was reluctant to stoop and scrabble in the shadows among people's feet. So what if they found the remains of the shell later? By that time they were bound to know a gun had been fired.

She turned, with the idea of observing to no one in particular that at least with the established religions one knew what to expect, when she realized that there was no one to observe it to. The affair had divided into riot and rout, with those guests who were not participating in the former fleeing by every exit. From now on the Grand would be more careful to whom it rented its facilities, Miss Melville thought. She spotted a small door half hidden by draperies and marked, "No Admittance—Employees Only." She blissfully passed through unnoticed.

✧✧✧ XVI

Mr. Tabor had given Miss Melville careful instructions on what she was to do next, but she could not make herself follow the procedure he had laid out for her, especially since nothing else was working according to plan. Instead of going upstairs to the ladies room she walked along a narrow passageway and down a flight of service stairs, colliding at the foot with a man in hotel uniform.

For a moment she felt panic, but quickly recovered. "There's a riot upstairs in the main ballroom. Could you tell me how I could get back to the lobby?" she asked, although she knew the way perfectly well.

The man pointed mutely in the right direction and turned as if to go back up the stairs to see for himself. The sounds of shrieks, screams, and crashes came clearly from above. He paused, gave her a weak smile, and plunged back into the recesses of the hotel.

The news seemed to have traveled fast, she noted, as she reconnected with the guests eddying in the lobby. More cameras were there as well as representatives of, she supposed, the print media, accosting selected departing guests.

Ignoring Mr. Tabor's instruction to "saunter," she marched directly to the Chomp House that he had chosen as a rendezvous—partly, he told her, because of its anonymity, and partly because of its convenient location vis à vis the Grand.

He was reading, or pretending to read, the *Times* and eating what she recognized from General Chomsky's commercials as a Grand Slamburger, complete with sesame seed roll, two kinds of cheese, pickle, the General's special dressing, French fried potatoes, and onion rings.

He sprang to his feet. "I didn't expect you so soon. Did anything go wrong?"

She sat down opposite him. "Nothing went wrong, mission accomplished . . . Good Heavens," she said, looking around, for she had never actually been inside a Chomp House before. "There are pictures on the walls even *here*!"

"I believe they have them in all the Chomp Houses," he said mechanically. "It was the first fast food chain to decorate its restaurants with so-called fine art, but I understand Wendy's is following suit."

"How interesting," she said.

"I fear I am unable to understand this type of art, and I gather you do not, either."

"Oh, I understand it," she said. "It springs from a creative nexus that concerns itself less with representational objecthood than with attitudinal function. Reality has metamorphosed into metaphor. Objects and space are destroyed and reassembled into a kinetic continuum that resonates psychologically within the consciousness rather than being recorded passively by the retina. It's just that it isn't what I myself would call art. I suppose I am old-fashioned. Just the same—"

"—Please," he interrupted, "enough of this aesthetic chit-chat." He was perspiring slightly. "Did everything go all right? Did you do what you were supposed to?"

She was feeling a curious sense of elation, lightheadedness, almost as if she were drunk. More than that, almost as if she were someone else, born again.

"Piece of cake," she said. "I just stood behind the television lights and shot him. Like that!"

She was about to point her finger and say "bang," but she realized that this would not go down well just then.

"You were *televised*?"

"Oh, *I* wasn't televised. I kept well out of the cameras' way. You shouldn't be so surprised they were there. They're everywhere these days, and the Reverend Bliss always makes—made, that is—news. And the cameras made things easier for me. The lights create such a glare it's next to impossible to see anything behind them," she said.

"I wish I had thought to bring a radio," he said.

Suddenly she was angry. "What's the matter? Don't you believe me? Don't you think I did it?"

"Please keep your voice down," he begged. "Of course I believe you did it, but I would like to have the details from a—shall we say more objective point of view."

It must have been the levitation that bothered him, she decided. "I need a drink," she said.

His courtesy, although strained, was undiminished. "Don't you think it is possible that you may have had . . . ah . . . a little too much to drink already?"

"You gave me his dossier. You should know that the Reverend Bliss doesn't approve of alcohol. Nothing but mineral water and vegetable juice have passed my lips tonight."

"Regrettably, the Chomp Houses do not have liquor licenses. How about a Kreemishake or a Frosty Froot Float? You could also have plain soda or coffee."

She chose coffee, although it wasn't what she'd had in mind. When she tasted it, she discovered it wasn't what she'd had in mind when she asked for coffee, either. Disappointment made her blunter than she might otherwise have been. "Do I get paid now, or do you want to wait until my story is confirmed?"

"No, I trust you, of course."

He reached into his pocket and handed her an envelope. She tore it open, examining the check with satisfaction.

"You must not be so obvious. Glance at it quickly to make sure I have not cheated you, then put it in your bag."

She had changed already. Never before when she had been given a check—for a gift, for her salary, for a painting—would she have looked at it while the giver was present.

Her embarrassment was only momentary. She was a businesswoman now; it was only natural for her to be crude and vulgar. "Oh, I almost forgot. Here's your gun."

"I told you: never, never hand the gun directly to me. Slip it into my briefcase. Next time, sit down next to me, instead of across the table. No, don't get up now, let me have it under the table."

He gave an exclamation as the cold steel hit his hand. "But why is it naked? I thought I told you to wrap it in something."

"I did. I brought it in a stocking."

He looked at her.

"A stocking mask, you know."

She tried to explain, but it didn't make too much sense now, although it had seemed perfectly reasonable at the time. "I must have been confused; it should have been I who wore the stocking mask, except that it would have made me rather conspicuous. A scarf would have been better. For the gun, I mean."

"Much better," he agreed.

"I'd planned to rewrap it afterward, just as you told me, but I thought it would look funny to stop at the powder room in the middle of a riot. Anyhow, when there's a general stampede, you're not conspicuous if you leave the place in a hurry . . . Oh, stop looking at me like that, as if you thought I just got out of there as fast as I could. Considering this was my first assignment, I thought I did pretty well."

He sighed and mopped his forehead. "You did very well, very well, indeed. My congratulations. I didn't mean to carp. It is just that—well, in a way I suppose I was more nervous than you were.''

As well he might be, she thought. His future was probably riding as much on the outcome of her performance as hers was.

In spite of its taste, the coffee must have had all the right chemical components, because she was beginning to feel more like her old self. ''I'm sorry I didn't bring your painting with me. I had a nice one picked out, but it was a little large to carry conveniently. Besides, they would probably have made me check it—''

''Believe me, Miss Melville, I did not expect you to bring the picture along with you tonight. There is no hurry. I can get it when I bring you the gun for your next assignment.''

''Oh, but I insist you get it this week. I want your employer to have it as soon as possible. Otherwise, I'll feel you're not taking me seriously.''

''I assure you, Miss Melville, I am taking you—we both are taking you—very seriously indeed.''

He did not offer to take her home. In fact, the way he looked when they parted made her wonder whether she should have offered to escort *him*.

But she forbore. Men tended to be sensitive about such things.

When she got home and turned on the late news, she found she'd been mistaken about having evaded the television cameras. One long shot showed her as part of the fleeing crowd . . . but there was nothing to indicate that she was anything other than another guest on the run.

At that time it was still believed that the Reverend Milton Bliss had been trampled to death by the crowd. It wasn't until the next day that the coroner's office discovered he had been shot, whereupon at least a dozen organizations claimed credit for the deed, including some that Miss Melville disapproved of as much as she had the Reverend Bliss.

No way of knowing which, if any, had actually subsidized his removal. Mr. Tabor had refused to divulge the name of her sponsor; that was privileged information, he'd said. And, of course, if it was a respectable organization it probably wouldn't be in a position to accept public responsibility.

The employees of the hotel were interviewed on TV and in print. Several reported having run into fleeing guests in places where guests, fleeing or otherwise, should not have been. No one mentioned seeing anyone like her.

Well, that was one of the reasons why she had been hired, she thought.

Ten days later, she met Mr. Tabor at a restaurant in Soho, where everything looked seedy except the prices on the menu. She gave him a large flat brown paper parcel. "If your employer doesn't like it, I can bring you some others to choose from."

"I am sure that the choice you have made will be excellent."

"Just make sure that your employer sees it."

"No need to worry, he will not only see it, he will treasure it. Now that he has set up the corporation, he will need your paintings to justify the checks."

Which meant that her painting would be preserved and perhaps someday, even if not now, appreciated.

◊◊◊ XVII

Her second assignment was to do away with the bestselling author of *Back to the Kitchen* at an afternoon book-signing party in one of the chain bookstores. Although the author was eminently qualified as a candidate for elimination, being also the author of *Adam's Rib Roast* as well as other unspeakable crimes against humanity and the English language, she refused to accept unless Mr. Tabor would give her some means of reaching him in an emergency.

Finally he gave in and gave her a number, stressing that she was to use it "only if there is actual need, not because you need someone to hold your hand."

"I never need anyone to hold my hand," she said.

"It is nothing to be ashamed of. Each one of us needs support at one time or another. However, for people in our line of work, it is never a good idea to seek comfort on the telephone. If you do call, you must observe the greatest discretion. If you get the answering machine, do not say anything more than 'Susan wishes to speak to Alex.' You may add, 'at his earliest convenience,' if the matter is truly urgent."

Whom did he expect to answer his phone? Or pick up his messages? The Boss, as she persisted in thinking of their employer? More likely a colleague or a girlfriend, possibly even a wife. He might even have children. Perhaps his father or, to be even-handed, his mother had been a hired killer and he himself an infant assassin, brought up to the family trade.

Was he simply afraid of eavesdroppers? In that case, wouldn't she be equally vulnerable?

Better not think about it, or she would become like poor Louanne Comstock, who thought strange men were always following her and came to a bad end.

Aside from the fact that this time she did need to use a silencer, the job was ridiculously easy. Although security guards were posted at all the doors of the large midtown bookstore sponsoring the event, their purpose was to keep customers from carrying out unpaid-for books, not to keep them from killing each other. As for the sales clerks, it was difficult to attract their attention at the best of times.

Affecting to browse along a route that led her away from the table where the author, surrounded by his admirers—mostly female, of the suburban persuasion—was busy scribbling fulsome sentiments in the volumes being handed over, she stopped and stationed herself behind a rack of self-improvement books that stood a few feet to the rear of the crowd.

The top row of books was level with her head. Making a gap between *Power Jogging* and *Starve Your Way to Success,* she pushed the barrel of her gun through, sighted on the bald spot on the back of his head and fired.

The author fell forward onto the table, amid an anxious twittering.

She dropped the gun back into the Bonwit Teller bag in which she had brought it and put both into the Channel Thirteen tote, purchased at a thrift shop especially for the occasion, then walked calmly to the door and showed her sales slip to the guard.

She'd felt she owed it to the store to buy a book, so before carrying out her assignment, she had purchased a copy of the *World Almanac*, reasonably priced and always useful. Ignoring the commotion and screams that were now coming from within—so many rock stars and their adherents had written books that he probably thought the noise was a normal concomitant of autographing parties—the guard waved her out with a smile and an "Enjoy your book."

She met Mr. Tabor at a Burger King on Sixth Avenue, where she found him consuming a Whopper ("I always choose the *specialité de la maison*," he explained). She gave him the gun, made an appointment for their next rendezvous, and that was that.

Miss Melville refused the next assignment Mr. Tabor offered her. It wasn't because she didn't feel that the intended target, a well-known criminal lawyer who had saved many a malefactor from receiving his just desserts, among other crimes, was undeserving of her attention, but that she didn't care for the modus operandi Mr. Tabor had chosen. She was to pose as a dog walker in Central Park and pot her quarry when he came jogging past. This did not seem feasible to her, even though the Organization had undertaken to supply an appropriate animal.

"In the first place, it would require more confidence in the dog than I could possibly muster on such short acquaintance. In the second, I doubt that I know the terrain well enough these days to be able to make an effective getaway. I haven't gone into the park for years; it's become much too dangerous. He's associated with so many causes. Surely he must go to benefits or dinner dances or premieres."

"He is a health enthusiast. Early to bed, and so forth. Megavitamins, seaweed, sprouts. Contributes to the appropriate causes, but rarely goes to public festivities."

"How about poisoning his yogurt?"

Mr. Tabor shook his head. "Obviously, in many cases it would be much simpler to poison the intended target or push him or her under a train or out of a window than to shoot him or, in extreme cases, blow him up. But that's another department entirely. The death must be unmistakably an assassination. It is important for media purposes that a definite statement by made. Natural causes may be sufficient to make an impression on those who hold strong religious beliefs, but the unbelieving masses need to have it made clear to them that the chosen one was punished for his sins through a human agency."

Not only that, she thought, but if a death appeared to derive from natural causes, there might be some question about payment, even though she supposed the Boss required payment in advance. Good will was so important to the small businessman, especially the one who had to rely on word-of-mouth advertising. How did the Boss get his clients? she wondered. Probably through having the right contacts, like everyone else.

A few weeks later she heard that the lawyer had been dispatched by a speeding bicyclist, who had not made a neat job of it at all. But what could you expect from someone who rode a bicycle? The lawyer, too, received his quota of commercials: "An educated consumer is our best customer" . . . "Share the fantasy" . . . "Reach out and touch someone" . . . "I personally guarantee it" . . . "Chomp House take-outs are the best; just pick up your phone, and we do the rest . . ."

Her next target was a woman, a magazine editor who had brought new dimensions to the publishing world by combining soft-core pornography with knitting patterns. But it was her ruthlessness in dealing with rivals, as well as other crimes so disgusting that even the weekly tabloids could do no more than hint at them, that made her obliteration seem right and necessary.

"And we do hope you'll be able to undertake this assignment," Mr. Tabor said, "because you are our only female, er, operative, and the others are reluctant to assassinate ladies."

"That sounds bigoted to me."

"It is bigoted. We all have our prejudices—even you, Miss Melville. But we try to keep the members of our Organization happy. Within reason, naturally."

Unfortunately, her first attempt—which was to be made at the Women in Communications Award Dinner at the Waldorf—failed through no fault of hers.

She had gone to a cocktail reception on the *Intrepid*, in honor of somebody she'd never heard of, sponsored by an organization equally unknown to her. Afterward, unable to get a cab to the East Side, she was forced to take the Fiftieth Street crosstown, expecting to be let off at Park Avenue.

Instead, the bus lurched past what should have been the

Park Avenue stop and carried her to the far side of Lexington Avenue. Later she found out that the Waldorf had arranged for the Transportation Authority to discontinue that stop because disembarking passengers interfered with the smooth flow of limousines. Still, she had lost time in making her way to the Waldorf, and to make matters worse she ran into Felix, who was on his way to join some of the other crashers at a festivity at the Summit. On discovering whither she was headed, he attached himself to her so that she was forced to cancel her own plans.

"We'll gladly poison *his* yogurt for you at no charge," Mr. Tabor offered when told the cause of the aborted mission—whether in jest or not, she could not be sure.

"No, thank you. Anyway, he doesn't eat yogurt."

Which was not true. Felix would eat anything. And although he had no redeeming social value, he was too insignificant to merit assassination. The world would not be a better place without him, although it would be no worse off either.

She carried out her mission handily some days later at a reception at the Ephemeron Club, sponsored by the Amelia Bloomer Association in aid of oppressed women's magazine writers behind the Iron Curtain. There was much public mourning and private glee, although this time no one claimed credit, probably because the victim was a woman. Even our crackpots are chauvinists, she thought.

It was at this point that she summoned up the nerve to tell Mr. Tabor she felt she should be raised to ten thousand dollars per removal. He agreed so readily, she had a feeling that once again she had sold her services too cheap.

Of course, even though her income still came nowhere near what her allowance had been in the old days of affluence, she was making more money than she had ever earned before. Still, she should be making even more. Because I'm worth it, she told herself, echoing a familiar hair-coloring commercial.

* * *

Miss Melville and Madeleine Jackson had been writing to each other regularly. Madeleine was doing very well, Miss Melville gathered, although Madeleine was careful to refer only casually to her success, not wishing to draw too great a contrast between her own happy state and Miss Melville's presumed precarious one. Miss Melville wished she could write and tell Madeleine how well she was doing but, of course, that was impossible—one of the drawbacks of her new profession. She did write to tell Madeleine that a distant relative had died and left her a legacy, so that Madeleine shouldn't keep worrying about her and offering to lend her money which she could ill afford to spare.

But luck did not continue to smile on Miss Melville. Her next assignment was to dispose of a male fashion designer. "Not Calvin Klein?" she asked hopefully, having seen Mr. Klein's television commercials.

"I'm afraid not. For now it's Mr. Guy. He is going to be given a 'Donnie' at the Adonis Awards dinner."

"Whatever for?" Miss Melville asked. She had seen Mr. Guy's fashions, as well as Mr. Guy himself, on TV.

"Who knows? Perhaps to keep him from putting the judges on his lists. He makes lists, you know—the world's ugliest women, sloppiest men, most offensive children; in addition to which he has done other things which I would not sully your ears."

She smiled indulgently. The poor boy still had the old-fashioned attitude that there were certain things that should not be mentioned in front of a lady, although apparently it was all right for her to read about them. The dossier he gave on Mr. Guy really shocked her, hardened as she was by this time to dark deeds that boggled the imagination. As someone who could conceivably be classified as an artist, he combined depravity with a creativity that would have made the Marquis de Sade sit up and take notice.

The Adonis Awards, sponsored by the manufacturers of Adonis toiletries for men (as well as Venus toiletries for women) were to be given out at the Metropolitan Academy of Fashion, in the venerable building that had once housed the High School of Vocational Arts, from which the Academy had descended. According to the program, Mr. Guy was to be fifth in sequence of the dozen or so award-winners. Since, despite the Academy's efforts to keep the length of the speeches to a minimum, there was no way of telling in advance how long each speech would take, she had to make plans for a wait of indefinite duration.

The presentations were being held in the main exhibition hall, formerly the gymnasium. Only the honorees and important guests had reserved seats, so she was free to pick her own location. Earlier she had reconnoitered the place on a visit with Amy Patterson, who was on the Academy's Board of Trustees and delighted by the interest her old schoolmate appeared to be taking in one of her pet projects.

"I can never get any of the children to come near the place," she complained. "Baldwin, Junior, thinks it's his fate to keep on getting mugged—it does seem to happen to him more often than most. But he's so narrow-minded. The Academy really isn't that kind of school any more, in spite of all the graffiti outside."

"At least it's chic graffiti. I understand that some of the hottest young artists today started out in graffiti."

"Come to think of it, I believe I did see a graffiti course listed in the spring catalogue, but I didn't have my glasses, so I got the idea it was on how to *remove* graffiti. I must tell Baldwin, Junior."

Miss Melville was tired of hearing about Baldwin, Junior; anyhow, she should express a courteous interest in Amy's other offspring. "How is—" what was the girl's name?— "Tinsley."

Amy beamed. "Although she won't be getting her MBA until June, she's already been invited to join Patterson, Pennypacker, Baldwin & Snook as a broker trainee. We're all so proud of her."

There might have been some cause for pride, Miss Melville thought, if the current Patterson, Pennypacker and Baldwin hadn't been father-in-law, grandfather and uncle respectively. She wasn't sure about Snook. Probably an in-law. Hardly necessary for Tinsley to get a degree in order to join the firm, but then, she probably would have felt naked without it.

"I only wish I could be as happy about Hebe," Amy said. "She's coming out in the spring, you know, and she insists she is not going to do anything about her hair. 'Hebe,' I keep telling her, 'you simply cannot make your debut with green hair,' but she doesn't seem to understand."

"Oh, well, she'll grow out of it."

"But she keeps retouching it," Amy complained. "Children are such a burden sometimes. You give them every advantage—why, mine have had the same father and mother ever since birth, which, you'll have to admit, is unusual these days, and they don't appreciate it."

"And how is Baldwin, Senior?" Miss Melville asked.

"I wouldn't know. We haven't spoken for years. But we're together, and that's what's important. And how is that charming brother of yours?"

"Brother?"

For a moment, Miss Melville was puzzled; then she remembered that chance encounter at the Stanhope. Just like Amy to have remembered. "Oh, you mean Alex Tabor. Honestly, Amy, he is not my brother."

"Well, nephew, cousin, whatever you want to call him, but really, Susan, don't you think you're being a little old-fashioned? I can't say I approve, but lots of people don't bother to go through a marriage ceremony these days, and their children are considered practically legitimate, although, of course, I don't know how it is in Brazil."

Wherever had she gotten the idea that Miss Melville was repudiating Alex Tabor as a sibling because he was illegitimate? But there was no point in trying to convince Amy of the truth; it would only renew the question of what he had been doing in her life to begin with.

"You must come to Tinsley's graduation party. And bring Alex with you."

"I'd be delighted," Miss Melville said.

When the time came, she would think of some excuse for not bringing Alex. She could always say that he had gone back to Brazil or, better yet, was dead.

The quondam gym had a shallow gallery or series of balconies running around the sides and back, designed to keep the spectators safely removed from activities on the floor below. At one time the balconies had been encased in wire netting, giving the effect of a series of chicken coops. The netting had been removed, but the vaguely rococo frames that had supported them remained intact, no doubt the work of preservationists who seemed to feel that anything old and ornate was a landmark. Fortunately that had not extended to the original benches, which had been replaced by what the MFA would probably call "faux leather" banquettes.

The whole area had been fitted out with a collection of the large potted weeds that had become so popular in modern interior decor. On the balconies, the MFA's decorator had set a series of shrubs which had grown to such majestic proportions that an Arab shiek could have placed his whole harem behind them, unveiled with perfect propriety.

Taking a drink and a plate of hor d'oeuvres upstairs for plausiblity and sustenance, Miss Melville made herself comfortable on a banquette just above the platform on which the presentations were to be made. No one joined her in her area. Participants at the Adonis Awards liked to be in the thick of things. It was possible too, that those unfamiliar with the building were not even aware that there were roosts behind the shrubbery.

The presentations were quickly under way. In fact, she was almost too late. Standing on the platform beneath her was the designer—she recognized his ferret face—stretching out a manicured hand to receive the statuette.

She fired so quickly she was afraid she had missed. But, no, there he was, a crumpled heap of gold lamé, innovative even in death, on the platform floor. She looked around in case someone had come onto the balcony during her torpor, although what she could have done in that case except shoot the intruder, she didn't know. But she was alone.

She was alone, too, in the upstairs' ladies room, where she carefully wrapped the gun in a quilted nylon Venus cosmetics bag and left via the route she had mapped out after Amy's guided tour. She met no one on her way out but a couple of youths engaged in furtive transaction, who took to their heels at the sight of her.

Remembering to saunter, she strolled along Fifty-seventh Street, pretending an interest in the windows, and down Lexington Avenue, where she joined Mr. Tabor in the Atrium of Citicorp Center. He sat at a small table, earphones and headset on the surface before him, an unforthcoming expression on his face.

She sat down on the chair at right angles to his and slid the gun into the opened briefcase at his feet.

"Everything went perfectly," she said.

"It did," he agreed. "Except for one small thing. You killed the wrong man."

"No! There must be some mistake."

"There was. You killed Mr. Phlemming instead of Mr. Guy."

"Are you sure?"

He was sure.

"From overhead he looked exactly like the pictures of Mr. Guy. So many of these designers are cut from the same cloth," she said.

She wondered whether he would laugh if she added, "Ha, ha," but decided not to chance it. "Wasn't he the one who showed his entire women's spring line on models wearing Mohawk haircuts? And the one who was involved in that awful S and M case? And wasn't he mixed up with Mr. Guy in—?"

"Please," Mr. Tabor interrupted, "there's no need to go into detail, especially since he was not a client of ours. Yes, I believe he was concerned in all those matters you mention."

That made her feel better. No need for regret over his demise except, of course, that she wouldn't be paid for it. "I suppose I don't get any money. Not even a kill fee, the way the magazines do it?"

"You are very merry tonight, Miss Melville."

Ominous, she thought. That's the word for his tone. Ominous. "Tell the Boss—tell our employer that he can have a painting free of charge, to help make up for my mistake tonight. I mean, to make up in some measure. It was entirely my fault."

He grunted. However, when he called her up to arrange their next rendezvous, he informed her that their employer had decided to accept her peace offering and she should bring along one of her pictures. He likes them, she thought. Or, more likely, he's just acquisitive.

◇◇◇ XVIII

Miss Melville carried out her next few assignments successfully, although enough unforeseen contingencies kept cropping up to keep her from getting too complacent. There was the evening she had to make her escape from the Thanksgiving Ball at the Stuyvesant Research Institute by a window, when she discovered all the doors had been boarded up by angry antivivisectionists, unaware that the object of their obloquy would never put another animal to the knife. And the night she was trapped after putting away a South American ex-dictator at a dinner dance intended to kick off his return from well-deserved exile. That one was held on board a private yacht cruising the Hudson, and Miss Melville most certainly would have been caught had not Mr. Tabor made a timely appearance in a rowboat.

She refused to kill a corrupt union leader who had been accused of mob connections at the Christmas Party for the children of members killed in the line of duty. He had been scheduled to play Santa Claus.

"It's not that he doesn't deserve extermination," she explained, "but I couldn't bring myself to kill Santa Claus in front of the kiddies. Another time, perhaps."

As it turned out, he was terminated by one of the orphans who was never caught but was believed to have been a midget in disguise. She wondered if he were a colleague of hers or whether he had been employed by a rival agency.

In between jobs she continued to go to parties and other festivities, partly for research purposes, partly because it had become a way of life. Even though she could now afford to pay her way into some of the less pricey charitable events when she was not there on business, she never did; it took away from the sport and would render her contemptible in the eyes of the other crashers, should they happen to observe her actually paying to get in.

She knew that some of them were beginning to wonder about her, their usual furtive snoopiness enhanced, she suspected, by the tales Rhonda must have spread about her "ritzy" connections.

"You seem to know an awful lot of these people," Shirley observed one evening at the Mid-Atlantic Archaeological Society's Gala for the benefit of impecunious Egyptologists. It was held at the galleries of Schliemann-Wooley, which specialized in overpriced antiquities.

Miss Melville had been bagged by Elvira Turlough, who

had been a moving spirit at events of this kind ever since Miss Melville had been a little girl; ever since Miss Melville's mother had been a little girl, in fact. As far as anyone knew, Elvira had never done anything in her life but sponsor charity affairs. Nobody had ever seen her any place else, and although Miss Melville's elders had chided Susan for suggesting that Elvira spent her days reposing in a coffin, they could not hide their amusement at the suggestion.

Mr. Turlough had vanished so long ago that nobody could remember what his first name had been. A noted yachtsman, he was presumed to have perished in a storm off the coast of Newport, although the more romantic among Miss Melville's schoolmates preferred to believe that he had eloped with a mermaid (a barmaid was more like it, her father had said).

Since Elvira was fabulously wealthy, with no known heirs, she was much courted by the various charitable organizations and begged to act as chairman of virtually every benefit or gala that came along. By this time she was too tottery to perform any of the actual duties of the post, but her photograph among the dignitaries almost always ensured space in the society pages.

So far Miss Melville had managed to avoid her, but tonight the decor was such that she mistook Elvira for a whimsically clad mummy. Before she could make her escape, she was pounced on and subjected to Elvira's usual monologue about how times were changing for the worse.

On this occasion Miss Melville was relieved by the approach of Shirley, who was not only wearing a black Cleopatra bob to suit the ambiance, but had clad her rotund body in a long white evening skirt topped by a sequined halter attached to an imitation Egyptian collar.

Elvira broke off her harangue as Shirley bore down on them to demand, "Who on earth is that extraordinary-looking creature, and how did she get in here?"

"That is my friend, Shirley Mont St. Michel," Miss Melville said. "Let me introduce you."

"It would have been a pleasure," Elvira said hastily, "but my car is waiting. So lovely to have seen you again, Susan. I'd heard you were in a bad way, but I hadn't realized things were quite this bad."

"Funny-looking old duck," Shirley observed after Elvira's retreating back. "I've seen her around a lot at these things. Surprising how spry she is; she's practically sprinting."

It was right after the encounter with Elvira that Shirley brought up the subject of Miss Melville's dubious associations as she stuffed food and, Miss Melville was grieved to see, several small items of tableware into her wrap cum tote bag.

"What I mean is, you seem to know these people not from just meeting them at parties, but from outside." It was as if, running into an acquaintance at a museum, she had discovered her mingling on familiar terms with the exhibits.

"Well, if you've lived all your life in New York, you're bound to run into an old acquaintance every now and then at these affairs."

"I have lived in New York all of my life, and I've never run into people I knew at these affairs. Except people like us, of course."

Even though Miss Melville had been trying to convince Shirley that she was not one of those others, she couldn't help wincing at the "us." "I do a great deal of social work, and you get to meet a lot of people that way."

"Oh, so that's what you do. I've often wondered but I didn't want to seem nosy. Some people are always coming up to perfect strangers and asking them what they do, which I think is so gosh."

"Gosh?" Miss Melville repeated. "Oh, yes, I agree, it's very *gauche*—gosh, I mean."

"What type social work do you do, if I may ask?"

"Er . . . I work in the area of demography."

Shirley looked blank.

'You know, population control.''

"And I'm sure you do a lot of worthwhile, uh, population controlling," Shirley said graciously. "I, myself," she added, to show there were no secrets in her life, "am unemployed."

Hilary had already informed Miss Melville of Shirley's status in a previous conversation. "B-b-b-b-but nobody seems to kn-n-n-now what she's employed at. She m-must d-do something, though, b-because she keeps g-g-getting unemployment insurance."

Miss Melville, who had been unable to get unemployment insurance herself because Sophie had kept her on the books as a free-lance employee, felt a momentary wish that she could have met Shirley long before so that she, too, could have learned how to get unemployment insurance without having had a job. She supposed it wasn't too late to learn, but she did have a job now, even though she was sure the Boss wasn't paying any unemployment insurance taxes on her behalf.

Most of the other crashers appeared to be gainfully employed, although it was difficult to conceive of them in the sober surroundings of an office. Felix had told her that he was an editor on a computer trade journal; this was borne out by his name on the masthead. Apparently, in order to be computer literate, you didn't have to be a human literate. Rhonda taught physical education at one of the city colleges. Hilary worked for the state in some unspecified capacity. Dana was a dental assistant. Even Freddy Makepeace who, if he ever had been ordained as he claimed, must certainly have been defrocked by now, worked as a proofreader for a law firm.

It was important for Miss Melville to stay on good terms with them because she needed the protective coloration they gave. A number of her old friends and acquaintances who might otherwise have asked her to join them at their tables were undoubtedly deterred by the fact that common courtesy would oblige them to ask her outlandish companions to join them as well. As an employee of the Organization, she felt far more comfortable in the company of the crashers, who seldom noticed what was going on amongst themselves, they were so busy watching the exalted ones on the dais and in the front tables.

When it came right down to it, Susan preferred that her old friends avoid her. If ever she should be exposed as a crasher, she did not want her embarrassment to take place in front of them, although the idea did not appall her as much as it once might have. Knowing that you had killed and could kill again made you far more tolerant of life's petty inconveniences. Most important of all, those sitting up front among the elite, in the limelight, did not have the mobility of those sitting in the obscurity of the tables allotted to the hoi polloi, who could move about and even disappear from time to time without attracting notice.

Of course people she knew well were not always shaken off quite so readily. Fortunately, there were few left, and by making an effort to keep in touch, she was likely to get an idea of where they would be likely to turn up and make her plans, either for crashing or killing, accordingly. Since art was Mimi's chief interest and wildlife Oliver's, by avoiding festivities that were connected with either and passing up Fitzhorn Foundation events—except when she went as an invited guest—she could reduce her chances of running into them.

Amy Patterson, she knew, was most likely to be found at educational events. Moreover, she was fairly easy to avoid because she didn't like to wear glasses in public and never could get used to contact lenses.

Mimi had gotten over her pique at Susan's refusal to accept the job at the Fitzhorn Foundation—she had located an even worthier candidate for the post in the shape of Dodo Pangborn, newly released from the Bedford Hills Correctional Facility and in need of respectable employment as part of the conditions of her parole.

"We feel we must do all we can for her, Susan," she told her friend at the Fitzhorn Foundation's annual Mother's Day Dinner Dance for the benefit of Unplanned Parenthood, held at the Foundation's opulent headquarters on upper Fifth Avenue.

"You were always so good-hearted, Mimi," Susan said. After all, she was there as the Carruthers' honored guest; it was the least she could say.

"And it's worked out very well. Dodo's always had such a good business head. Oliver says he doesn't know how he ever got along without her."

Since Oliver had been head of the Fitzhorn Foundation for only a few months, this tribute was not as overwhelming as it might otherwise have been. Miss Melville glanced over to where Oliver and Dodo were greeting the guests. It had been Mimi's own decision, she'd said, not to join the welcoming committee; receiving lines were "so boring."

"Besides," she said with a smile, "since I have no direct connection with the administration, it looks better if I stay in the background."

Miss Melville couldn't help wondering about this latest development . . . it wasn't like Mimi to choose to stay in the background. And Dodo really did look well, considering that she'd been incarcerated for the last few years; but then the first thing she'd done when she got out, she'd confided to Susan earlier that evening, was to have her face lifted.

"It's a great morale builder, but perhaps you don't feel you need to have your morale built, Susan."

Miss Melville smiled and made a noncommittal remark. She remembered now that she had never really liked Dodo.

"Mimi tells me that you're still painting."

"That's how I make my living."

"I never heard of you. As an artist, I mean."

Miss Melville had not thrown off the ingrained habits of

a ladylike lifetime sufficiently to be able to punch Dodo in the nose. "Perhaps art isn't your field," she suggested.

"Oh, but it is. I had quite a collection before it was sold to pay my legal expenses, and I'm planning to get back into art as soon as I can."

"Model agency, something like that?" Miss Melville could not resist asking, although she knew it was unworthy of her. "Do you think your parole officer would approve?"

"Oh, that kind of agency's old hat," Dodo said. "And so are you. You're so out of date, Susan. The way you look, the way you dress, the way you think. No wonder you never made it as an artist—or in any other way. You were always out of step with the times."

"I'm certainly not trendy," Miss Melville acknowledged, handicapped by the fact that she had also been brought up not to insult people flagrantly to their faces. So had Dodo, but then she'd been in prison.

"Trendy!" Dodo sniffed. "You're positively archaic. You have no sense of self-image, and it's image that matters, not actuality. You've got to remember that today the packaging counts for more than the product; it's the artist that's important, not the art."

That might explain a good deal of contemporary art, Miss Melville thought, but it didn't explain the artists.

"You might still be able to make it if—" Dodo regarded her critically "—well, you could never be packaged as young, but you could at least go for glamorous." She paused. "Well, elegant, anyway, if you did something about your hair."

Observing Oliver and Dodo from across the room now, Miss Melville wondered how long it would be before the inevitable took place. She tried not to look behind her to where Rhonda, festively garbed in a bouffant pink ball gown, sat glaring. At least she isn't going to come up and speak to me, Miss Melville thought. None of the other crashers seemed to be around, probably because Miss Melville had given Oliver a few extra security tips beforehand, which he had accepted with gratitude and without wondering how she happened to be so well informed. Oliver was a simple man and she liked him.

ㅇㅇㅇ **XIX**

By this time Miss Melville had dropped into a regular routine, painting steadily, going to parties several times a week, now and again killing some deserving person. To the outward eye, it might have seemed as if she were leading a full, rich life, but something was missing. She wouldn't have admitted that she was lonely, but sometimes, especially after one of their target practice sessions in what she had finally determined was Westchester County, she found herself wishing that Alex Tabor really were her nephew.

Not her brother, though. Even in her imagination, she refused to go that far. Still, he was the only person in the world in whom she could confide, to the degree that she could confide in anyone at all. They had a shared vocation and shared interests up to a point. She enjoyed talking to him, but she couldn't talk to him about Peter or anything personal. And while he seemed to like talking to her, he never touched on anything personal.

She wondered whether he had someone to whom he could talk freely. Once when she'd called him, a female voice had answered instead of the machine. After Miss Melville left word, according to form, for Alex to call her, the voice had said, "Oh, absolutely." She seemed about to say more, then contented herself with "Bye-bye."

So at least he had a girlfriend, although of course it could be his cleaning lady. It might even be the Boss. Although Mr. Tabor had always referred to their employer as "he," is was possible that the pronoun was used in its generic sense. For some reason, the voice had sounded vaguely familiar.

Somehow the thought of Mr. Tabor with a girlfriend made Miss Melville feel lonely. She missed Peter more than ever.

He did write regularly, at least once and sometimes twice a week; however, the letters came only every two or three months, in great batches forwarded from the Institute. Some appeared to have been attacked by some form of insect life before reaching her. "Everything is very carefully fumigated before it's passed on to you," the young man who represented the Institute in such matters assured her. So that accounted for the strange odor. She was glad to know, because she'd been afraid it might be some kind of tropical fungus.

Although Peter had promised he would be coming back for a few months early that year, he wrote now that he could see no chance of getting back to civilization in the near future. ". . . I've really made a breakthrough in winning the natives' confidence. If I disappeared for a couple of months, I'd run the risk of losing all the headway I've already made. I know you won't understand, but please try to." Almost as an afterthought he added that he missed her and repeated his invitation for her to join him in the jungle.

She thought about getting a dog for company. Her father had always had dogs, but Mr. Tabor discouraged her. A dog, he said, would need to be walked at regular hours. "Your hours, from what I understand, are most irregular. And I can't see you using a—what do they call it?—pooper scooper. How about a nice cat?"

He was like a cat himself, she thought, a sleek, beautiful animal neither domestic nor feral but posed between the two, ready to jump in whichever direction the advantage seemed to lie. No, she did not want a cat; it would not provide the uncritical adoration she needed right then. Besides, she couldn't see herself emptying a litter box.

"What you need is a change of scene. Why not go on a cruise or to a resort? If you'll let us select your destination, we will gladly pay your expenses as well as your customary fee."

But she refused. A buswoman's holiday would be no holiday at all. And she did not care for the idea of mingling socially with her prospective victims. It would detract from her professional detachment. In addition, a hitman or woman was, in effect, a hit and run man or woman. Mobility was a vital part of the operation. Both ships and resorts were, in effect, closed societies. Although in a resort she would not be trapped in the same way as on a boat—she remembered her experience on the yacht with a shudder—her sudden disappearance afterward would be bound to cause comment.

She thought of going down to South America to visit Peter, but her contact at the Institute vehemently vetoed the idea. "Even if we could manage to get you down there, it would be months before we could get you back. And, believe me, Miss Melville, you would not like it down there, no matter what Dr. Franklin says."

Her next idea was to take a week or two off and go visit Madeleine Jackson in Santa Fe. It would be nice to see Madeleine again. Before she had a chance to formulate any plans, Madeleine herself telephoned one evening, full of excitement.

She'd gotten married again on the spur of the moment before a Justice of the Peace, which was why Susan hadn't been invited to the ceremony. And she and her new husband, a philosophy professor on sabbatical from his university, were on their way to a honeymoon in India. They expected to be there for at least a year.

Susan wished them both the best and said she looked

forward to seeing them when they returned. "By that time," she said, "Peter should be back and we can all have a reunion."

"Is he going to be back permanently?"

Miss Melville could not stretch fact beyond the breaking point. "I hope so," she said. "But with Peter, you never know."

Miss Melville bought herself new clothes, but this time they failed to elevate her spirits. She experimented with acrylics, found them unsatisfying, and returned to oils. No more bargain brands now: Winsor and Newton, plus the best canvases, the finest brushes.

In June, Tinsley Patterson had her graduation—if the acquisition of an MBA counted as a graduation—party, in the guise of a cocktail reception and dinner sponsored by Patterson, Pennypacker to establish scholarships for needy tyro entrepreneurs, so the whole thing could be written off as a business expense. Miss Melville was not, after all, invited. She read about it in the *Times'* schedule of coming events and was surprised. It was not like Amy to have forgotten to invite her.

Miss Melville wondered if she had offended Amy in some way, but couldn't see how. Even though she wasn't particularly fond of Amy, she'd been brought up never to offend unless you did it on purpose.

In any case, she wouldn't have been able to attend, for her services were required on the same day at a garden party to be held on the ground of Chilon College, a small but prestigious institution in Riverdale, for the benefit of the scholarship fund. Scholarship benefits were very big in June.

Miss Melville considered it fortunate that the two events happened to overlap. Otherwise, Amy would probably have been in attendance. Actually, if Miss Melville had known how closely Amy was connected with that particular educational facility she would have begged off the job—and been the better for it, for it was at that garden party that disaster struck.

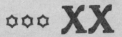

Even if she had been willing to make the requisite five-hundred-dollar contribution, Miss Melville would have been unable to buy a ticket. The garden party was sold out. This was the event of the season. One of the recipients of an honorary degree on this occasion was to be a superannuated pop singer who had been a legend in his own time; and, turning to politics, bid fair to become even more legendary in this one. The grounds on which Lennie Shannon was getting a degree were, as far as she could tell, that Chilon College was in Riverdale, which is geographically part of the Bronx, and he had been born in the Bronx. These days, that was enough.

Security would be very tight. The Pied Piper—as Lennie Shannon had been known ever since the day, a generation and a half before, when his press agent had hired a mob of screeching pubescent females to follow him wherever he went—was popular only with the public. Those who knew him did not love him; those who had worked for him hated him.

"Usually he's surrounded by at least a dozen bodyguards," Mr. Tabor informed her. "However, he tends to be thrifty where it doesn't show. If he buys tickets for all of his bodyguards, they'll get the tax deductions, which would mean he'd actually be paying the full price for them. So he's taking only two."

"Two could be enough. I assume the regular campus security will be on hand."

"That's why we're counting on you. If anyone can get near him, it would be someone like you."

"Someone whom the bodyguards wouldn't pay any attention to, you mean?" She knew the chip was showing on her shoulder, but she couldn't help it.

"Someone whom the bodyguards wouldn't be likely to look at as a threat, true, but also someone capable of carrying out the job."

Which must be true to some extent, she thought, or they would hardly have entrusted her with the job.

"I must warn you, though, this will be more dangerous than any of the other assignments you have undertaken thus far."

"Does that mean I get hazard pay?"

"You have become mercenary. Good. It's what we like to see in our operatives. Greed is the only motive that can really be relied on. Yes, there will be a substantial bonus after you've pulled it off."

She wondered where they were going to rendezvous afterward, for she was not too familiar with the terrain of Riverdale except for the ice cream parlor where they stopped after their shooting sessions, and that would never do. By now they were old customers and would certainly be remembered if the question ever came up.

It didn't matter, though, as this time, it seemed, they were not going to follow their usual procedure. "I'm afraid I won't be able to meet you afterward," Tabor said, "as I have an assignment of my own to carry out that same afternoon. The day after, I'll call you and arrange to pick up the gun and, of course, give you your check. You're going to be completely on your own, Susan. Think you'll be able to handle it?"

"I'm sure I can handle it," she said.

And, of course, it really made no difference whether he would be waiting for her after her assignment was completed or not. It was merely that it was comforting to be able to unwind a little with someone with whom she could discuss the day's work. Still, his presence was to be regarded in the light of a luxury rather than a necessity. To be unable to carry out her work without the knowledge that he would be there afterward would be very unprofessional, to say the least.

The only way she could be sure of getting into the garden party was to conceal herself beforehand in a place that was not likely to be frequented. Early in the morning, therefore, she hid herself in one of the bays in the library that overlooked the rose garden where the party was to be held, along with a supply of sandwiches, a few books and an alarm watch to prevent a recurrence of November's unfortunate incident.

No chance of her mistaking anyone else for the Pied Piper, though. During the past week alone, she had seen him on TV at least half a dozen times, appearing on all the talk shows to announce his impending doctorate. "Pretty good for somebody who never even finished high school, hah!" he said on each show.

Buried in the mountain of flesh, the impertinent face of the boy who had made her friends' mothers and older sisters' hearts throb (and whose appeal had even extended to some of the more backward bosoms of her own generation) could still be made out. It really was a shame, she thought. Not what was going to happen to Lennie Shannon, but what had already happened to him.

She spent a pleasant late morning and early afternoon in the library without being disturbed. Around two o'clock, the strains of the school band floating through the open window indicated that graduation ceremonies had started—in the grounds beyond the rose garden, so that the sounds were mercifully filtered by distance.

She had elected not to do away with the Piper during the speeches and their accompaniments, tempting though it would have been, especially during the Piper's off-key rendition of the *Star Spangled Banner*. That would have been foolhardy. Too many people would be sitting there in broad daylight with their attention wandering from the stage. Far better, even if less dramatic, to kill him when the guests would be milling about, the wine flowing freely, and everyone much more relaxed if not actually merry.

She lazed there on the top floor of the library, listening to the faraway mellifluities of T. Harrison Baldwin, Chilon's charismatic (according to the publicity handouts) president, welcoming Lennie Shannon and the other honorary degree recipients. Then Lennie made a speech, stumbling over only a few of the longer words, acknowledging the honor that had been done him and announcing the huge sum he was contributing to the scholarship fund (although, of course, it was Uncle Sam who would, in the end, foot most of the bill).

Dr. Baldwin thanked him again. There were speeches from other, lesser recipients of honorary degrees and dignitaries who were not getting degrees, as well as the class valedictorian, almost lost in the shuffle. The afternoon wore on . . . and on. . . . I must not fall asleep, she told herself, resetting her watch once again.

At last the sounds of a march that was either the school song or one of the lesser-known opera of John Philip Sousa indicated the cessation of ceremonies. She made her way down the stairs in a leisurely manner and left through a side door that led directly into the sun-filled rose garden.

The campus had seemed a charming place on a preliminary visit she's made some weeks before as part of a guided tour (sponsored by the Hudson Valley Gourmet and Fitness Society), with its ivy-covered stone walls, wide green lawns, and ancient-looking trees. On that visit, the rose garden had seemed especially appealing. Its clusters of small, old-fashioned blooms, most still in bud, had perfumed the air delicately with the scent that modern roses had largely sacrificed for size and perfection of shape. Today most of the roses were in bloom, and the scent that hung in the warm, humid air was no longer delicate but almost cloying.

The party was being held in the rose garden because it could be shut off by tall, wrought-iron gates from the rest of the grounds where the graduates and their guests milled about, occasionally peering through the grillwork like lost souls anxious for a glimpse of Paradise. At least she wouldn't have to worry about being seen by any of the regular crashers. Not one was visible, not even the indefatigable Rhonda, a long-time fan of the Piper who had boasted that she would make her way in, no matter what the obstacles, to see her beloved Lennie. Pity she wouldn't be able to gloat over Rhonda later, Miss Melville thought, but that was one of the penalties of her profession.

Miss Melville made her way toward the elaborate ornamental fountain—featuring Niobe weeping for her children, along with a bevy of water nymphs, dolphins, and winged cherubs—in front of which the Pied Piper was holding sway, glass in hand, surrounded by admirers. As Miss Melville approached, he was dispatching one of his two bodyguards to fetch another drink, although there were plenty of waiters around. Either he didn't trust the waiters or he simply was accustomed to using his bodyguards as gofers.

Even to a casual observer it would have been apparent that the Piper had had more than enough to drink already.

"Oh, Mr.—or should I say 'Doctor'—Shannon," she gushed, "I've always been such a great admirer of yours . . ."

"Gwan, beat it," the Piper broke in. "With all these young college chicks around, I should talk to an old broad like you?"

The "young college chicks" giggled, and the remaining bodyguard guffawed. A portly middle-aged man whom she recognized from photographs as President Baldwin gave a deprecating murmur.

". . . Ever since I was a little girl," she finished.

Dr. Baldwin turned as if to speak to her, but with a gallant little wave of her hand, she left, melting into the crowd.

"You shouldn't have spoken to him," Mr. Tabor told her later. "You never spoke to any of the others."

Why had she done it? She didn't know—except, perhaps, in a way to give him a last chance. Apparently she hadn't been as immune from him in her formative years as she had supposed. In any case, as she reminded Mr. Tabor, what happened afterward would have happened anyway, whether she had spoken to him or not.

Shielded by the crowd, she circled the fountain, stepped behind a group of bushes backing it, which served to screen a row of garbage cans—vegetation has always been my friend, she thought—and shot him neatly in the back.

She was wrong about vegetation. The bushes might have been her friends, but it was a tree that betrayed her, a tall oak that stood against the stone wall separating the rose garden from the street, a tree that overlooked the fountain, the bushes, the garbage cans, the corpse and, of course, Miss Melville herself.

"She killed him! She killed him!" a voice screeched from its branches, and Rhonda's face appeared between the leaves like some demented dryad's. She had sworn that nothing would keep her from reaching her beloved Lennie, and she had kept that vow. If only they could have died together in the grand tradition, Miss Melville couldn't help thinking, it would save her a lot of trouble.

She sidled toward the statue of Niobe, and under cover of that bereaved mother's copious tears, which provided the fountain's water source, tossed the gun to the goldfish. She then strolled forward to mingle with the guests, who were coagulating into horrified groups around the corpse without getting too close, accustomed as they were to keeping their distance from unpleasantness.

"She did it! She did it!" Rhonda screamed, pointing a claw at Miss Melville. "I saw her!"

Several members of the campus police fetched a ladder and hauled her down from the tree.

Everyone turned to look at Miss Melville, who was wearing an ankle-length flowered georgette dress with a filmy picture hat, an outfit she had last worn at Ascot, aeons ago. How fortunate, she'd thought as she dressed that morning, that the style had been revived, or perhaps it had never gone out of fashion.

Then, almost as if part of some macabre tennis match, the crowd turned as one to look at Rhonda, hair shrunk into sweaty draggletails, face swollen red and streaked with bark dust and emotion, her drab jumpsuit ripped in several places to reveal the festive royal blue satin with which she had planned to dazzle the guests, one hand still clutching a pair of pruning shears. Apparently she had propped a ladder against the other side of the wall and climbed it in the guise of a gardener engaged in horticultural activities.

"Murderess!" she shrieked, lunging in the direction of Miss Melville with the pruning shears; then gave a yip of pain as one of the campus police twisted her arm behind her back, forcing the shears to drop to the ground.

Another campus policeman carefully picked them up in a large clean white handkerchief. Good Heavens, Miss Melville thought, did he think the Piper was pruned to death?

"Murderess!" Rhonda hissed again, adding several obscenities before lapsing into dribbling incoherence.

"Now, now," T. Harrison Baldwin said. "Now, now."

"Poor woman," Miss Melville said, "Obviously she isn't responsible."

By this time the bodyguard who had been sent for refreshment returned with a glass in his hand. He and his fellow bodyguard exchanged glances; then both drew their guns—at least one did, the newcomer following suit only after it occurred to him to put down the glass.

"Call the cops," he ordered. "The real cops."

"We've already notified the local precinct," a campus policeman said, with the contempt of the man wearing an authorized uniform for the man in private service.

"And make sure nobody leaves—especially this dame," the other bodyguard ordered, gesturing at Miss Melville with his gun.

"Don't you tell us how to do our job," the campus policeman said. "And both of you better put those guns away before somebody gets hurt, most likely *you*."

His eyes were appropriately narrowed. He, too, must be a television watcher, Miss Melville reflected.

"I'm sure this lady will have no objection to staying," Dr. Baldwin said, "and our police have already been posted at the gates, asking the guests to stay, although we can't hold them by force."

"Why not?" the bodyguard demanded, pointing his gun in a sweep at the guests generally.

Someone gave a genteel shriek.

"I told you to put that gun away," the campus policemen said. "Otherwise I'll have to arrest you. Both of you." He sounded as if it would be a pleasure.

"There is no necessity for any of this," Dr. Baldwin protested. "The committee has a record of everybody who purchased a ticket."

Oh, *dear!* Miss Melville thought.

"If you wouldn't mind staying until the police arrive, madam. It will only be a formality, of course." He looked at her more closely. "Why, it's Susan Melville, isn't it?"

Rhonda paused in her struggles with the campus police. Three of them were holding her down now, and the blood was running down one's hand where she had bitten him. Miss Melville hoped he wouldn't get rabies.

"That's right—that's her name! Susan, Susan Melville! She's a murderess!"

"I don't suppose you remember me from those old days at the Farnsworth Baldwins. You were such a great friend of my little cousin Amy's—Amy Patterson, she is now."

"She shot the Piper!"

"Why, you're Amy's big cousin Tim. Of course I remember you!"

As well as anyone could remember Tim the Dim. By this time she had already placed him. Timothy Harrison Baldwin had been a vague, wimpy figure. Eight or nine years older than his teen-aged cousin and her friends, he had continued to go to graduate school, amassing assorted degrees, because his parents couldn't figure out what to do with him. He'd appeared to have neither aptitude for, nor interest, in anything. They should have guessed he was destined to be a college president.

"Why don't they arrest the lousy murdering bitch?"

"I'll bet you never guessed what a crush I had on you," Susan said, smiling up at him. "But then all of us girls did."

He beamed. "Well, of course, it was only natural at your age."

"Murderess! Murderess!" Rhonda screeched, following this with a profusion of obscenities that surprised even Miss Melville; she hadn't thought Rhonda could be so creative.

This time Dr. Baldwin pretended not to hear them, but he was clearly relieved when the police arrived, bringing an ambulance which took away Rhonda, who was foaming at the mouth by then.

Dr. Baldwin placed his hand on Miss Melville's shoulder. "I've known this lady for years," he assured the detective in charge. "I'm sure she couldn't possibly have anything to do with this terrible tragedy."

"It hardly seems likely," the detective agreed, "especially if you vouch for her, Dr. Baldwin. However, we've got to follow the rules. So, if you wouldn't mind letting yourself be searched, ma'am."

"Surely you can't subject this lady . . ." Dr. Baldwin began, outraged.

"It's his duty, Tim. I quite understand."

She went into the library and submitted to the indignity of a rather perfunctory search performed by a policewoman, reflecting that after all the Piper had suffered a much greater indignity.

"If you'll just leave your name and address with the sergeant, Miss Melville," the detective said, when she emerged again, "we'll be in touch." He gave her a reassuring smile. "Just another formality, of course."

She gave him her name and address; no help for it, since Tim Baldwin knew who she was. Even if he didn't, she wouldn't have known whether or not to lie and how. For the moment, she was safe, but what was going to happen when they found her name wasn't on the list of those who had purchased tickets?

She went directly home as soon as she was able to get clear. What a time for Mr. Tabor to have withdrawn his supporting presence. Not, she reflected, that there was any practical need for a meeting, since she had no gun to give him. If he wants it, she thought, he'll have to get it from the fishes.

She phoned him, anxious to tell what had happened and to ask him what, if anything, she should do. Only the machine answered.

Then she remembered: he was out on a job of his own. She turned on the news. No report of anyone's having been killed that day but the Pied Piper. Of course the news of his death would overwhelm all other stories; still, was it possible that Mr. Tabor had eliminated someone so obscure that the slaying would not even have been *mentioned* on the air?

Or perhaps he hadn't completed his assignment yet. She kept the news on until the early hours of the morning, but the only assassination reported was that of the Piper's (and a Bulgarian dignitary in Dubrovnik; and she hadn't gotten the impression that Mr. Tabor was leaving the country to carry out his assignment).

It was the first time she had been even remotely connected with one of her hits. What was worse, she had not been able to escape the photographers when she left. Fortunately it turned out that the picture hat obscured most of her face, and the press got her name as Susan Neville, but Tim Harris was bound to talk about what had happened— to Amy, at least—and so was Rhonda, to anyone who would listen.

People were hardly likely to credit Rhonda's allegations. Still, the "where there's smoke there's fire" adage held as true now as it ever had. People always liked to believe the worst, no matter how improbable.

Mr. Tabor seemed almost as shaken as she was when they finally did meet the next day. "Be thankful that they didn't put your hands through any chemical tests, which could have shown that you'd fired a gun. I only hope they won't be able to get any fingerprints from the gun in the fishpond."

"I thought water obliterates fingerprints."

"Not necessarily. They've developed methods by which fingerprints can sometimes be taken from an object even when the object has been under water. However, there is nothing to link the gun itself to you—or to anyone else. What concerns me more is that your name will not be on the guest list."

"I thought about that myself, so since I couldn't reach you, I called Tim Baldwin and confessed that I'd been so anxious to go to the party that, when I found it had been all sold out, I simply decided I'd crash, the way we'd used to when we were young."

Not that it was likely that Tim the Dim had ever done such a thing, but it gave him a chance to feel he'd been a hell of a fellow in a small way.

"He was very nice about it and said of course he'd say he'd invited me as his personal guest."

"Do you think he'll stick to that?"

She was surprised by the question. "Of course he will. It would be beyond his comprehension to think that I had come there to do . . . what I did do."

And, even if he had suspected, he would have lied anyway, because she was a Melville and he was a Baldwin.

She didn't tell Mr. Tabor that T. Harrison Baldwin had also said, "If I had known you wanted to come, I certainly would have asked you, so it's not really a lie. The wonderful thing is that it enabled us to meet again after all these years."

According to the paper, Rhonda was released from police custody when the autopsy revealed that the Piper had been shot in the back, which would have been impossible from her roost. In addition, she had been subjected to the paraffin tests, with no signs of her having handled a gun. She also proved to have a past record of mental illness. As she had gone completely berserk her relatives—Miss Melville was surprised to hear she had any—had had her removed to a psychiatric facility, from which Miss Melville couldn't help hoping that she would never be released. From the accounts in the papers, Rhonda had gone berserk several times before and been committed and then released. Moreover, nothing criminal had been involved and, if "mentally ill" rapists and wife-beaters could be let loose after a few months of "therapy," Rhonda had almost as good a chance.

Mr. Tabor seemed unperturbed by the prospect. "But when she comes out, she'll go on telling people I killed the Piper," Miss Melville pointed out.

"No, she won't," he said, "not if she ever expects to get out of that place. She'll be given to understand that as long as she keeps on accusing you, she'll be considered to

be suffering from hallucinations and therefore won't be released.''

"How do you know?''

He smiled.

"Meaning I shouldn't ask questions?''

"Meaning you can ask all the questions you like, as long
as you don't count on having them answered.''

Miss Melville lived in apprehension of the time the police
would get in touch with her, as they were bound to do;
however, the young man who eventually did interview her
was very nice, asking only if she knew why Rhonda had
picked on her to be the killer.

Miss Melville said she had never so much as laid eyes
on the woman before, and hoped there were no party crashers inside the police department to give her the lie.

"She seemed to know your name.''

"Evidently she heard Dr. Baldwin call me by it. He
turned out to be an old family friend. Pity we had to meet
again on such a tragic occasion.''

"Life is like that,'' he agreed, closing his notebook.
"Well, thank you for your cooperation. I doubt that we'll
be bothering you again.''

After that, the police appeared to lose interest in her.
They kept announcing they had new leads in the case, and
suspicion rested heavily on another pop singer of the *an-
cien regime* who had happened to be on the grounds (though
not, he claimed, at the garden party) to attend his son's
graduation, but that came to nothing. In the end, a fresh
crisis in the Middle East drove the death of the Pied Piper
off the air, the front pages and, ultimately, from the papers
entirely.

◇◇◇ **XXI**

For the next few months, Miss Melville firmly refused to accept any new assignments. "I just can't do it," she told Alex Tabor. "I don't think I'm ever going to be able to kill anyone again. I'll forever imagine someone is going to leap out at me from behind a tree or a pillar and shriek, 'She did it! She did it!' "

"You must not take such a negative attitude. Admittedly you had a close shave, but you knew when you accepted this job that there would be risks involved."

"I didn't know that there would be the risk of having Tim Baldwin keep calling me up and asking me to have dinner with him," she said petulantly.

She was glad now that Tabor had presented her with an answering machine of her own, even though she had resisted it at first, because it enabled her to evade Dr. Baldwin.

"Why not go out with him? Just as long as you are discreet about your work, there's no reason why you should not enjoy his company."

"I am always discreet, and there is every reason why I shouldn't enjoy his company. He's a bore and a fool."

"You're being too hard on the poor fellow . . ."

She could see Tabor was about to say more, but was deterred by the expression on her face. She did not take kindly to being offered advice on her social life from him. People of his age seemed to think a woman of hers should jump at any offer of a date, no matter how dull and boring it might be.

Besides, he must know about Peter. The most superficial investigation of her background would have disclosed his existence in her life.

She received the bonus she had been promised, and it was a handsome one. But she was still shaken from her narrow escape. Tabor had told her from the start that if she were caught she would be on her own, but she had never fully realized what being alone in a situation like this might be.

He had also warned her, although not in so many words—he was far too civilized for that—that, if she tried to tell anybody about the Organization, she would, in the vernacular of fiction, "be taken care of." Wasn't it possible that if she fell into the hands of the law, she would be "taken care of" even if she didn't speak, on the general principle that dead women tell no tales?

She tried to reassure herself. After all, how much did she know? Her only contact with the Organization was through Alex Tabor, which was probably not his real name anyway. Let the law try to find him, and he would probably dissolve into smoke.

Just the same, she began to think it might be a good idea to get out while the getting was still good. She didn't actually make up her mind at this point that she wasn't going to do any more work for Tabor or his boss—at this juncture, she couldn't afford to stop. She still hadn't made much of a dent in the principal of the loan she'd taken out to pay for the apartment. But she kept turning down job after job for reasons that became increasingly unconvincing.

Since summer was the slow season, at first he didn't press her to go back to work. However, when Labor Day came and went and she refused to do away with such unexceptionable candidates for extermination as a sleazy international publisher, a foul-mouthed disk jockey, and a sadistic

African dictator embarked on a fund-raising tour "for cultural purposes," he started getting insistent.

"You must go out in the field again, unless you want to lose your nerve completely. It's like riding a horse. You—"

"—Have to get back on right away," they finished together.

"I've fallen off horses. It's not the same thing at all," she said.

"Very well, then, let me put it another way. If you keep turning down assignments, how will you pay the interest on your loan? The maintenance on your apartment?"

At least he didn't threaten her with anything but poverty. Not that poverty wasn't threat enough. In order for her to quit there had to be some alternative occupation she could take up. She hadn't been able to think of one before, but now she had a lot more work experience.

She tried to figure out ways she might be able to put that experience to use. Could she find a job as a bodyguard?

It wasn't likely that anyone would hire her without references, and she could hardly expect Tabor, let alone his employer, to provide her with testimonials to her character and ability, nor would it be feasible for her to draw up a résumé listing her recent accomplishments and submit it to potential employers.

"You could, of course, marry Dr. Baldwin," Tabor suggested.

What on earth had put marriage into his mind? It wasn't a conclusion people normally leaped to anymore.

"May I remind you that Dr. Baldwin only asked me to go out with him, not to marry him? For all you know, he is married."

"My dear Susan, would a man as upright as Dr. Baldwin, the president of a college, ask you out if he were married? Besides, he's a widower."

"How do you know?"

He didn't reply. But, of course, that efficient secret service of theirs must have checked Dr. Baldwin out, as they probably checked out everyone she had anything to do with. As for Peter, they were probably not only aware of his existence but had pinpointed his exact location and checked out the natives to make sure they were authentic. I'll bet they could get my letters to him a lot faster than the Institute does, she thought.

Tabor was persistent. "But if you did go out with Dr. Baldwin and he *did* ask you to marry him, would you find that an acceptable solution? Does the life of a faculty wife appeal to you?"

It might, she thought, if Peter were on the faculty. She sighed. "All right, whom do you want me to kill next?"

Her next slayings came off successfully, but she never regained the confidence that had buoyed her through her earlier jobs. "That means you're a seasoned professional now," Tabor complimented her.

He seemed to think she should be gratified by such an accolade. While she failed to appreciate the honor, she did seize the opportunity to ask whether that meant she was going to get another raise. "This time the honor alone will have to do," he said.

But it did nothing to raise her spirits. If she had derived any pleasure from killing, she would have said her own brush with disaster had taken all the fun out of it. It made her think again about preparing herself so that some day, the sooner the better, she would be equipped to earn her living in a safer, if less lucrative, way.

She wondered whether Alex Tabor also had dreams of escape to an alternative career—writing plays or composing symphonies or something else that didn't pay. No, if he had any artistic bent, she would have sensed it. He might have been an actor, though a failed one. There was something very theatrical about him.

As for herself, now that she had the means and the time, she thought that perhaps she should go back to school and get a degree after all. Many middle-aged and even elderly women were doing it these days.

Still, what would she study?

Amy's suggestion—grantsmanship? Absurd. Grant givers, like everyone else, tended to favor the young, unless the subject of the proposal was something like surrounding Manhattan Island with rusty tin or correlating the decline in the birthrate with the sale of overpriced sneakers, to qualify the recipient as young in spirit. A degree in education? Now that she had some sort of choice, she certainly didn't want to go back to teaching. Besides, teaching wouldn't pay enough.

The only way she would be able to achieve financial independence would be in her own line of work, her original line of work. While she still had regular employment, she had to make an all-out effort to bring her paintings before the public. Surely, with the indiscriminate nature of art collecting today, there must be a market for them.

But why be so self-deprecating? she asked herself. She knew she was a good painter; it was merely that her work was old-fashioned by contemporary criteria. Rather, it wasn't so much that her work was old-fashioned—some of the younger artists were creating more or less representational work, she noted—but that she herself was old-fashioned. Dodo had been right. She was not properly packaged for today's high-powered art business, and she could see no way she could be. Or would be. All the same, she felt that if only people could see her work, they would buy it— even though they might not pay as much as they would if she were a work of some publicist's art herself.

◦◦◦ XXII

Although she was unwilling to make a spectacle of herself, she was more than willing to make a spectacle of her paintings. Once Mimi had promised Susan she would arrange a show of her work. Whether or not Mimi's promise had been sincere, Susan decided she would remind her about it. It was certainly worth a try.

Susan felt that by this time she had achieved a degree of self-assertiveness, even pushiness. But once she had succeeded in getting Mimi to invite her to lunch—easy to do, as Mimi was eager to show off her new apartment—that assertiveness deserted her. The luncheon began with Mimi's having drunk several martinis while Susan nursed a glass of white wine. The chatter had been inconsequential, mostly on Mimi's part. It wasn't until they were sitting on the terrace, eating off heavy pottery plates, that Susan could bring herself to broach the object of her visit.

The terrace was on the fiftieth floor of a building slightly north of midtown on the East Side and, depending on which side you sat, offered a spectacular view of either the East River or the Hudson. It also seemed to be at the nexus of all prevailing air currents. Susan felt as if she were sitting in the path of a permanent hurricane.

"It is a bit windy up here," Mimi acknowledged, grabbing the floral centerpiece from the table just as it was about to take flight from the silver bowl in which it had seemed so solidly ensconced. "I keep telling the florist he must always *anchor* his arrangements, but I can't make him understand how it is up here. Bessemer, what is that large flapping thing?''

"It appears to be the remains of a kite, madam,'' the maid said as she picked up the shredded object by its edge in aggrieved, gingerly fashion.

Susan wondered whether Bessemer had a degree in Applied Economics. Somehow she doubted it.

"Everything seems to get blown up here,'' Mimi said. "Newspapers, balloons, hats; once we even got some poor man's toupee.''

Bessemer left, carrying the remains of the kite, her back the embodiment of disapproval. "The servants don't care too much for serving meals on the terrace,'' Mimi said. "They don't like anything that requires the least bit of extra work.''

"I suppose it is difficult for them,'' Miss Melville said, trying not to espouse the staff's point of view too enthusiastically. She was there, after all, to ask a favor of Mimi: she didn't want to rain on her parade.

"But tell me, Susan, why have you decided you want to show your paintings? I thought you were already working exculsively for one collector?''

Miss Melville had forgotten about that. ["Oh, what a tangled web we weave . . .''] She thought fast. "I haven't been working for him *exclusively*, just steadily. There was nothing in our agreement to keep me from showing my paintings, and the arrangement was only for a limited time, anyhow.''

"You mean he doesn't want to buy any more of your pictures?''

"Oh, he does want them; he wants all I can paint. I think he wants to corner the market on them; then wait until I'm dead so their value will soar.'' She laughed.

Mimi nodded seriously. This was no joke; it was sound business practice.

"Anyhow, I've come to the conclusion that you were

right when you said he was exploiting me. I'd be able to make more money on the open market."

"You are still working for him, then?"

"Yes, of course. After all, I do have to earn a living."

Important to stress this every chance she got, to account for her own modest prosperity. Not that Mimi would ever question it—to her, anyone whose income was less than six figures was below the poverty line—but she might talk to someone who would be more curious. Also, in view of Miss Melville's purpose in approaching Mimi it was important to establish the fact that her work was selling. In Mimi's circle, you gave benefits for lost causes; you didn't back them.

Mimi looked thoughtful. "I'll try to see if I can get you introductions to some other collectors. That would be a start, although it would help if I could just whisper to them the name of the one you've been working for."

Miss Melville shook her head. "I promised I wouldn't tell anybody. And he is still buying my pictures, so I couldn't afford to offend him."

"I don't see why your telling *me* would offend him," Mimi pouted. "But I certainly don't want to try to persuade you to do something that would go against your conscience."

"I knew you'd understand," Susan said.

"We'll also have to work out some way of getting people to see your pictures, so that he'll know he can't go on exploiting you."

When Susan had first come into Mimi's apartment and been given the grand tour—and grand it was—she had been gratified to see that Mimi had hung the painting her friend had given her for a wedding present in her new boudoir, along with correlating draperies and upholstery as promised. However, only Mimi's intimates were admitted to her boudoir. If only Susan's pictures could be exposed to Mimi's circle. But she could not ask Mimi to rearrange her carefully ordered decor in order to put on a private showing of Susan's pictures.

Susan wished she could figure out some way that more of her pictures could become an integral part of that decor. She tried to think of other occasions on which it might be appropriate to bestow pictures on Mimi.

A little too late, after all these years, to suddenly start remembering Mimi's birthday. Surely she could give her a painting for Christmas, but that was many months away. Thanksgiving Day, with a note, "Many thanks for all your kindness"? Maybe. Halloween? No.

"Of course you already know Tim Baldwin," Mimi said.

Had she missed something, or was this just a non sequitur?

"I did happen to run into him recently," she said. "I didn't know he was a college president now. I must really have been out of touch."

"Come on, Susan, don't act so innocent. You must have known the Chilon Alumni Association just set up a fund to become the nucleus of a contemporary art collection. Amy tells me the student association was livid because they wanted a sports stadium, but art is less expensive and more enduring. Anyhow, this way you're in on the ground floor, so to speak."

"Honestly, Mimi, I had no idea they were starting an art collection at Chilon."

"Oh, don't be coy, Susan, why else would you have gone to the Chilon commencement party. . . ?"

Why else, indeed? She had better stop protesting, unless she could come up with some better explanation for her presence there.

". . . Instead of Patterson, Pennypacker's party for Tinsley? I remember Amy's telling me how hurt she felt when you didn't even so much as answer the invitation."

Susan had done enough things for which she could be fairly blamed. This was not one of them. She felt righteously aggrieved. "Mimi, I never even got an invitation.

As a matter of fact, I admit I was a little hurt at the time
that she hadn't asked me, but I assumed she must have had
her reasons . . .''

"Hold on to your plate!" Mimi cried as a gust of wind
swept over the terrace, depositing a thin film of soot on the
table, the food, and their persons. The dishes—Susan saw
now why such heavy earthenware had been chosen—rattled
but held firm.

"Isn't eating out on the terrace *fun!*" Mimi cried, her
hazel eyes (either she had changed her contact lenses or
she wasn't wearing them today) sparkling. Although her
coppery hair had moved in the wind, not a strand was out
of place now, while Susan could see herself reflected in
the side of the silver bowl as a middle-aged female Strew-
elpeter. Mimi probably does it with magnets, she thought.

"Oh, it is fun," she agreed politely. "If I lived up here,
I would—" she gulped "—I would eat out here a lot." She
picked some leaves out of her salad that hadn't been there
when she started to eat it. "I didn't know you went in for
pets, Mimi. Or does that bird belong to Oliver?"

"The pigeons, of course, are a drawback," Mimi acknowledged, turning to see what particular bird Susan had
in mind.

"Oh, my goodness!"

She hitched her chair around to Susan's side of the table.
"That isn't a pigeon; it's a vulture. Do you suppose it
knows something we don't know?"

"It's a hawk, Mimi," Susan said, looking more closely
at the large, red-tailed bird perched on the parapet close to
where Mimi had been sitting, "and it appears to be tame.
See, it's wearing little bells."

"It may be tame, but it doesn't look *friendly*." Mimi
clapped her hands. "Shoo, bird, shoo!"

The hawk shook itself all over. Feathers showered over
them and the little bells tinkled.

The maid came to remove their salads. "Oh, Bessemer," Mimi said, "would you chase away that bird?"

"No, madam," Bessemer said.

The bird sneered.

"I wish Oliver were here. He'd know how to deal with a hawk."

Mimi didn't make it clear whether that was because of Oliver's masterful nature or his wildlife expertise.

"But he's always so busy these days with the Foundation and the Venturers. It seems to me I see less of him now than when I was here and he was in Kenya. I don't see how you can stand Peter's being away so much, Susan."

"Well, I'm more or less used to it. Besides, he shouldn't be away too much longer, just until he's finished his preliminary study of the tribe he's working on—working with," she amended.

"But that could take him years. And then he'll just go back to the jungle and start researching another book."

"But it would be years before he'd finish the first one," Susan told her. "He's a very slow writer."

When he did come back, she would definitely have to close down her career as a killer, she thought. With Peter around all the time, there would be no way she'd be able to keep it from him—and no way she'd be able to explain it to him, either. She'd have to figure out how to handle Tabor and company when the time came.

Still, she couldn't understand why Mimi didn't seem happier that her Oliver was there, living in the same city as she was, the same apartment, even if he didn't give her as much of his time as she wanted. She pointed this out to Mimi, who said petulantly that of course she was glad Oliver was there *with* her. "It's just that—well, he isn't as much fun anymore. I mean, he doesn't just administer and arrange parties and make speeches. He goes and *investigates* the organizations we contribute to. He's actually turned down groups we've been contributing to from time immemorial. He's antagonized so many of my dearest friends, I have to spend half my time apologizing. It's embarrassing."

"You've got to give him time to adjust, Mimi."

"He's had plenty of time!" Mimi snapped. "And that's not all he does. Sometimes he just gives the money directly to an organization he feels needs it, instead of going through channels. Or tries to, anyhow. The trustees have complained to me about that. In fact, they even asked an accountant to look into things."

So that was what Mimi had been working up to. Susan wasn't surprised, but she was a little saddened. "Of course they didn't find anything wrong," she said, prepared to hear the opposite and make soothing noises.

"No, they didn't!" Mimi sounded almost disappointed. "In fact, old Mr. Vanderpot congratulated me. He said Oliver was doing admirable work, and together he and Dodo had really reorganized the whole place, cutting out deadwood and rearranging the records and—and doing all sorts of things like that—" she made them sound faintly disreputable "—so the Foundation was in better shape than it had been for *decades*."

Susan was pleasantly surprised, but she could see that Mimi was not pleased, at all. She'd always had a weakness for scamps. It must have been a bit of a shock to find she had inadvertently allied herself with a solid citizen.

"You should be very proud of him," Susan said.

"Oh, I am, I am, only I thought that once I got him away from the wildlife he wouldn't be so dedicated. It's the duty of those who are privileged to help the less fortunate, of course, but you can't let it get out of hand."

"He means well, Mimi, you know that."

"I know, I know," Mimi said. "But it has played hob with my social life. The only reason I didn't go to the Castellans' lunch today was that I loathed the idea of all those old biddies clustering around me and telling me what a wonderful man Oliver is."

She met Susan's eye and turned a pretty pink under her

maquillage. "Of course I much prefer having lunch with you, dear, but I have a responsibility to the Castellans. . . . Now, what were we talking about before we were interrupted?"

"Introducing me to collectors," Susan said firmly.

"Tinsley Patterson's party, and why you didn't go. I suppose your invitation must have gotten lost in the mails. You hear all sorts of horror stories about the post office and say, 'Oh, no, it must be an exaggeration; things can't be that bad,' and then they turn out to be worse. Life has been getting more and more like that these days."

Susan said yes, things were certainly changing. "Take the art world, for instance . . ."

"Pity you missed meeting Tinsley's new beau, such a charming young man. Palmer was heartbroken; he had quite a thing for Tinsley. So did Potter, poor lamb, but of course he was born five minutes earlier, so he's going to be the Comte de la Fleur one day, and it's expected that he'll marry into the *noblesse* . . ."

So the formidable twins, whom Susan had seen—from a distance, fortunately—at a number of social events were Mimi's own offspring. Potter, Comte de la Fleur . . . but probably he had been christened with a long string of alternate appellations, one (or more) of which he would choose for formal purposes upon his accession to the title.

They must have been living in France with their father during their formative years, which was why Susan had never met them while they were children, although she supposed Mimi must have mentioned them. She was surprised to hear that Tinsley Patterson was such a femme fatale. I really must be out of touch with current standards of beauty, she thought.

Mimi rattled on, "But you wouldn't have been able to come, anyway, because you were busy buttering up poor old Tim—"

"Mimi, I was not buttering him up. I just happened—"

"—which was a very sensible thing to do. Frankly, I

wouldn't have expected you to be so practical . . . But it must have been dreadful, being there when the Pied Piper was killed."

Mimi sighed. "Do you remember how crazy all the maids used to be about him? And not only the maids. I must confess, I was a little bit thrilled myself when Joe brought him around once or twice back in the old days, although he did turn out to be rather obnoxious. The Piper, I mean, although I know there were some who thought Joe was obnoxious, too . . ."

"Well, he's dead now," Susan said, wishing Mimi would get off the topic. "I mean the Piper. Well, both of them, of course, but Joe died a long time ago."

"Have you noticed how many people are getting killed these days?" Mimi observed. "It seems to me there never used to be many assassinations, or maybe they're getting more attention now. It's all the fault of television. But whatever possessed that madwoman to pick on you—you of all people—to accuse?" She laughed merrily. "The idea of you killing anyone. It's ridiculous."

Susan couldn't help feeling a little peeved. "Maybe it was my hat," she said.

The maid placed a tray of crackers and cheese and fruit on a side table. This seemed to be what the hawk had been waiting for. With a cry of triumph, he seized a wedge of aged cheddar and bore it off in his claws, soaring away on the gust of wind that had swept across the terrace at that moment, toppling the table and a couple of small potted trees. The crash of crockery and the clatter of silver was followed by the tinkle of distant bells.

"Thank goodness, he's gone," Mimi said. "Now we can talk."

Bessemer came out and surveyed the disaster scene. "Coffee will be served in the living room, madam."

"What a good idea!" Miss Melville said before Mimi

had a chance to say anything. From the expression on her face, she was about to say a lot.

"Well, of course, if that's what you'd like," Mimi said, ever the gracious hostess, although it was clear she felt this was rather poor-spirited of her friend.

They trooped inside. "Isn't it wonderful to have a little oasis of peace and tranquility high above everything?" Mimi said as, after a short struggle, Bessemer managed to slide the doors shut against the tempest raging outside. "You'd hardly know you were in the city."

Bessemer snorted and stomped out.

"She acts as if she'd been with the family for ages," Mimi explained, "but I hired her only last week."

"About those other art collectors you were mentioning . . . ?" Miss Melville persisted before Mimi could get launched on the servant problem.

Mimi sipped her coffee thoughtfully. "Let me see. There's Philip Johnson, but I barely know him. Henry Geldzahler, of course . . . Heini Thyssen . . . only he spends most of his time in Europe. There's General Chomsky, a dear man, but, just between you and me, a bit uncouth."

"Not the Chomp House Chomsky?"

"Don't sound so surprised. He's supposed to have one of the finest collections of contemporary art in the country."

"I've seen the fine art in the Chomp Houses, if that's what you mean."

"Well, that doesn't truly represent his collection, although I understand there are some very good things there, too. You mustn't be such a snob, Susan. Remember cigar store Indians were once outside cigar stores. I met the man only recently at the Venturers Club; he's been a member for some time. Probably started out by hunting down his own hamburgers."

She laughed merrily.

"Whatever were you doing in a Chomp House, Susan?

Oh, I keep forgetting, you're poor now. Not that that's anything to be ashamed of. Someday you must take me to lunch at a Chomp House. I'm sure the food is very good. *Cuisine bourgeois* and all that.''

"You were talking about collectors . . . ?"

". . . Collectors, collectors, let me see . . . There's General Chomsky, and then there's General Mills.''

"General Mills isn't a person, Mimi. It's a conglomerate.''

"Well, so is Philip Morris and he collects art.''

Although meeting collectors would certainly be useful, it wasn't what Susan had come for. She wanted a wider audience than a few collectors, no matter how acquisitive, would be able to provide. A little later, as she rose to go, she made a final try. "I wouldn't expect to have a show all of my own, of course''—she said with false humility, because, although that might not be her expectation, it was certainly her hope ''—but as part of a group exhibit, perhaps . . .''

Mimi looked as if she found this a striking and original thought. Susan took a more direct approach. "Don't you know any gallery owners who might at least look at my work?''

"Nobody below Fifty-Seventh Street, really, and the uptown people don't seem to be interested in an artist unless he—or she, of course—is a big name or dead, preferably both. And the downtown scene has always been a mystery to me, even though Bud was such a big part of it. Although music was his thing rather than art. I don't believe I've completely recovered my hearing yet.''

The downtown scene was still a mystery to Miss Melville as well. At one time the area that was now somewhat self-consciously known as Soho had been a manufacturing district. A number of artists she knew in her youth who did not have her financial advantages had surreptitiously set up combined working and living quarters in lofts zoned for business.

Those studios, although illegal, had been cheap and spacious and, in a way, Miss Melville had envied their "Bohemian" atmosphere. Still, as she returned from visiting her less affluent friends' places, she couldn't help wondering how anyone could bear to live down in that neighborhood.

Today, Soho was supposed to be an art center, although priced far beyond the reach of all but the exceptionally well-heeled. And every time she visited it—which was not often—she still couldn't understand how anyone could bear to live down in that neighborhood.

"But galleries aren't the only answer. There are lots of other places where artists show their work. It's a pity you're not an ex-offender or a member of an oppressed minority; there are always shows for people like that, in model homes and people's apartments. Roy Cohn used to have exhibits of ex-offenders' work in his place, and Ariel Slocum is big on oppressed minorities."

"I am a member of an oppressed minority," Susan said hopefully.

"But not a fashionable oppressed minority," Mimi pointed out.

If they had shows for current rather than ex-offenders, Miss Melville thought, then she certainly would qualify.

"There's always the Whitney Biennial, but they're getting more and more difficult, and every time you approach them, it always seems to be the other year. Besides, I think you have to have been exhibiting in galleries recently for them to consider you. Perhaps we could set up a little show at the Venturers Club for you. Would you like that?"

Susan said she would, indeed. And she resolved that, if Mimi forgot this promise, she would grit her teeth and remind her. If necessary, she would even *nag*.

Bessemer was opening the front door for her when Mimi called, "Oh, I meant to tell you, there's going to be a

Spring Gala at the MAA in May. General Chomsky is
going to be the guest of honor.''

She paused and added. ''He's sponsoring a new wing. I
think you should be there.''

Susan thought she should be there, too. ''I'd be delighted to come,'' she told Mimi.

Maybe Peter would be back by then, she day-dreamed,
and they could go together.

✡✡✡ XXIII

Later that month Miss Melville, while attending—at her
own invitation—a cocktail reception at the Pierre to benefit
superannuated racehorses, ran into Shirley, who told her
that Rhonda was on the loose again. Miss Melville nearly
choked on her caviar, which would have been a shame
because it was nearly the best imported Beluga; then she
recollected that Shirley was not the most reliable of infor-
mants.

Since, like so many of the crashers, Shirley seldom read
the papers—except to look for news of potentially crashable
events—and listened to the news on radio and television
with less than rapt attention, she had not only a confused
idea of life in general but a very hazy impression of what
had happened in the rose garden at Chilon that June. That
had not stopped her from telling Miss Melville and the
others all about it at a buffet dinner on a barge a couple of
days after the actual event.

Lennie Shannon had been shot to death—that much she
had grasped accurately—''at a very exclusive party at a

swank college in Riverdale, probably by the mob; you know how those colleges are. Anyhow, there was a gun moll named Neville something or other—that's a pretty name, Neville—who, Rhonda claimed, did it. But she couldn't have done it or she'd be in jail, right?''

"Not necessarily," Emmett Greensteen informed them. "Today it doesn't matter whether you're guilty or innocent; it's how good a lawyer you can get, and gangsters have the best lawyers money can buy. It's first class all the way with them."

Since Emmett was a newspaperman—he worked in the classified advertising department of one of the suburban papers—his words were always listened to with respect.

"It was a terrible thing, wasn't it!" Miss Melville said. "As a matter of fact, I was at the Chilon party myself," she admitted, having decided that this would be the best way to forestall any dark hints that Rhonda might drop in the future. "I'd been a fan of Lennie Shannon's since I was a girl, so I thought I'd see if I could crash." She wondered what they would think if they knew that she herself was the infamous Neville.

"And you actually got in!" Shirley was impressed. "How did you manage it?"

"I was just lucky," she said modestly. "Matter of walking in the wrong door at the right time."

"I guess you know, then, that Rhonda managed to crash the party disguised as a plumber . . ." Shirley said.

"A gardener," Miss Melville murmured apologetically.

"Oh, that's right, you were there and saw the whole thing."

Miss Melville was not about to let herself be trapped into details that might prove an embarrassment. "I didn't actually see it happen. I was at the other end of the garden, at the buffet table."

Her listeners nodded solemnly. That was where they would have been, too. "I heard a bang, and a commotion, and I went over to see what was going on. But they wouldn't let me get close. I didn't even know the Piper had been killed, at first. I just saw the police taking Rhonda away, and I though she'd been caught crashing—''

"I'll bet that made you nervous," Shirley said.

"You can't begin to imagine how nervous. It was only afterward that I heard what had happened to Lennie Shannon."

"But what happened to Rhonda?" Dana wanted to know. "I mean, where is she now? Is she all right?"

Shirley opened her mouth to answer, then remembered she must defer to the one who had actually been there.

Miss Melville shook her head, indicating ignorance.

Beaming, Shirley took over. "They've locked her up in an institution for the mentally disabled where she prob'ly will stay forever, because the Piper was a very important person."

"But the papers said she couldn't have done it," Dana objected.

Emmett smiled a wise newspaperman's smile. "You can't always go by the papers," he said.

At the time, Miss Melville had hoped Shirley would be right about Rhonda's fate, even though in her heart she knew better. Hadn't Rhonda been incarcerated in "institutions for the mentally disabled" and released several times before, according to Freddy Makepeace, who had himself been let loose from similar institutions time and time again? Why should this time be any different?

So when, several months later, Shirley told her that Rhonda had either been released or had escaped—she had been seen on the party circuit—Miss Melville managed to convince herself after her initial startlement that this information was as confused as the rest of Shirley's reports. Rhonda couldn't possibly have been let go so soon, and if she had escaped, surely it would have been in the papers, if only because of her connection with the Piper's demise.

Miss Melville really hadn't been prepared to run into the

woman at the Grand the evening when she went to kill the
ambassador, although she knew she should have been.
Rhonda had been subdued and avoided Miss Melville, no
doubt still intimidated by the Boss's psychiatrist or psychi-
atrists. Miss Melville was glad, of course, that the Organization had chosen to frighten Rhonda rather than get rid of
her in a more permanent way, but she would have felt a
lot more comfortable if she could have been assured that
Rhonda would be off the scene forever.

Late in the year, a big batch of letters arrived from Peter.
As always, she read them in chronological order so that
she was half asleep by the time she came to the last one,
and at first didn't grasp the good news. In fact, she had to
read the words twice before she finally took in their import.

". . . I think I've gone about as far as I can on a preliminary study; and now that I've become fairly fluent in the
language, I am beginning to suspect that I may have worn
out my welcome to a degree. I have discovered that the
words the Oupi have been chanting when they dance around
my hut every morning waving their spears and gnashing
their teeth are not, as I first believed, an invocation to the
rising sun, but a warning to the unwelcome stranger.

"I should be back home in six months, give or take a
month or two, and I will want to start working on my book
right away, so clear out a room for me to use as a study
and make sure there's a good reading lamp. You might
also look into the possibility of buying a good second-hand
word processor cheap or, better yet, see if you can borrow
one from somebody."

The letter was dated only a month back, so unless he
changed his mind, or circumstances changed it for him,
she could expect him some time around the summer of the
New Year. That meant she would need to get out of the
assassination business as fast as she could, no more shilly-
shallying. It did cross her mind that, once Peter got im-
mersed in his book, she could carry out an occasional

assignment without his noticing. Although it was highly unlikely that she would want to.

She reminded Mimi of her promise to arrange for an exhibition at the Venturers. Mimi was distressed, not because she had forgotten her promise—that wouldn't have bothered her—but because, for perhaps the first time in a life devoted to achievement through influence, she had actually tried and been unable to deliver.

"I'm still working on it, but some of the members are very stubborn. They say it's a club, not an art gallery. When I pointed out that they've shown pictures there before, they said it was only of people performing heroic deeds. Or killing animals. Or animals alone, not doing anything in particular.

"Personally," she burst out, "I think it's because you're a woman. They're such chauvinists, the old dodderers!"

Miss Melville would have been touched by her friend's apparent distress on her behalf, if Mimi hadn't gone on to say, "Besides, you're the same age as I am, even if I don't look it, and anyway I don't see why being young is so important, especially for an artist. You only have to look at her pictures; you don't have to look at her."

The wicked old neo-Victorians on the board of the Venturers wanted to discover new young talent; they didn't want to resurrect an old middle-aged one. She could see them licking their chops at the idea of a show of nudes by a nubile young lady artist, under the impression that those who painted nudes were easily denuded themselves.

"But I'm going to keep on plugging," Mimi vowed. "Meanwhile, paint bigger pictures. Big pictures are what's in these days."

So Miss Melville painted bigger pictures for a hobby and went on killing people for a living. She disposed of a few politicians, a comedienne who got her laughs by denigrating her own sex, and the head of a giant entertainment conglomerate, but refused to handle the government official whom Mr. Tabor proposed for her next assignment. Although the circumstantial evidence was strong, she explained to Mr. Tabor, the allegations against him of sexual harassment, accepting bribes, buying votes, covering up crimes and fixing traffic tickets had not been proven.

Later she heard on the news that he had been duly disposed of at a street rally by a sniper who wounded two policemen in making his getaway. Slipshod work, she thought severely. "No more ring around the collar . . ." the commercial following the news story said.

◊◊◊ XXIV

Alex Tabor had tried to make her change her mind about the last job, but his efforts seemed perfunctory. She couldn't help worrying. Had she lost ground in their employer's esteem? Had they found someone to supplant her or, at least, make her less useful to the Organization?

It didn't seem likely, judging by the way her replacement had botched the job. Could it be simply that Tabor had other things on his mind?

She resolved to see if she could bring up the subject tactfully when next they met in order for her to give him the painting for her last job and him to give her the weapon for the next. (After all, she thought, he *had* offered her another job, so she must still be giving satisfaction. She knew she was being inconsistent, but she wanted the option of quitting rather than being fired. It was a matter of pride. And, of course, money.)

Battery Park was the site he'd chosen for the rendez-vous. She hated making the long trip downtown just to deliver a picture and get a gun. "Really," she told him on the phone, "there's no reason why we need to meet all over town. You could just as well come up to my apart-ment or I could come over to your place."

She had no idea of where he lived, but, since there was no area code to dial, it had to be either Manhattan or the Bronx, and she could not visualize him in the Bronx.

"No, no, and please remember we are talking on the phone. We're not supposed to go to each other's houses. We're not even supposed to know where each other lives."

"But you do know where I live."

"Yes, most irregular. Please don't ask me to explain. It's the way we've always done it."

Like every other profession, conspirators had their rules and regulations, she supposed.

The day was chilly and the breezes from the bay made the park seem glacial. "I'm freezing," she said, shivering as she handed him the picture, neatly wrapped in plain brown paper as if it were something obscene. It would be difficult for a picture to be obscene these days, she thought, unless it actually leaped out of its frame and violated the viewer. For something like that, she thought, I probably could get a grant.

"Is it that cold?" he said. "I hadn't noticed."

He took the painting from her as if it were a surprise, as if he had never before seen a large flat brown paper parcel. He stared at it for a moment. "Thank you," he said. "Thank you very much."

There was an awkward silence—awkward, that is, for her; he appeared to be communing with some beautiful inner voice.

"You seem preoccupied," she ventured. "You must be in love."

"Love!" he repeated, turning scarlet and dropping the

picture. He picked it up and brushed it off with meticulous care. "I'm sorry. I hope it isn't damaged. How did you know? Did someone . . . ? I suppose a woman always knows," he finished.

Goodness, he really *is* in love, she thought, relieved to know he was not about to break the news to her that she was being dumped before her time (whatever had happened to Orson Welles and those wine commercials?), not that one conclusion necessarily ruled out the other.

She felt she should say something encouraging—young love should be encouraged—but anything she might have normally said would sound like prying if she said it to him. A young assassin in love could not be treated the same way as any other young man in love.

"Tell me about her," she was about to say, then checked herself. It was too cold to stand there and listen to a panegyric on the loved one's charms. It was too cold to stand there and listen to anything.

"Does she know what you do for a living?" she asked, shivering a little more ostentatiously this time.

She thought the question might get him going, but he merely looked sad. "Naturally not. Even if I were willing to breach our employer's confidence, she wouldn't be likely to sympathize. . . . She comes of a very good family," he added.

A less good family would presumably be more tolerant. "You think they wouldn't understand?"

"Oh, they'd understand, all right," he said drearily. "They might even wish to avail themselves of my services. But they wouldn't want me to marry their daughter."

Marriage? He was that serious? No matter how free-spirited modern youth might profess to be, in the end, they always returned to the basic conventions. Not that Alex Tabor had ever impressed her as being especially free-spirited. Criminal he might be, but never unconventional.

What had he told the girl's family—the girl herself—

about his background? What kind of plausible past had he given himself?

Of course he had the advantage of being a foreigner. He could claim he was a refugee, unable to divulge his background for fear of reprisals against loved ones back in the old country—always a useful ploy for a young man whose background could not bear investigation.

He suddenly seemed to become aware of the cold, cruel world around them. Probably, she thought, because I am turning blue. "You're right. It *is* cold. I shouldn't have suggested that we meet here. Most inconsiderate of me. Let's walk up Broadway and find a more sheltered spot where we can take care of our business in greater comfort."

But his gait, as he started uptown, was more suitable for a summer stroll than a brisk late-winter walk.

He must be thinking about his inamorata . . . Well, she thought, he might be willing to freeze to death but she was not, especially not for his love. She wouldn't even do it for Peter, although with him, she was more likely to be baked than frozen. No need to worry about the jungle any more, she reminded herself. He was coming home.

She quickened her pace so that Tabor was forced to follow suit. Still he did not speak, merely stared ahead with a silly smile on his face.

"What's she like?" Susan finally asked.

"She is very beautiful, very intelligent, very passionate—" He checked himself and colored. "Forgive me . . ."

"Believe me, Alex," Susan said gently, "I know what passion is."

"Of course," he said. "Of course. I didn't mean . . ."

"Does the Boss know about her?" Susan asked, to cover his embarrassment.

For once he let her use the word "Boss" without correcting her. "Why should he know? What business is it of his? My private life doesn't concern him."

She gave him a look.

"Well, you—you're still a rookie. And you're a woman. It's different with me."

Susan started walking even faster.

"If you've taken up jogging, I think you might at least have warned me," he complained.

"Sorry," she said, slowing down, "I was just trying to get warm."

"Naturally he would expect me to have girlfriends. Only . . ."

"Only he wouldn't expect you to get serious about any one of them?"

"I suppose not. I never have before."

"He probably has already had her all checked out," Susan said, a little meanly, but extremes of temperature always made her mean. It's a good thing I never did get down to that jungle, she thought.

"I never thought about that. I suppose it is possible."

Obviously he didn't like the idea, any more than she'd liked the idea of their checking up on her social life. What's sauce for the goose is sauce for the gosling, she thought.

"But it wouldn't matter," he said. "I can see now it wouldn't be right to go on doing the kind of work I do after we're married. It wouldn't be fair to her. Or to the children."

"Children!"

She hadn't realized things were as far along as that.

"The children we hope to have one day," he explained. "We both believe in large families."

They came to a halt outside Trinity Church. "How about going in here?" he suggested. "They encourage tourists to stop in."

A womblike warmth encompassed them as they left the icy street. She only hoped she wouldn't catch cold as a result of the sudden temperature change. A snuffle was a handicap to a hitwoman; people tended to remember you when they thought you might be infectious.

Inside, an unseen organist was practicing and the church was empty. Tabor slipped her the gun in the shelter of a pew, then whispered instructions for her next assignment.

As they rose to go, he looked sentimentally down the aisle. "We're planning to have a church wedding," he said. "I think one's wedding day should be a positive affirmation, don't you?"

"I hadn't really given the matter much thought," she said.

At the church door, he stopped. "This is in strictest confidence, you understand: I am thinking of quitting the business."

She forced herself to smile, trying not to show the shock she felt. "Going straight, as it were?"

"As it were," he agreed, without smiling back. "But you don't have to worry. Another contact man will take my place if I do. Things will go on as before for you. In fact, I think you're due for another raise."

The idea of a raise offered small comfort, especially since she was not planning to stay with the Organization any longer than she had to. But his leaving was going to make a big difference in the time that still remained. Absurd that such a sense of desolation should spread over her at his news, but she couldn't help it. If any sort of friendship had sprung up between them, she should be glad for his sake that he was getting out.

If he could get out. It might not be as easy as all that. He must know a lot about the Organization. He seemed to be in direct contact with the Boss. He could, if he was of a mind, "put the finger" on him.

"Do you think the Boss will let you quit?"

'I'm sure he won't make any difficulties."

But she could see he wasn't sure at all. Poor Alex. How old could he be? Twenty-six? Twenty-seven? He had so many years ahead of him. She only hoped he would live to enjoy them.

A month or so later, after she had successfully accomplished her mission of eliminating an activist who sat home and fiddled while his followers looted and burned, Alex Tabor introduced her to the new contact man. There was something different about Tabor, but she couldn't stop to figure out what it was at that moment; her attention was riveted on Mr. Skolnick.

She hated him at first sight. He was small, elderly and bald, except for a tuft of grizzled hair standing up at right angles on each side of his head. He had a Brooklyn accent and a face like an excessively ill-tempered Pekingese.

He doesn't look like an assassin, she thought. He looks like a revolutionary. It was obvious that he didn't like her any better than she liked him, and they glowered at each other across the table in the Chomp House where the three had met.

"He's uncomfortable in what he calls 'fancy, shmancy restaurants,' " Tabor had told her. Fancy, shmancy restaurants, she thought, would be equally uncomfortable with Mr. Skolnick. Offering him a tie would have done nothing to improve his appearance except cover the grease spot on the front of his shirt.

He pushed away the remains of the Double Grand Slamburger that he had consumed with noisy gusto. "So this is what I got to work with," he said. "Bad enough a woman, but a lady yet!"

"She's good, Skolnick. Our employer thinks a lot of her. And so do I."

"Well, maybe you know what you're doing. Maybe she is good. But good enough to be worth the money the Boss is paying her, that I can't believe."

"Believe it, Skolnick. For one thing, she knows how to take orders."

Mr. Skolnick squinted across the table at his young colleague. "Meaning that I don't?"

Tabor shrugged.

"Alex, Alex, have I ever let you down? Have I ever let the Boss down? He wants me to work with her, I'll work with her. He wants me to take a gen-u-wine hand-painted picture from her each time, I'll take a picture. He wants me to kiss her ass, I'll kiss her ass. As long as she takes orders from me like a good girl, everything is going to be okay.''

Miss Melville got up. ''I am not going to take orders from you and I am not going to work with you. Of all the rude, uncouth, vulgar . . .''

She stopped, not at a loss for words but reluctant to utter the words that came to mind.

Mr. Skolnick did not get up. ''See, what did I tell you? First she sits looking down her nose at me. Now she stands, looking like she would like to spit in my eye if only she wasn't too much of a lady.''

Miss Melville was silent.

Both men waited, Alex tensely, Skolnick with bright-eyed interest.

''You're right,'' she said finally. ''I *am* too much of a lady to spit in your eye. But—'' she turned to Alex Tabor ''—tell the Boss if he wants this old goat put down I'll do it for half price.''

And she stalked out of the Chomp House.

Tabor caught up with her just outside the door. She realized now what the change in him had been. He had shaved off his mustache. And he was less formally dressed than usual. Instead of a shirt and tie he was wearing a turtleneck sweater under his jacket. He still hadn't gone native—he wasn't nearly sloppy enough—but he was getting there.

''Aren't you cold without a topcoat?'' she asked. Today she could afford to be sympathetic; she had been careful to dress warmly.

''Yes, I'm freezing. Have pity on me and come on back inside.''

She shook her head and started to walk on. He kept up with her, shivering every time she glanced his way.

"I know Skolnick is difficult. But he and our employer go back a long way together. At least give him a chance."

She kept on walking.

"The arrangement isn't necessarily permanent. If you two really can't hit if off together, our employer will find somebody else to work with you."

"When he finds someone else, maybe, just maybe, I'll come back to work for him. But I will not work for Mr. Skolnick."

"Not for him, with him. He's unhappy because his hands are too shaky for him to do any more killing himself."

No doubt Skolnick was a pathetic case, but she simply could not make herself feel sorry for him. If that's a flaw in my character, she thought, so be it. I'm not perfect.

"Please give him a try. That's all I ask. Our employer will be upset if you walk out on us at this time. There's—there's a very important job coming up that only you can handle."

He caught her arm. "I'm asking you to do this—and I know I have no right—for my sake. It's vital for me to keep on our employer's right side just now."

He gave her a look from under his lashes. "You see, he has not only agreed to accept my resignation, he is actually going to back me—us, that is—in a little business of our own."

" 'Us?' Oh, you mean you and your girlfriend?"

"My fiancée officially now," he said, beaming. "We're getting married this June, and we want you to come to the wedding. It will mean so much to both of us."

Which one of her paintings, she wondered, would make a suitable wedding gift for a retired hitman and his bride? Not the one she had done of Alex—she was beginning to use more and more figures in her work—being crushed by a flowering vine. She had done it a couple of months before and it was one of her best, but hardly the thing for a new-lywed couple's wall.

"If you won't come back to the Chomp House," Tabor

said, "let us go some place else where we can talk. Here, for instance."

She let him lead her into a coffee shop on Lexington Avenue. Even this place had fine art on the walls, and not contemporary art, but Old Masters.

What is the world coming to, she wondered, with Corots in the coffee shops?

"What kind of business is he setting you up in?" she asked as they settled themselves in the middle of a group of unoccupied booths.

She couldn't see Alex Tabor as a shopkeeper, unless it was, say, a very elegant haberdashery. A restaurant, perhaps; she could envision him as a restaurateur. All kinds of people who knew nothing about it went into the restaurant business.

"Investment broker," he told her.

"I thought you were going straight."

"I refuse to dignify that with an answer."

Didn't you need a license or something to be a stockbroker? she wondered. Well, the Boss could probably take care of that. For all she knew, Alex already had a license.

A waiter came, took their orders and disappeared.

"How did you account to your fiancée and her family for the money that's backing you?" she asked.

"I told them a wealthy relative in another country was investing it in our firm."

Which was entirely plausible. A lot of foreign money was being invested in American enterprises these days, in the spirit of reverse colonization that characterized the times. And she didn't suppose the girl's family would ask too many questions. If the money were of dubious origins, they undoubtedly wouldn't want to know about it.

◇◇◇ XXV

High finance, more properly low finance, seemed to be in the air. A couple of days later when Miss Melville turned on the news to hear if anyone had been assassinated that day and whether it had been a neat, workmanlike job, she learned of the scandal that had rocked the financial world. Patterson, Pennypacker, Baldwin & Snook were in trouble. As their commercial promised, they had, indeed, taken care of their clients' money as if it were their own. They had, it was alleged, gambled recklessly with it, speculated, peculated, spent it on personal pleasures, padded their expense accounts, fraudulently converted, and embezzled what was left.

That is, Snook had apparently disappeared with the residue, leaving Patterson, Pennypacker and Baldwin holding the bag and shifting—or trying to shift—the entire blame to him. He was only an in-law, the husband—as closely as Miss Melville could figure out from the meager genealogical information given by the press—of Amy's oldest niece, whom she remembered vaguely as a spotty little girl with bad manners; and thus not part of the clan by blood kinship. He was entitled, certainly, to protection from the bulls and bears, but first meat for the wolves of Wall Street, should the necessity arise. It had now arisen.

It was he, she learned now, who had been the restlessly roving man in the commercial. Now he had roved completely out of sight, taking the firm's assets with him. I would never have trusted him, Miss Melville thought, but then she wouldn't have trusted General Chomsky either. Crazy Eddie she would have been inclined to give the benefit of the doubt.

The exact details of the firm's alleged malfeasances were no clearer to her than to most members of the general public. There had never been any need for her to understand the nuances of the financial world. Those were matters you paid others to handle for you, while you sat back and clipped coupons and, from time to time, went through the motions of consulting with your financial advisors, just to show you were on top of the situation.

In this case, she could see that Patterson, Pennypacker, Baldwin & Snook would not be able to survive the debacle. Its principals would be lucky if they stayed out of jail. (Snook would not be that lucky, provided the law were lucky enough to find him.)

Poor Tinsley, to have something like this happen on her first job. But she was young, she was an heiress, she would survive. Susan wondered whether to call Amy to commiserate. As it turned out, Amy herself brought up the subject when she called Susan later that week, although it was for another purpose entirely.

Her cheerfulness was explained when she told Susan that none of her money had been lost; she never let relatives handle her investments.

"It becomes so sordid if things go wrong and you have to take them to court, especially if your lawyers and their lawyers are cousins."

"Your cousins or cousins of each other?"

"Both. I'm afraid poor Tim Baldwin wasn't so lucky. He had quite a bit of money invested with them, but fortunately the bulk of his assets was tied up in a trust."

"How lucky for him," Susan said.

"Tim is feeling rather depressed about it, though, and it would be a positive act of mercy for you to have dinner with him some evening. I'm sure Peter wouldn't mind; that is, if you're still seeing him."

"Yes, I'm still seeing him, although not at the moment because he's still down in South America. But he expects to come back permanently in a few months."

"I'm glad to hear that," Amy said in an I've-heard-that-before tone of voice.

Susan changed the subject. "I'm sorry about Tinsley."

This was greeted with a blank silence.

"Won't she be out of a job?"

"A job?" Amy repeated, as if she had never heard the work before. "Oh, that! I thought you knew; she left the firm months ago. But it's taking time for them to set up their own shop; there's so much red tape involved."

For some reason, she seemed to assume Susan knew what she was talking about. Susan was about to point this out when an idea occurred to her, an idea so preposterous she dismissed it as absurd. It wouldn't go away, though.

Apparently thinking Susan's failure to respond implied some reflection on Tinsley, Amy got defensive. "I know people are saying things about rats deserting the sinking ship, but Tinsley was very junior. She hadn't the least idea of what was going on. If she had, she certainly would have reported it to the SEC. Tinsley is very strong on business ethics. She's so much more a Baldwin than a Patterson."

"I'm sure she is. Very ethical, I mean. When you speak of 'them' setting up their own shop—?"

"Of course Patterson isn't the best name to operate under right now, so she'll be using her married name for business purposes, although for social purposes she'll keep her own; just the reverse of how it used to be in our day, but things are so different now."

"Do you mean that—?"

"To give an aura of respectability to the firm, old Norbert Tinsley is coming out of retirement to head it—in name only, of course. He's senile, but his name's unblemished and that's the important thing."

Susan managed to grasp one fact firmly. "So Tinsley's

getting married?'' Her idea, although no less preposterous, began to seem increasingly plausible.

"It's all set for June, as you know. I'm so glad you broke down and decided to give them your blessing, so that's one thing off their minds.''

"Blessing?'' Susan repeated.

"Tinsley's opted to go the traditional route as far as the wedding goes, thank God. I was so afraid she'd want to get married on a bus like Hebe. Actually, Hebe wanted to get married on the subway, but Baldwin Junior talked her out of it. You wouldn't think anybody would mug a whole wedding party. Still, as he pointed out, what with the TV cameras and everything it would be a strong temptation.''

"Just how do you mean I gave them my blessing?''

"Well, not in so many words, perhaps,'' Amy conceded. "Alex said he'd finally confessed the whole thing to you. He knew you wouldn't be able to hold out once you knew how much they loved each other. And Tinsley's happy everything's out in the open; she's such a straightforward girl. She's very anxious to get to know you better. After all, you are going to be her sister-in-law. We must all have lunch very soon. Did you say something?''

Miss Melville choked.

So not only was Tinsley Alex's betrothed, but he had deliberately pretended to be Susan's brother in order to weasel his way into the bosom of the family. Of course the original mistake had been Amy's. He had simply gone along with it at the time just to annoy her, Susan had thought, and she had been duly annoyed. Apparently it hadn't ended there.

She was angry and also hurt. At the same time, she could appreciate his point of view. If she had know he was seeing Tinsley, she undoubtedly would have tried to put a spoke in his wheel.

"The reason I called,'' Amy was saying, "was to invite you to the shower Muffy is giving for Tinsley the end of the month. I don't think you ever met her. She's a Baldwin, Junior's wife. A Pennypacker on her mother's side, from the Pennsylvania branch.''

"For whose benefit is the shower going to be?''

"They aren't incorporated yet, so they can't take it as a business expense. Oh, you're joking. I must tell Tinsley. I'm sure she'll be amused.

Susan was anxious to hang up at this point, but Amy was constitutionally incapable of saying goodbye without passing on various items of gossip, including the rumor that Mimi and Oliver Carruthers were on the brink of divorce. "Didn't Mimi say anything about it to you?''

"Not in so many words," Susan said absentmindedly, "but I suspected something like that might happen, what with Dodo Pangborn working so closely with Oliver.''

"Dodo! What does Dodo have to do with it? Is that why she's leaving the Foundation? I thought it was because her parole was up and she wanted to start another business. How interesting.''

"Amy, I didn't mean—''

"So that's why she seemed to be throwing herself heart and soul into the Foundation's work, going around with Oliver and doing all sorts of Victorian things like visiting the poor. There was always a gaggle of P.R. people along wherever they went, which was why nobody so much as suspected anything was going on between them until you told me just now.''

"I didn't tell you anything, and there's probably nothing to suspect," Susan said, uneasily aware that she had just launched a rumor. "I simply jumped to conclusions, nothing more. Stupid of me.''

"What people are saying is that Oliver's divorcing Mimi because he caught her carrying on with a man who lives in the same building and raises birds of prey as a hobby. Years younger than she is, but then she was always attracted to younger men. But, let's face it, who is not?'' Amy sighed.

"If raising birds of prey is his hobby, what does he actually do?"

"I haven't the faintest idea. He must have pots of money, though, or he wouldn't be living in the same building as Mimi. Do you know how much those condominiums go for?"

What bothered Susan was that she now seemed to be stuck with a brother whom she didn't want but was unable to repudiate—any more than he would be able to repudiate her, if it came to that, she supposed.

At first she felt guilty about the Pattersons . . . but that was silly. Why should she feel she should have protected Tinsley and her kin—and what, indeed, was she protecting them from? They were very well able to take care of themselves. In fact, if Alex Tabor were marrying into that clan, very likely it would be he who needed the protection.

◊◊◊ XXVI

Which didn't mean she was not going to give that self-styled brother of hers a piece of her mind immediately. As soon as she was able to extricate herself from Amy's verbal clutches, Miss Melville called his number and told the machine she wanted to speak to its master *right away*—earliest convenience, forsooth! Then she prepared to occupy herself for the long wait that usually followed before Alex returned a call.

This time, however, less than an hour had passed before he responded to her message. She was painting away grimly at a picture of a giant decaying rose over which maggots were crawling when the doorbell rang. She looked through the peephole. Alex stood outside, wreathed in false smiles and carrying—for God's sake—a huge bouquet of flowers.

Without speaking, she opened the door and gestured for him to enter.

"Forgive the informality," he began with a breeziness that even he failed to make convincing, "but I had a feeling that this might be something that shouldn't be discussed on the telephone. And you have asked me so often to come to your place that I ventured to, er, drop in."

"You're right," she said, slamming the door behind him. "It's definitely something that should be discussed in person." If he expected words of welcome, he had a long wait ahead.

How was it that the doorman hadn't announced him? Had he, too, been somehow convinced that Alex Tabor was her brother?

Still, it was no excuse. He was supposed to announce everyone, including relatives. In the case of some of the tenants, especially relatives.

Alex looked around him, surveying the gracefully proportioned living room with its high ceilings and wealth of architectural ornament, so conspicuously lacking in the new high-rises, however expensive. Through his eyes, she could see the incongruity of the few bits of furniture she had not sold—either because they were shabby or too necessary—piled high with smaller canvases, while the larger paintings were propped against walls and bookcases and armoires. And the flowers: dozens, hundreds, of them in all stages of life, from near freshness to near dissolution, crammed into containers of every kind—vases, pitchers, bottles, pickle jars, even a pail, the sweet scent of their decay mingling with the sharp odor of paint thinner to create a unique atmosphere.

"I see these are somewhat superfluous," he said, tendering her his offering with a courtly bow, "but after all, it's the thought that counts, isn't it. So please accept these with my compliments."

She accepted them with a growl.

He let his glance rove over the paintings. "You're very prolific. A most impressive body of work."

He didn't know the half of it. He hadn't seen the rest of the apartment, with all the bedrooms save the one she slept in piled high with her *oeuvre*, as well as the paraphernalia of her profession and the boxes of memorabilia she still had not parted with more out of inertia than sentiment, plus the junk Peter had amassed on his journeyings.

Only the kitchen and dining room remained clear, thanks to heroic efforts on Nellie's part. "If the Fire Department ever saw what was in here," she said, "you'd be out on your ear, Miss Susan, even if you do own the apartment now."

Alex caught sight of the huge canvas that showed him writhing in the vine's clutches and gasped.

She hadn't planned on his ever seeing it. Now she was grimly glad.

"You have a—a real gift," he said. "It's a pity that . . ." He paused.

"That what?"

"That you never reached a wider public."

But she had a feeling that hadn't been what he'd intended to say.

"May I?"

Without waiting for an answer, he lifted a pile of small canvases from a chair, placed them carefully atop another pile of canvases on a table, and seated himself.

She felt it would be silly for her to remain standing while she confronted him. The confrontation could be a lengthy one. She sat down on the stool by her easel.

They eyed each other.

"You look so formidable and businesslike in that smock, with the brushes in your hair. I would feel almost afraid of you if it weren't for that streak of green paint on your cheek.''

Now he was being coy. The next time he'd roll over and wave his paws. It won't work with me, my boy, she thought, resisting the temptation to wipe her cheek. That would show weakness. Besides, the paint was probably dry.

''How dared you tell the Pattersons you were my brother?''

''If you will recall, it was Mrs. Patterson who told me I was your brother. I merely accepted the relationship.''

''You did more than accept it. You encouraged it.''

''At the time is was—well, sort of a joke. I saw it irritated you and sometimes, Susan, you ask for it, really you do.''

She remained silent. That might have explained his behavior at the time, but it didn't explain his subsequent actions. He would hardly have started going out with Tinsley just to annoy her.

''I was quite taken by Tinsley. I wanted to see her again. Since her mother had mentioned that she was going to the Columbia School of Business, I had no trouble tracking her down.''

He looked at Susan earnestly. ''Because she thought I was your brother, she accepted me right away. Was I to tell her it had all been a joke? Or even a mistake? I knew she liked me, but at the beginning I wasn't sure she liked me enough.''

''And afterward?''

He passed his hand over his hair. ''Afterward? Well, as a Melville, even on the wrong side of the quilt, I didn't have to account for myself, explain who I was or how I supported myself.''

She couldn't let that pass unchallenged. ''Even my brother would have to explain how he supported himself. Even when the Melvilles were riding high, they always had to eat. By the way, where is the 'Tabor' supposed to come from? Are you claiming my father changed his name to Tabor?''

He grinned. "Rest assured, I haven't gone that far. I've told them it's my mother's name. I am illegitimate." He assumed an expression of mock sadness. "It is a fact that I have learned to live with."

"You certainly are a bastard," she agreed, thinking he probably came of respectable, hard-working lower-middle-class parents—the kind of background that would have immediately disqualified him as a contender in the Pattersons' eyes.

"But how did you account for the fact that you haven't starved to death? Did you tell them that you had a job or an occupation of some kind?"

"Well, no." In trying to avoid her eye, his glance met the picture of himself and the vine again, and he shuddered. "There is nothing wrong with good honest work, of course, but then I would have to substantiate the lie. Tinsley might have wanted to come down and visit me at— at the ditch I was digging."

"What *did* you tell them then?"

The question was rhetorical. She knew the answer. "You told them you were living on my father's money, didn't you?"

He smiled beatifically. "I didn't tell the Pattersons anything. They're realists. They simply took it for granted that I was living on *our* father's money. They don't believe in blaming children for the sins of their parents."

"I should think they'd blame the parents for the sins they committed against their children, though."

"Believe me, Susan, I didn't let them think Father had forgotten you. No, no, I told them you had been living the way you were because you were too proud, too upright, to accept tainted money."

"Not all of it was tainted. Some of the money he made off with was family money. Didn't they want to know why I was too proud to accept that part?"

"Oh, I told them that part was already gone. Only the tainted part was left."

For a moment she wished he really had been her brother. Given the chance, she might have killed him in infancy.

"You can't believe how painful it was for me to stoop to all these subterfuges. As, for example, when I neglected to mail your invitation to Tinsley's party, after her mother had entrusted me with the invitations. Naturally I wouldn't have done it if I'd known that, by purest coincidence, there would be an assignment coming up for you the same day."

She didn't believe in coincidences, particularly not that one. The thought that she might have been chosen as Lennie Shannon's assassin only to make sure that she didn't go to Tinsley's party was a chilling one. Had she gone through that whole nightmare experience only to insure that the path of true love would run a little more smoothly?

"But you knew I was bound to find out about you and Tinsley sooner or later."

"I was shooting for later," he said. "I knew you wouldn't like it, and I wanted to spare your feelings as long as I could."

He never had cared much about her feelings before . . . the whole thing sounded fishy. Even if he was supposed to be living on inherited money, he still needed to have some ostensible profession. "Gentlemen of leisure" were objects of suspicion these days unless they were students, in which case he'd have to register at some school, or Amy would nose out the truth. Very likely he'd told them he had South American business interests, but still . . .

Even more baffling: if they had been seeing each other ever since she had played cupid by compulsion, why had she heard nothing of the "romance"? Why hadn't Amy mentioned it before? In fact, it wasn't like Amy not to have called her up specifically to discuss it in detail.

Alex had an explanation for this, too. According to him, at the beginning he had managed to persuade both Tinsley and her mother not to tell anybody that they were dating (he pronounced the word so that you could actually hear the quotation marks around it).

"But what reason did you give them?"

He looked very solemn. "I told them that until you acknowledged me as your brother, I didn't want to make our relationship public."

"And they bought that?"

"Mrs. Patterson had to be talked into it, but Tinsley said she honored the stand I was taking and said something—" he coughed "—which I'm sure she didn't mean, about your being—what was the expression?—somewhat of an 'old fuddy duddy.' "

"Oh, she did, did she? And I suppose you agreed with her."

His face was still solemn, but his eyes were laughing. "I told her we must not condemn you because you adhered to the prejudices of a previous generation."

She picked up the heavy copper vase in which she kept her watercolor brushes. He ducked with an exaggerated alarm that had, she thought, an element of genuine apprehension. He may be a killer, she thought, but so am I.

"Surely, Susan, you're not going to do anything so—so unladylike as to throw that at me?"

"Why, Alex, I'm just going to fill it with water, so I can put the pretty flowers you brought me in it," she said in dulcet tones. "No reason why they should die for your sins."

When she came back with the vase she found him staring at the picture of himself and was glad that the picture had gotten through to him, even if she herself couldn't.

He turned as she came in and would have taken the vase from her, but she resisted. "You wouldn't know where to put it."

She had some difficulty in finding a place for the vase herself. I really must start tidying the place up, she thought as she cleared away a few more canvases, thus liberating an armchair. She was tired of sitting sternly on the stool, keeping her back rigid. Somehow it would give him a moral advantage if she slouched.

"And so Tinsley went along with all this?"

"I think Tinsley enjoyed keeping our love a secret. Like most stockbrokers, she had a romantic streak."

He seemed to be serious.

Once they became engaged, they could no longer keep their relationship a secret, he explained, not unless they also kept their marriage a secret, which Tinsley had no intention of doing. So, as soon as Tinsley decided on her silver pattern, Amy let her family and friends know about the betrothal on an informal basis, no doubt dropping a few hints to Alex's "parentage."

"What about me?"

"Somehow, she got the impression that I had told you about it."

"I see."

"At first when we told Mrs. Patterson we were going to get married, she actually wanted me to change my name 'back' to Melville. Wouldn't you have loved that?"

"I suspect that you probably have as much right to it as to the name of Tabor."

"You are very suspicious, my dear sister. Then Mrs. Patterson—and Tinsley, too—decided that it was lucky after all that I chose to stick with my mother's name, in view of the fact that we are going into partnership in business as well as in life."

Of course, although the statute of limitations would probably apply as far as the money was concerned, the SEC would be likely to look far more closely into the finances of a Melville than a Tabor. And, skilled though the Boss might be in cover-up, it was probably better that Mr. Tabor's finances not be too closely investigated.

"Come, accept things as they are, Susan. Come to the wedding and join in our happiness. By that time the incorporation will be final, and there will no longer be any reason to conceal the fact that I am your brother."

"But you are not my brother."

"I know that, and you know that, but nobody else does, and there's no way you can prove it. So why waste your time trying?"

Was that a threat? Not really. Just a warning that if she persisted in denying him, she would simply be making a fool of herself.

"Oh, *no!* You didn't tell the Pattersons you were starting the business with my father's money?"

"Our father's money. Our late father's, that is," he added. "Why are you so angry? It isn't really your father's money, you know."

"I don't suppose it bothered the Pattersons to know that the money wasn't honestly come by in the first place, supposing it had been my father's."

There was a mocking expression on his face.

"No, of course it wouldn't."

Since there was no way she could see of stopping the charade, why not take advantage of it? If she could use their supposed relationship to retire from the extermination business, then the relationship would be almost worth it.

"If I acknowledge you as my brother and say I've forgiven my father for everything, wouldn't you have to share the money that's supposed to be coming from him with me? Supposing I said I felt time had removed that taint? Wouldn't it look odd if you didn't?"

He smiled. "Alas, owing to the financial situation in Brazil—inflation has been catastrophic, you know—Father's fortune dwindled to the point where it required all that was left to launch our little business. With your approval, of course, Susan. 'Alex,' you said to me, 'I want you and Tinsley to have it, and together you will make up for Father's mistake.' "

He didn't explain how using the remains of her father's money to found a stock brokerage would have atoned for the fact that it had been stolen originally. She couldn't help wondering whether, had the Pattersons known that Alex worked for a master criminal and that it was his money that was being used, they would have cared.

Only, she decided, if there was any chance that the connection might be made public.

No wonder Amy and Tinsley had agreed to keep the romance under their hats. Neither would have believed that Susan had nobly renounced her claim to her father's money (and, indeed, if it had been his money, they would have been right). They merely thought that it was in Brazil and she was in New York, without any way of getting her hands on it. Accordingly, they wanted to make sure that when the money moved north it would be securely tied up before she had any chance to lay claim to it.

"I hope you're not thinking of trying to blackmail me in order to get enough money to retire from the business," Alex said. "You wouldn't succeed, you know." She knew she wouldn't. And it wasn't that she'd really expected to get any money out of him; it had just seemed worth a try. She tried playing on his sympathies. "Don't you think you've been unfair, using me like this? You hired me as a killer, not as a—a front. At best, you've raked up old, painful memories, at worst . . ."

She was unable to think of what the worst might be in this connection, but Alex took her inability to speak as a sign of emotion. He looked sincerely disturbed. "Believe me, Susan, I am truly sorry. I didn't think of it as using you. It just seemed . . . convenient, that's all."

"Well, it seems to me you could persuade the Boss to do me a favor in return."

She waited for a sign of encouragement. None came.

She persisted nonetheless. "Artists are showmen in a way. They like to have their pictures exhibited so the public can see them. Even you said I should have a wider audience. I would like to have a show of my work, so I could feel I'm a legitimate artist, not just a hitwoman."

She attempted a winning smile. "Even if I don't sell my

pictures, it would make me happy, and you said the Boss likes to make his employees happy.''

She waited. Although he must have known perfectly well what she was getting at, he didn't pick up on it—which boded ill for her attempt to take advantage of this particular connection. Maybe this wasn't the place to try networking. She took one last stab: "The Boss obviously has all kinds of influence. He's arranged all sorts of things. Couldn't he get an art gallery to show my paintings?''

The issue, of course, was not could he, but would he? He could even pay a gallery to exhibit her work. There was a time when she would have been too proud to entertain such an idea. Now, she had no pride left—especially if the gallery were one of the big uptown ones.

"I'll speak to him," Alex said finally. "I'm sure he'd like to help you if he possibly can.''

He didn't even make any promises. She was disappointed, but not really surprised. A polite ''no.''

Why should the Boss do anything for her? After all, *he* wasn't pretending to be her brother. She wasn't a longtime employee. No matter how little he knew about art, there was no way he—or anyone else—could tell what impact her paintings might have on the public. If they were exhibited and sold, she could gain financial independence and he would lose her services as an employee. Clearly, not a scenario he would want to see played out.

Were she of a paranoid turn, she could have made herself believe that he had already exerted his influence, which was why the Venturers had turned her down and Mimi could do no more for her than arrange an introduction to General Chomsky.

That was ridiculous. If the Boss had that much influence, he would never have needed her. If he had wanted someone killed, he would simply have ordered the heavens to open and strike him with a thunderbolt.

But there was nothing she could do about it now. She couldn't discredit or even try to discredit Alex without bringing herself under scrutiny; and perhaps, with the Boss backing him, something more. She would have to go along with whatever Alex told her to do until after the wedding. She would even try to work with Skolnick. After all, he was just a hired hand like herself.

After that, if things didn't work for the better, she would simply refuse any more assignments. Alex could hardly leave his "sister" destitute; it would be bad for his image. And, once Alex and Tinsley were married, she would be a member of the Patterson clan, who would never let their new in-law's half sister become a bag lady.

If she didn't try to rush it, things just might work out for her after all . . .

⬦⬦⬦ XXVII

In the middle of April Mimi called to say that General Chomsky was going to dedicate his new wing at the Museum of American Art on the second Sunday in May.

"That's Mother's Day," Susan observed. "Or Mom's Day, as the General himself would say in his commercials," she explained. " 'Get Mom out of the kitchen, away from the heat, and take her to a Chomp House for a Mom's Day treat.' "

"How clever of him," Mimi said. "Anyhow, I would like you to be there as my guest, and I'll introduce you. Who knows, history may be made."

"Nothing could keep me away," Susan vowed.

This time she intended to carry plenty of cash on her, just in case Mimi forgot to leave a ticket. Of course Susan had a viable checking account now, but in case one or all of the witches she had encountered on the previous occasion—years ago, but the episode was still vivid—was again haunting the reception desk and recognized her, it would be as well to be prepared with actual bills which could be waved in the face or, if need be, flung in it.

Once the mere possibility of such an encounter would have been enough to keep Susan awake for nights beforehand. Now she regarded it as one of the routine hazards of life. Interesting, she thought, how having the power of death in your hands changed your way of looking at life.

A few days later Alex called. His purpose was to put Mr. Skolnick on the phone and monitor the conversation to make sure Skolnick behaved himself.

Somebody must have been speaking sharply to Skolnick. He wasn't exactly polite—she didn't think he knew how to be—but he was subdued and, for him, almost conciliatory.

Both of them had to be placated until after the Patterson-Tabor nuptials were concluded, and so she forced herself to be civil in return. Undoubtedly courtesy came more easily to her than to Mr. Skolnick, but it wasn't easy, all the same.

He had called, he informed her, to ask where they should . . . he bogged down. "Rendezvous, rendezvous," Alex's voice prompted.

"Rendezvous, shmendezvous. Where do you want to meet?"

Her first suggestion for a meeting place was Union Square, which seemed to her to represent the essence of Skolnick, besides being far from the haunts of anyone she could possibly know. Being seen with the crashers on occasion hadn't bothered her too much. She had learned to accept them. Skolnick was another matter. She felt it would be utterly mortifying to be seen in such company as his by anyone.

Alex, however, vetoed that choice. There were both a Greenmarket and a drug market there, he pointed out, without specifying whether they were simultaneous or alternate. The place was constantly under surveillance by the Police Department and the Department of Markets. If the Police didn't think Skolnick looked suspicious, she thought, Markets would surely tag him as unwholesome. Alex was right.

Finally, after Mr. Skolnick had made some unreasonable suggestions—one was in Brooklyn, for Heaven's sake, and not even Brooklyn Heights—they arranged to meet in Riverside Park at the unearthly hour of seven in the morning.

Once there would have been little danger of running into anyone she knew on the West Side, but these days all sorts of people not only went there to visit museums and other cultural institutions (this would be too early in the day for that, at least), some went so far as to live there. She also had warned against choosing a spot too far uptown, because Columbia University was engaged in colonizing the areas adjacent to its campus, driving out the indigenous inhabitants and replacing them with academic types. She knew, of course, that where there were academic types, you were likely to find Baldwins and Pattersons, and sometimes even Pennypackers.

The early hour was no guarantee, either. These days all sorts of people were up at the crack of dawn in ridiculous costumes, jogging their silly little hearts out. Well, every religion to its own rituals. At least it was better than walking barefoot over live coals.

They finally arranged to meet at the Soldiers and Sailors Monument on the West Eighty-ninth Street.

"Can't we meet some place where I can at least sit down?" Mr. Skolnick asked plaintively.

Alex's voice, off telephone: "You can sit on the steps. It won't be for long. She's very punctual." And, in response to a series of mutters, "I'm sorry if the damp makes your rheumatism worse. Bring a cushion. We all have to make sacrifices."

Alex then spoke directly into the phone: "Goodbye, Susan, I'm glad that's all settled."

She tried to cheer herself with the thought that this could be her last job. The date of the wedding was less than month away. After that she would be tied to Alex far more permanently than Tinsley. You could always divorce a wife, but never a sister.

If worse came to worst, she thought, she could always threaten to move in with the two of them. The handsome East Side condominium that was the bride's parents' wedding gift had ample space in expectation of Tinsley's displaying the standard Patterson-Baldwin fecundity, so there would be plenty of room for one more.

The day was sunny, but there was a chill in the air when she arrived at the little Greek temple. Mr. Skolnick huddled on the steps like some malignant guardian spirit. "You're late," he growled.

"I'm precisely on time."

She stopped him as he reached inside his coat. "We'd better go down into the park. Here we're overlooked by the houses on the Drive. We don't want anyone to see you give me the gun."

"But it's in a bag."

"We don't want anyone to see you give me anything."

Groaning, he got up and hobbled down the steps that led to the path below, emitting a wheeze with every breath. She would have felt sorry for him if he hadn't been such a vile old man.

"Look," he said, stopping when they had gone only a few yards, "in case you're planning to go to New Jersey, maybe you hadn't noticed there's a river in the way."

"I'm an excellent swimmer. And we should go a little further into the park just to be sure nobody's watching."

"This is far enough," he said, sinking onto a bench. "Nobody will even look at us. If anybody happens to pass by, they'll think we're such a beautiful romantic couple we must be lovers, so they'll leave us alone." He chuckled roupily.

She sat down on the bench as far away from him as she could, without getting out of earshot, and tried to look as if she had nothing to do with him.

The brown paper bag that he handed her appeared from its odor to have originally been used to carry something that had garlic as one of its main constituents. "This is your gun. Alex tells me you know how to use it."

"I know how to use it."

"All right, then, these are your instructions . . ."

"First, tell me who it is I'm supposed to kill."

"What do you mean 'first tell you'? What business is it of yours? The Boss says kill somebody, you kill him. You don't ask questions."

"Didn't Alex tell you I have the right of refusal?"

"He made some kind of joke on the subject which naturally I didn't take seriously. Whoever heard of right of refusal in our line of work? This is not grand opera. We don't have prima donnas."

"I have always had the right to refuse to kill anybody who I did not think deserved to be killed. It was a stipulation I made before I signed on, and the Boss agreed to it."

Mr. Skolnick shook his head. "I don't know what the world is coming to. Hit ladies with stipulations! All right already, I'll tell you who it is, but if you think you can get out of doing it because you like the color of his eyes, you got another think coming."

The candidate was unexceptionable—a well-known travel writer and TV personality who also prepared commercial brochures for the very attractions he "disinterestedly" touted, and had grown so rich through these and other activities that he owned a private South Sea island, where he was reported to utilize slave labor, as well as to have committed other acts too nefarious to contemplate.

The cause and the sponsoring organization were suitable: The Suburban Empty Nesters' Other Side of America Benefit for children who had never crossed the Rockies. Even the place where the assignment was to be carried out, the West Side Wanderers Club, was conveniently located near all forms of public transportation.

Only the date was wrong. "I can't make it," she said. "That's Mother's Day."

He stared at her. "So it's Mother's Day. You got some kind of prejudice against killing people on Mother's Day?"

"Hardly. It's just that I have another engagement on the same day at the same time. Anyway, what are the Suburban Empty Nesters doing holding a benefit on Mother's Day? They should be home waiting for the birds to fly back to the nest."

"Lady," he said, "like most ladies, you talk too much. Whaddya mean you got an engagement? You got a date? Break it."

"Nonsense. I'm a freelancer, not a serf."

"You talk too fancy, too."

No use continuing the discussion further. She saw there could be no meeting of the minds; how could there be when he didn't have a mind? He was just a grizzled old bundle of emotions.

She got up from the bench. "Well, I'm sorry you had to come all the way out here for nothing, but I'm sure the fresh air and exercise will have done you a world of good."

"Listen," he snarled, "you may think you're safe because you've got a gun, but you haven't had a chance to load it. My gun is loaded and ready to use."

He patted his pocket. The mean little eyes behind the thick-lensed glasses were pink-rimmed and watery. He seemed to have difficulty focusing. She doubted he could see well enough even to aim. She doubted that he had another gun.

She also doubted her own judgment. And there was no point taking chances. She began to back up the path slowly so that her retrograde motion would not be immediately apparent to him. "If you kill me then I'll never be able to work for your organization again. And the Boss wouldn't like it."

"Girlie—" she wondered whether that was a step up or a step down from *lady* "—you're getting too big for your pantyhose. If you don't work for us, you don't stay alive."

Absurd to let herself be cowed by such a melodramatic threat. It was laughable, really. Still, she hadn't known Skolnick long enough to know if there really was a loose nut in that foggy brain of his.

"The Boss let Alex quit," she said, continuing to glide backward, wondering what she was going to do once she got to the steps. Going upstairs backward was not one of the skills she'd acquired at boarding school.

Skolnick laughed unpleasantly and tottered to his feet with an audible creak. "Alex didn't quit. He got promoted. Now he's on the managerial rather than the exterminatorial end, but believe me, he's still part of the Organization and will be until the day he dies."

He waggled a shaky finger at her. "Anyhow, there's no danger Alex will ever talk. The Boss's got too much on him. But you—you're something else. If you don't do what we tell you, you're no use to us—or to anybody else, either," he said, adding vindictively, "silly old bitch."

She gave up any attempt to keep the conversation on a civilized level. "If I'm old, what would you call yourself, you—you halfwitted old mummy!"

"It's different for a man. And stop dancing away like that. You're making me nervous. And when I'm nervous, my trigger finger gets itchy."

"Why don't you ask the Boss to get you a flea collar?"

He had his hand in his pocket. Maybe there actually was a gun there. Only a madman would try to kill her right there in Riverside Park, but by now she'd concluded that Skolnick was crazy as a bedbug.

* * *

"Sue, Sue!" a familiar voice called, and Shirley Mont St. Michel came tripping—in every sense of the word—down the path, her face flushed, her hair, now a radiant red, in disarray. She was wearing a raincoat over a sheer black nightgown. Since the raincoat was of transparent purple nylon, the effect was one which would have caused even Peter Paul Rubens to blink.

"I saw you from the terrace. Felix and I are staying in Freddy Makepeace's apartment. We're taking care of his cat while he's in jail for disorderly conduct. That is, Freddy's in jail, not the cat. I got up early and went outside to look at the sunrise . . ."

"The sun doesn't rise over the Hudson River," Miss Melville couldn't help pointing out, ever the pedagogue.

"That's what Felix claimed. But I thought there was no harm taking a look anyway—you never can tell—and I saw you and this gentleman here . . ." she smiled at Skolnick, who glared at her ". . . down by the monument. So I said to Felix, 'That looks like Sue Melville.' And he took a look and said, 'It sure does.' And I said, 'It is Sue.' And he said, 'It sure is.' So we rushed right down to tell you the news."

Felix, coming down the path behind Shirley, smiled vaguely in Miss Melville's direction. It was the first time she had ever seen him without glasses, and his face looked naked.

So did Felix. Except for sneakers, his only garment appeared to be a raincoat, mercifully opaque but devoid of either belt or buttons. From the way he held it clutched about his pudgy body, she rather thought that was all he had on. If only he doesn't fall over something, she thought as he stumbled nearsightedly down the path. If only he doesn't lose his grip . . .

Up until that time, the park had been virtually deserted. Suddenly it seemed to be thronged with dog walkers, joggers and women with baby carriages, people on their way to work (or not on their way to work) and children on their way to school (or not on their way to school), park attendants and balloon sellers and food vendors. It was Carnival time in Riverside Park, with her little group the chief midway attraction.

And they say New Yorkers are blasé, she thought.

Shirley grabbed Felix's arm, either to keep him from wandering off or to establish territorial rights. "We're going to be married in June. Isn't is wonderful? I hope you don't mind," she added anxiously, remembering, it seemed, that Miss Melville was once supposed to have had a *tendresse* for Felix.

"It's the best news I've heard in a long time," Miss Melville said with genuine sincerity as she saw the look on Mr. Skolnick's face.

"And I wondered whether you would be my maid of honor? Or matron of honor, whichever? I have to admit I asked Rhonda first. I've known her so much longer it seemed only right, but she's leaving the country. She answered a singles ad and she's gone to the Philippines as a mail-order bride."

Miss Melville was even happier to hear that.

"I do hope you'll be able to come to the wedding, too," Shirley said to Mr. Skolnick. "There's going to be a three-tier wedding cake and everything, but if you want champagne you have to bring your own bottle."

"He'll be delighted," Miss Melville said as Mr. Skolnick stood there making odd, gobbling noises.

"Now, I do hope you'll forgive me but I've got to run. I'm late for a very important appointment. Do give Mr. Skolnick all the details, and he'll pass them on to me."

With a wave of her hand she was off, literally running up the path before Skolnick realized what had happened.

Behind her she heard a bellow of rage and the sound of ancient feet clomping uncertainly after her. Even without her head start, he couldn't possibly overtake her, she assured herself. With luck, he'll fall over something.

There was a crash . . . then the sound of a police whistle.

Curiosity overcame prudence. She ventured a backward glance. Mr. Skolnick had indeed fallen over something. He had fallen over Felix. Either that, or Felix had fallen over him.

The end result was the same. Both men sprawled on the path. Felix's raincoat had opened wide. He was, as she had surmised, not wearing anything under it.

To complete the tableau, in a vain attempt to give him covering, Shirley had torn off her raincoat and cast its purple diaphaneity over both men. In the early morning sunlight, the nightgown barely shadowed the vast pink bulk of her body.

I must give them a really nice wedding present, Miss Melville said to herself as she fled.

✧✧✧ XXVIII

The first thing she did when she got home was load the gun. Common sense told her that Mr. Skolnick was hardly likely to come after her. A complaint—to Alex, to the Boss, to God—would be more his style. In any case, although the doorman might have let himself be talked (and tipped) into letting Alex into the building without announcing him, he would never be persuaded to admit the likes of Skolnick without authorization.

She told herself all this, she knew it was true, but the loaded gun gave her a greater sense of security than any amount of rational thinking.

Her next step was to call Alex. Only the machine answered. She wanted to leave a message that said a lot more than the approved words, but she knew now why precautions had to be taken. It was Tinsley who might pick up his phone and get his messages, although if all his communications were as cryptic as Susan's were required to be, the girl must have started wondering what he was up to a long time ago. But love is often as deaf as it is blind.

Susan was too restless to simply stay near the phone and wait for him to call, so as soon as the hour grew reasonable, she called Amy to see if she had any idea of her prospective son-in-law's whereabouts.

As it happened, Amy had. "He and Tinsley are out with their decorator, looking at carpets."

The world was running amok. Passion and bloodshed were on the rampage. And Alex and Tinsley were out looking at carpets.

"Is something wrong, Susan?" Amy asked solicitously. "You sound a little short of breath."

"I've been running."

"I didn't know you were into physical fitness. We must have a talk about it some time. My exercise coach thinks it's a mistake to start running at our age. Jog if you must, he says, but running is too strenuous, especially if you've been leading a sedentary life. If you're interested, I can give you his name. He's an Indian and he combines the physical with the metaphysical in a way that's—"

"—Do you know to which carpet places they went?" Susan interrupted, then checked herself. They could be going to wholesale firms, antique dealers, auction houses, even thrift shops. She couldn't trudge from one to the other, trying to track them down. Even if she succeeded, she couldn't just drag him away from his fiancée and their decorator. Decorators had been known to kill for less, and even a fiancée might take it ill.

"No, don't bother, but if they come back to your place

or if either of them calls, would you ask him to call me
right away? It's important.''

"Nothing wrong, I hope?'' Amy asked greedily.

"Nothing serious. Just a little family matter.''

"Well, can't I help? I'm practically family.''

"Sweet of you, Amy, but there's no need for you to
bother. Just tell Alex to call me as soon as he possibly can.
That would be a big help.''

She hung up before Amy could attempt to catechize her
further. But she couldn't stay home all day waiting for
Alex to call. Suppose when she picked up the phone the
next voice she heard was that of the dreaded Boss himself,
announcing her doom?

Which was ridiculous, she told herself. The Boss didn't
announce doom; he just ordered it, and somebody else carried it out.

She tried to keep herself busy, but she didn't feel like
painting. She couldn't force herself to read, and daytime
television tended to remind her too forcefully of her own
situation. Some people watched soap operas, she thought;
others lived them.

Finally she decided to go out and have lunch at a restaurant instead of preparing one of the scratch meals she usually got together for herself. Before she went out, she left
a message for Alex on his machine that she would be back
in an hour or so, but that it was no less urgent that he get
in touch with her as soon as he could.

She chose a small French restaurant near her apartment
which had been favorably reviewed by several food critics.
There she was seated too close to the kitchen, served only
after everybody else had been taken care of, insulted by
the waiter, and experimentally overcharged—in short, given
the usual treatment accorded a middle-aged woman dining
alone.

She wondered whether they would treat her like that if
they knew she had a loaded gun in her purse. It didn't

matter, she wasn't going to let her plans go to ruin for such contemptible creatures as these.

She dealt with the inflated bill, informed the waiter that he did not deserve a tip, and told the manager that she was the food critic for a major metropolitan publication in which he might soon expect to read about the shortcomings of the establishment which he served so ill. You didn't need a gun to solve the world's problems, she thought, but it was certainly quicker and more convenient than sweet reason.

By the time Alex did call, early that evening, her capacity for rational thinking had diminished to the point where she heard Skolnick sniffing at the doors, creeping up the side of the building, and lowering himself from the roof on a rope, even though she was aware that the latter two were well beyond his capacity.

"What's this I hear from Skolnick?" Alex demanded. "He said you lured him into Riverside Park and had him set upon by naked thugs, then they all got taken to jail after a dog walker identified him as the Riverside Flasher."

He sounded as if he didn't know whether to laugh or not.

"Was he able to prove he wasn't the Riverside Flasher? Or is he still in jail?"

Poor Shirley and Felix. She really had to do something nice for them. She wondered whether there was anyone they would like to have killed . . . probably, providing the champagne for the entire wedding party would be enough. She was afraid that after this she would actually have to go to their wedding, though she resolved that she would not be Shirley's maid of honor; that would be carrying contrition too far.

Tabor obviously had little sympathy for his irascible colleague. "Oh, Skolnick managed to clear himself somehow. Perhaps by proving he had nothing to flash. What I want to know is what really did happen? How much of his story was true?"

She tried to explain. It wasn't easy.

At the end he finally did laugh, but his laughter was not completely wholehearted. "I'm afraid Skolnick does come on a bit strong. He'll know better next time."

There isn't going to be any next time, at least not as far as I'm concerned, she thought, but she had the sense not to say anything.

"And what did you mean by telling him that you couldn't carry out this assignment? Don't you realize how important it is?"

"As I told Mr. Skolnick, I already have an appointment for that day which is very important to me."

"Susan, you've simply got to do it."

"Am I supposed to dedicate my entire life to the Boss?" Bad question even though intended rhetorically. "Why can't somebody else do this job?"

"We simply don't have anyone else who can pose as an Empty Suburban Nester, or a Suburban Empty Nester—whatever."

"Do I look like one?"

"More than I would. More than Skolnick would. More than any of our other operatives would. They're all men, and all of the Empty Nesters are women. Men don't have empty nests, at least not for very long. They go out and feather new ones."

"I don't work under threat. Don't you understand? Mr. Skolnick threatened to *kill* me!"

"Skolnick always threatens to kill anyone who disagrees with him, which is one reason he's on the inactive list, though obviously not the main one. I'm told that back when he was an active agent he held the title for Mr. Uncongeniality ten years running."

He wasn't taking her seriously; at least, he was pretending not to.

"But he said in so many words that he'd shoot me right then and there, in Riverside Park, if I didn't do the job."

"Come on, Susan, I'm surprised that you of all people

should have let that old scarecrow intimidate you. He doesn't even carry a gun anymore. He can hardly see well enough to cross the street, let alone aim a gun. Anyhow, do you think the police would have let him go if they'd found he was carrying a gun?''

Good point. And she didn't think Mr. Skolnick would have had the time or the wit to ditch a weapon. Perhaps his threats *had* been empty. It didn't matter. The very fact that he had threatened her was more than enough. She did not like to be threatened.

Well, she supposed, actually nobody like to be threatened, but she was a Melville. In Black Buck's day you did not threaten a Melville with impunity. Black Buck would have hanged Skolnick from the yardarm. Unfortunately, this was no longer Black Buck's day.

"Skolnick just talks. He has no authority. Our employer only uses him as a go-between, rather than pension him off outright. Of course you can turn down any job you want to, any time you want to. Except this one. If you go through with it—" she thought she heard him gulp "—I swear we'll arrange to have your pictures exhibited. Even if our employer has to open an art gallery of his own."

"Oh, come on, Alex!"

"Honestly, he was talking to me about doing something along those lines. I've never told you, Susan—he was afraid you would raise your prices if you knew—but he really likes your pictures a lot. He's actually thinking of buying some without . . . without any strings attached."

Opening an art gallery, buying her pictures, indeed! Did he really think she was stupid—or gullible—enough to swallow bare-faced lies like that?

The Boss probably had her pictures piled up somewhere in a closet. No, a closet wouldn't be big enough to hold the quantity he had by now. A cellar, where they would molder away until he no longer had need of her services. Then he would dissolve the corporation, get rid of the pictures, and . . . what would he do about her? If she had remained faithful in his employ, would she be pensioned off like Skolnick and detailed to instruct the field operatives (women's division)?

She felt now that she'd been naive in attempting to deal with her problem in a straightforward manner. Deviousness was the line to take in dealing with these people—in dealing with most people, she had discovered. It took years to undo the bad habits of a blameless lifetime. Or, had hers been a merely complacent one?

She tried to correct her current mistake; the misapprehensions of a lifetime could not be so readily amended. "All right, all right, I'll do the job. But I will not have any further dealings with Mr. Skolnick."

Alex's sigh of relief was as audible over the wire as if he had been standing next to her. "I'll give you the details right now over the phone. We've been so indiscreet already I doubt it will make a difference now. And it'll spare Skolnick another brush with you. Believe me, he is more frightened of you than you are of him."

That gave her a few days' grace. If they were convinced that she intended to carry out this assignment, they wouldn't bother her again until Mother's Day. Then she would make some kind of last-minute excuse for not going to the Westside Wanderers.

She could pretend to have had some kind of accident to her shooting hand—that was it—and call Alex in the morning, no, in the afternoon, when she could simply leave a message on his machine that she was *hors de combat* and go. She had failed assignments before—though not many, it was true. Nothing awful had happened to her on those occasions, except she hadn't gotten paid that one time she'd killed the wrong man. Why, for heaven's sake, was it so important that this pernicious travel writer be eliminated on Mother's Day?

The Boss had grown too accustomed to having everything his own way, Miss Melville decided. Once the Nester's benefit was over, the whole thing would blow over. The Organization would simply have to pick another date for the job. And, she hoped, someone else to do it.

Just the same, on the second Sunday in May she took the loaded gun to the Museum of American Art with her, in case one of the Boss's minions was lying in wait to make sure she carried out her mission. She wasn't sure whether she carried it in order to demonstrate her good intentions in case someone suddenly appeared to escort her to the Westside Wanderers, or to shoot anyone who tried to stop her from going to the MAA, but it made her feel warm and comfortable inside. I'm carrying it for good luck. At least, that's what Miss Melville told herself.

⬦⬦⬦ **XXIX**

She arrived at the museum early. There was no reason for her to contrive to be late, now that she was a legitimate guest. And she didn't want to hang around the apartment not answering the phone if it did ring, listening to it take messages she didn't want to hear. She was looking her best, she knew: new dress, new shoes, even a new bag— dressy, but still large enough to hold a gun. She wondered if she would ever again be able to buy a bag without taking that into consideration?

The day before she'd had her hair done at a beauty salon that Mimi had recommended, and was interested to note that its walls were hung with etchings and aquatints. At first she had thought they were for sale; however, as Mr. Michelangelo pointed out huffily, he would never be so crass as to sell anything but his services. "All these are part of my own personal collection," he confided. "I want to share them with my clients. Besides, my apartment is too small for them all. He sighed. "I know collecting art is the in thing these days, but it does make for so much *clutter!*"

"I know," Susan said, "I'm an artist myself."

He did not seem impressed.

She was surprised when her cab stopped outside of the museum to see no evidence of new construction outside. Had the Chomsky Wing been built in the back? But that would mean they had given up most of the parking lot . . . Astonishing. Artists had made greater sacrifices than that for their art, but never trustees or curators.

The women at the reception desk were strangers to her, but greeted her with a deference that was explained when she discovered that the ticket that was waiting for her this time was for the head table. She would be sitting on the dais along with the other guests of honor. How kind of Mimi, she thought, a little surprised. Mimi was not one to give honor where honor was not advantageous.

In the foyer, set up on an easel, was a badly designed poster commemorating the evening's event. From it she learned that tonight's dinner was not only to dedicate the new Chomsky Wing, but for the benefit of young artists throughout the world. Of course she'd known it had to be for the benefit of something, but she had assumed it would be for the museum itself. The museum was forever in need of funds, having long since been outstripped by the bigger, newer, more glamorous institutions that were more successful in attracting those with deep pockets. But wouldn't you know it would be for *young* artists . . .

She was about to go into the Hall of Primitives and get herself a drink when she sighted a familiar figure at the bar. Amy Patterson. That came as no surprise; Mimi had undoubtedly roped her in. Amy was accompanied by a chicly dressed, dark-haired young woman whom it took a moment for Miss Melville to recognize as Tinsley transformed. She could see now that Tinsley was a very attractive girl by any standards, except maybe those of the Oupi.

Suddenly Miss Melville stiffened, then turned away quickly. At Tinsley's elbow stood Alex, elegant in slightly too well-cut evening clothes. Of course once she saw Tinsley she should have expected to see him, but she was hit by momentary panic.

Before setting out she had thought of bandaging her hand to lend credence to her tale, but had decided against it. That would only have inspired more questions from Mimi and probably others wanting to know what had happened.

At the moment it did cross her mind to try to whip up some sort of bandage before he caught sight of her, but it was too late for that. She had little more than a packet of tissues in her handbag. She would just have to keep out of way, at least for the early part of the evening. Even though there was nothing he could do about her defection from the Empty Nesters, he could make the atmosphere decidedly disagreeable.

If only she could manage to avoid him after the speeches, until after Mimi had introduced her to the General. . . . Perhaps he would be gone by then. Surely he and Tinsley had better things to do that to eat an inferior dinner (she wouldn't put it past the museum to serve Slamburgers in honor of the general and their budget) and listen to a lot of dull speeches. She was surprised that the two had come at all. But, of course, they probably viewed General Chomsky as a prospective client, assuming that anybody who would invest in the kind of art he hung in his Chomp Houses would invest in anything.

Best to keep away from the bar, she decided. Later, when the guests were all seated, she would come into the dining room at the last minute and take her place unobtrusively, or as unobtrusively as it was possible to climb up on the dais and seat oneself at the head of the table.

Or maybe she would pass up the meal entirely and join

the bigwigs afterward, explaining that she had been late and hadn't wanted to make herself conspicuous by arriving during dinner. Mimi would buy that. It was the sort of thing she would have expected from Susan.

That gave her at least an hour and a half to kill, probably more. What on earth would she do to occupy herself in the museum for an hour to two? She could look at the exhibits . . . she hadn't been in the Melville Wing for a long time. It would be nice to see the old family collection again.

She turned left, heading past the telephone booths, around the corner past the bench where the bag lady had been, under the arrow that said "To the Melville Wing."

Only . . . the bag lady was gone. The arrow was still there. But it no longer directed patrons to the Melville Wing. Instead, it bore the legend, "To the Chomsky Wing."

She closed her eyes and opened them again. The words hadn't changed: "To the Chomsky Wing."

General Chomsky had not built a new wing. The old hamburger-monger was too chintzy for that. He had stolen her wing, the wing that had been built and endowed by Melville money, *in perpetuity*.

And he couldn't have done it alone. The treacherous MAA had aided and abetted him. In fact, they had probably instigated the whole thing. There was no way he could have known that the Melville Wing was going to be up for grabs. Someone had to tell him. What kind of people were they letting on the Board of Trustees these days!

Perhaps they were the kind of people they had always been. It was only that now she was seeing them in a different light. And Mimi—Mimi, her old friend, her girlhood chum—Mimi must have known about this. Why hadn't she done something about it? Or at least warned Susan so that she would have been spared the shock of hearing the news announced after dinner was over, while she was sitting up there with all the notables?

The answer was all too obvious. It must have been Mimi

herself who had sold her down the river. The MAA's Board must have been afraid that, if Susan found out in advance what was being planned, she would go directly to her lawyers, which was what Susan would most certainly have done.

Not that she was likely to have gotten anywhere. The museum wouldn't have deaccessioned the Melville Wing without first getting expert legal advice. They always made sure to have members of some of the most high-powered law firms on the Board so that advice would cost nothing and discourage lesser legal lights from coming up against them. However, she could and certainly would have created a stink and gotten plenty of media coverage. The media doted on scandal in the art world. That really cut the culture mavens down to size, which was one of the things contemporary journalism was all about.

The whole thing—the invitation, the seat on the dais— was a set-up. The MAA, briefed by Mimi, figured she would be too much of a lady to do anything but accept what was a fait accompli.

And Mimi had probably arranged for General Chomsky to show an interest in her work. Much cheaper, he would have been advised, to buy a couple of pictures—which he could always hang in some out-of-the-way Chomp House— and utter a few gracious words than to build a new wing. *Et tu*, Mimi, she thought sadly.

Would Black Buck Melville have stood tamely by and let someone steal his wing? No, he would have marched right in and told everyone exactly what he thought of such despicable behavior.

And that was what she was going to do, but not right away. Nobody who was anybody would be there yet, not even the television cameras that turned up at events like these on a slow news night or when enough pressure was put on the stations. If she tried to say her piece now, she probably would be hustled out before she had a chance to make any real impact.

No, she would stick to her original scenario, not joining Mimi on the dais until after the meal was over. Then she would get up and denounce the museum for its crassness, Mimi for her perfidy, and General Chomsky for everything she could think of, including his commercials. She remembered having planned to make a similar speech once, two— or was it three?—years before at another time in another place. She hadn't gone through with it then. This time, she would.

She opened the door to her one-time haven, the utility room. This time it was occupied by a woman in blue overalls who looked up from the sink where she was washing what looked to be a small exhibit, thought it could have been one of the hideous vases the museum used to hold the floral arrangements on these occasions.

"Sorry, I was looking for the ladies' room."

"There's one on the second floor, in what they're calling the 'new' wing. That's where they expect guests to go, so they've fixed it up, with a maid to hand out towels. You have to tip her," she said sullenly. People who worked behind the scenes, in places like utility rooms, never got tipped. "There's another ladies' room down on the ground floor, but nobody goes down there much."

It sounded like just what she was looking for. "Thank you," Miss Melville said, giving her a tip large enough to evoke gratitude but not so large as to arouse suspicion.

She went down to the ground floor, which looked as if it hadn't been painted since her last visit there . . . nearly three decades before. Before entering the ladies' room she noticed, purely out of habit, that there was a fire exit next to it, which, so far as she could judge, must lead out to the parking lot. She didn't open the door to see. There used to be alarms attached to all the exits, and some might still be working.

The ladies' room gave her space for meditation, but she couldn't spend an hour and a half in there. Not having anticipated such a need, she hadn't brought anything with her to read. She didn't suppose the museum's gift shop was open, although she wouldn't have put it past them to try to grub a little money on the side by extending the hours. Anyhow, the shop opened right off the entrance hall and she wasn't going to go back upstairs and risk being seen by anyone until the time was ripe.

Miss Melville wandered out to see if there was anything on the rest of the ground floor of interest. She found a group of mothseaten Indian handicrafts, which seemed to be rather tentatively on display.

The solitary guard, a weary old man who, like the exhibit, had seen better days, seemed glad at the sight of what he took to be a friendly face. "It isn't much of a collection," he said apologetically. "They didn't start collecting Indian art until after it became fashionable and it was too late to get the good pieces cheap. When they started doing the place over, they tried to give what they had to the Museum of Natural History and the Museum of the American Indian, but both of them turned it down. So it's just occupying space until they get the money General Chomsky's promised, then I guess they'll get rid of it. Maybe give it to a small museum in the sticks, the way they did with a lot of the stuff they couldn't sell."

One phrase caught her ear . . . so the museum *wasn't* letting the General off so cheaply after all. "Is the General giving them a lot of money?"

"Funny? What's funny about it—?"

"Money, money," she mouthed, realizing that the old man was hard of hearing.

"We're not allowed to take tips," he said, extending his hand.

She shaped the words carefully with her lips: "Has the General promised them a lot of money?"

"Pots. We're to have new uniforms, they say, and they're going to paint the rest of the place and put a new rug in the trustees' room, maybe even sandblast the outside of the building. The last time it was sandblasted, I remember—"

"Aren't they going to buy any new art work?" she interrupted.

"Car works?" he repeated, puzzled. "Oh, art works. You should learn to speak up, young lady. Oh, they've got plenty of those already. Besides, the General's promised to leave the rest of his art collection to the museum when he passes on. They say it's very fine, if you like that sort of thing."

She spent as much time as she could looking at the Indian artifacts. Even though they were third-rate, they would have served to pass the time had not the guard kept following her around, insisting on explaining everything to her. Poor man, she supposed he was lonely—and it was his job, after all, to watch over the wretched objects on display.

Finally she went upstairs earlier than she had planned, though she knew the guests would probably still be eating. She didn't want to go into the Statuary Court through its formal entrance via the Hall of Primitives. There were always a few diehards who never left the bar, one of whom might well be an acquaintance. She could go in far more unobtrusively, as well as less circuitously, if she went through the janitor's room. She prepared herself with a little story to account to the woman in blue for her reappearance; however, this time the little room was empty.

◦◦◦ XXX

She pulled open the door into the Statuary Court and stood thunderstruck. All the statues that had been there before—the Indian brave, the Roman warrior, the bag lady, even the bulging statue of Motherhood that had caused so much controversy when the museum first acquired it—were gone. Not just moved out of the way for the occasion, but gone for good. The enormous nonobjective pieces, either in the drab hues of their original materials, or in livid color, that had been placed there were obviously permanent. The whole place looked like some strange geological formation that had been hit by a cataclysm, after which little tables had sprung up like mushrooms among the ruins.

She slipped inside, intending to take a seat at one of the tables in the no man's land where she had dined the first time she had ever crashed, where it had all begun. Those tables were squeezed tightly together now, due to the spatial limitations enforced by the new exhibits. Tonight, to her surprise, most of those back tables were filled—with young people who seemed out of place at a museum benefit. They were not a new breed of crashers. They were too conspicuous-looking, too outré—not only by her standards, but by comparison with the rest of the people in the room.

Miss Melville settled into the only empty seat at one of the back tables. Her new-found dinner companions were very friendly, welcoming her into their midst and offering her one of the cigarettes they were passing around among themselves—which did not, she knew, contain tobacco. She hated to think that this could be the cause of their warmth; it was certainly the origin of a certain miasma that hung over the entire area.

She declined politely and tried not to inhale. Still, she didn't want to be stuffy, so she accepted a glass of what looked like wine but tasted a lot stronger. She hoped it had merely been augmented with brandy, or something of the sort.

A spiky-haired youth seated next to Miss Melville seemed to feel their presence needed explanation. "You're probably wondering what we're doing in a place like this."

Miss Melville was about to deny that such a thought had ever crossed her mind when she realized that he was not apologizing; he wanted to make it clear that they were all slumming.

"As a rule we never go above Fourteenth Street," he said, "but Dodo said to me, 'Biff, no matter what kind of crap it has on its walls, it's a museum. Remember, the next piece of crap it hangs might be yours.' "

These were, it turned out, some of the young artists the dinner was supposed to benefit. Usually the beneficiaries of such events were not invited to attend them—none of the homeless, she recollected, had been present at the fatal dinner that had launched her career—but apparently tickets had not been selling well, so a representative group of artists had been shipped in at the last minute to fill the empty seats. "Sure you won't have a joint?" asked a young woman with a haircut similar to Biff's.

"No, thanks, doctor's orders."

As the young woman was wearing skimpy leather shorts, an even skimpier leather bolero, and nothing else but leather boots, a lot of clanking jewelry, and paint everywhere except on her face, Miss Melville wondered whether she provided the kind of representation best calculated to appeal to the museum membership, an idea Biff immediately expressed in much earthier terms.

The others seemed amused by the whole thing. Many had been persuaded to come, she gathered, by gallery owners. Among them Biff's Dodo seemed to figure prominently. Miss Melville couldn't help wondering . . . surely it was mere coincidence . . . but ownership of a Soho gallery seemed so right for the Dodo she knew.

One young man (she assumed that was what he was; except for a pair of bluejeans, he was covered entirely by hair) had been dispatched by his art teacher. Another—whose beard was divided into three parts, each plaited with a different, coordinating color of ribbon—claimed to have been sent by his mother. His confession was greeted with derisive hoots, either because it was some sort of inside joke or because the idea of motherhood was considered ludicrous in and of itself.

"What we have to go through just for the sake of our art," the young man with the braided beard sighed. "Of selling our art, that is. I hear that in Holland, if your art doesn't sell, the government buys your pictures. Why don't we all go to Holland?"

"I think you have to be Dutch before they'll buy your pictures," a girl whose hair was orange on one side and red on the other suggested.

"I can't believe the Dutch would be so narrow-minded. There are a lot of other advantages to working in Holland, too."

He explained what they were. Most had to do with the Netherlands' (supposedly) enlightened attitude toward use of illegal substances.

"I vote that we all go to Holland immediately," the hairy young man proposed. "All in favor say 'Aye.' "

The resulting "Aye" was so thunderous that one of the museum ladies hurried up and begged them to keep their voices down.

She looked at Miss Melville snugly ensconced among her new friends in polite disbelief. Miss Melville smiled affably and said nothing.

Some of the group started to get up, presumably on their way to Holland.

"Have a heart, guys," Biff protested. "We can't leave now. We promised to stay until the speeches were over, remember? We wouldn't want to get Dodo mad, now would we?"

Apparently this was a powerful threat. After some muttering, all had subsided in their seats except for Braidbeard. "What do I care about Dodo?" he asked. "She doesn't handle outdoor sculpture. I work in masonry," he explained to Miss Melville.

"He's a Concrete Expressionist," someone giggled.

"Well, the rest of us are staying," Biff said, "so you might as well, too. You'd never even be able to find Holland on your own."

"He'd never be able to find his way out of the museum on his own," the hairy one said.

Several of the others suggested activities, ranging from the mildly scatological to the astonishing, that Braidbeard wouldn't be able to do on his own.

"It doesn't mean changing our plans," said the young woman in skin and leather, "only postponing them. So we stay and get introduced to General Chimpsky. ["Chimp, chimp, chimp," a couple of the other chanted and dissolved into laughter at their own wit.] We bow and curtsy and maybe scrape a little. That fulfills our obligations. After that, we get to work on the place with our marking pens. Then we go to Holland."

The others at the table applauded. The museum lady flashed a fierce look at Miss Melville from across the room.

"It sounds like an admirable plan of operations," Miss Melville said. "What this place needs is some living art. But it would be a shame for you to go to Holland. We need you here."

They beamed at her again and urged her to change her mind and have a cigarette or perhaps a toke. Again she refused and accepted another glass of the fortified wine instead. She was having a better time that she had expected. She found herself telling the young artists about the problems she was having in bringing her own work before the public. They were most sympathetic.

It was Mimi herself who finally rose to introduce the General and speak about "this glorious occasion" on which they had gathered together to do homage to something Miss Melville could not quite make out. "We had hoped," Mimi said, looking severely at the empty chair that Miss Melville assumed she had been destined to occupy, "to have the last of the Melvilles here to, er, pass on the torch to the first of the Chomskys . . ."

Oh, you did, did you, Miss Melville thought. Perfidious Mimi, treacherous Mimi. Why had she ever trusted her?

In point of fact she never had, she reminded herself. But how wise she had been not to take her allotted seat. She could envision herself sitting up there on the dais with a fixed smile on her face, while the press took notes and the cameras rolled. Not that there were any television cameras present, she noted. The museum's P.R. man was going to be dragged over the coals for sure.

". . . But, alas, circumstances prevented her from joining us tonight, as we had hoped. However, although Susan Melville's physical presence is not, er, present, she is here with us in spirit. And now, without further ado, let me introduce our benefactor and my dear, dear friend, General Winthrop Chomsky."

General Chomsky arose and cleared his throat. In person he was even more revolting than on the little screen. His face was coarser and redder and his wattles wiggled disgustingly when he spoke. And he was old, older than time, older even than Mr. Skolnick. The first of the Chomskys, indeed! He looked like all the last days of Pompeii rolled into one.

She half expected him to begin, "Folks, I want to tell you about the best finger-lickin', lip-smakin', foot-stompin' art collection in the world that we've got waiting for you right here in this little old museum today.''

But he began, ''Fellow art lovers,'' which was worse, and plunged into a speech that was even more awful than his revolting commercials. ''. . . We must put the old behind us and look only to the new, for it is the hands of the young that the future of modern art lies. It is they who are blazing new and hitherto undreamed of trails, opening our eyes to new insights and interpretations of a multidimensional and oft formless reality . . .''

No use *her* getting up and making a speech, Miss Melville thought. She would never be able to compete with that. ''Oft formless'' indeed! She would put the old behind once and for all: she would put an end to General Chomsky.

How provident of her to have brought the gun along! She took it out of her bag and got up. By this time, all the young people at her table seemed to have sunk into a stupor.

Only Biff lifted his spiky head. ''Atta girl,'' he said. ''Way to go, but you'll never be able to hit him at this distance. Circle around behind the art and pop him from close up. You can't miss.''

Whereupon he dropped his head on his arms and returned to his own multidimensional reality.

It was good advice and she took it. She sidled past the wilted lettuce and the pregnant jelly bean, climbed around the blob from outer space and the distended diatom, skirted the pornographic rhomboid and came to a halt behind the hollow cucumber. She was now very close to the dais, just beyond the door to the janitor's closet.

No one seemed to have noticed her stealthy progress. Most of the audience was half asleep anyway, lulled by the General's soporific prose.

She sighted through the hole in the cucumber and fired. General Chomsky became part of a three-dimensional and very finite reality.

◇◇◇ **XXXI**

Without looking back, she pushed open the door to the janitor's room—still empty, fortunately—dropped the gun in a bucket full of soapy water, and glided out the other door. She passed through the entrance hall and into the Hall of Primitives, where the bar was doing a brisk trade. Most of those present were too absorbed in the pleasures of alcohol to notice the commotion starting up in the Statuary Court beyond. The bartender, however, seemed alert and interested. "Know what all the fuss in there is about?" he asked as he handed Miss Melville the scotch on the rocks she had requested.

"I have no idea," she said. "I've just come from the ladies' room."

She wasn't going to run this time, she thought, as she heard the sound of distant sirens. They might, of course, have no connection with the General's demise. The sound of sirens was an omnipresent background noise in New York, and this would constitute an abnormally quick response for the police.

But respond they would, sooner or later. The young artists—Biff, at least—had seen her set out to kill the General. The police would be bound to question him and the others. After all, she had been sitting at their table . . . It would be easy enough to track her down from their description. What would be the point in running? She would wait until they came for her. That was what Black Buck would have done, she told herself. At the same time a little inner voice said no, it isn't. He would have left the place as fast as he could, as so many of the other guests were doing, and set sail for the Spanish Main. However, she had no sail to set, and no acquaintances on the Spanish Main to give her safe harbor except the Trowbridges in Nassau, and she'd been out of touch with them for years.

Those of the guests who were not attempting a getaway were streaming into the bar now. Among them was a weeping Mimi, supported by Amy on one side and Tinsley on the other. They didn't see Miss Melville, who rose from her stool on seeing them and concealed herself behind a monolith.

However, Alex Tabor saw her. His face, which had been ashen to start with, turned chalky white. As soon as the ladies had been supplied with strong liquors, he came over to Miss Melville.

"What are you doing here?" he demanded in a fierce whisper.

"Cheers!" she said, lifting her glass and draining it. "As you can see, I didn't go to the Suburban Nesters'. I came here instead. The Boss can do whatever he wants to me. I mean," she amended, "he can think whatever he likes." The Boss might take carte blanche, but there was no sense in giving it to him.

"The Boss can't do anything to you or to anybody else," Alex said flatly. "He's dead. Somebody just killed him."

She stared at him, speechless.

He looked at her. "And suddenly I have a very good idea of who that somebody must have been."

He put the flat of his hand against her shoulder. "Let's get out of here."

And, when she didn't move, he shoved her out of the Hall of Primitives into the entrance hall.

It was still difficult for her to assimilate the news. Could it be that good old General Chomsky, upholder of Mom's Day and Dad's Day and all the national virtues, friend and dispenser of lollipops to kiddies, had been the Boss of an Organization of assassins, the local version of the Old Man of the Mountain—only his mountain had probably been a skyscraper, and he was infinitely more dangerous than the original Old Man had ever been?

She began to laugh. "You—you mean *General Chomsky* was the Boss? That's the funniest thing I ever heard . . . !"

She laughed and laughed and couldn't stop laughing.

His hand cracked sharply against her cheek. Never before in her life had she been slapped. If the gun hadn't been back in the utility room soaking in detergent, she would have shot him, too.

"Thanks, I didn't need that!" she snapped. "And, if you try it again . . ."

"You're getting hysterical. People are starting to look. You don't want to draw attention to yourself, do you?"

But nobody in the crowd milling about in the foyer seemed to have noticed the episode, perhaps because she was far from being the only one engaged in unseemly and unmuseumlike behavior. Several of the women and even a few of the men were showing signs of hysteria as the guard at the front door, having become aware of what had happened, tried to keep them from leaving.

Some were even getting violent. When the chips are down, Susan thought, there is a beast in all of us, mixing its metaphors.

Alex took her by the arm again and pulled her back, around the corner, past the telephone booths to the bench under the abominable arrow. The sound of sirens was right outside. No mistaking their destination now. Ask not for whom the sirens shriek; they shriek for thee.

"We've got to get you out of here," Alex said. "We could try to push past the guard, but the police must be outside by now, and they'll just herd us back in. There must be another way out."

"Several of them. There's a fire exit by the downstairs

ladies' room. The only guard on duty down there is deaf.
He probably doesn't even know anything's happened yet.''

"Show me.''

They hurried down the steps. The guard wasn't visible.
The fire exit, as she had surmised, was unattended.

He pushed open the door. A distant alarm rang somewhere, but it didn't matter. Alarms were beginning to go
off all over the place as guests found other exits. This one
led, as she had supposed, into the parking lot—a hive of
activity as fleeing guests piled into their cars and drove off.

Alex hurried her into the side street, from where they
could hear the police cars out front and the sound of other,
self-important vehicles. Television camera trucks, no doubt.
The event was going to get full, if belated, coverage after
all.

Alex urged Susan in an easterly direction. ''I killed him,''
she said. ''I killed him with his own gun. Don't you think
that's terribly amusing?''

"Let's go this way,'' he said at Park Avenue. ''And
stroll, as if we were out for a walk.''

"Nobody strolls on Park Avenue,'' she said. ''They send
for their limousines or call a cab.''

"We're visitors from another borough,'' he said, ''another planet. We don't know any better. Tell me, how did
you know General Chomsky was the Boss? And why did
you do it? Did somebody put you up to it?''

She began to laugh again, stopped when she saw the
look on his face. She didn't want to get slapped again,
especially not on Park Avenue.

"I didn't *know* he was the Boss, not until you told me.
I killed him because he was General Chomsky who made
those awful commercials and stole my wing and because
his wattles wiggled in the most disgusting way.''

He didn't say anything.

"I left a message on your machine,'' she said inanely,

"to tell you I wouldn't be able to carry out the assignment tonight."

"Did you, indeed? I'm afraid I haven't had a chance to pick up my messages. Did you by any chance give some reason why you wouldn't be able to carry out the assignment?"

"Yes, I hurt my hand and wouldn't be able to shoot."

He glanced at her hand. "You seem to have made a miraculous recovery."

Suddenly she felt tired and cross and put upon. "Stop playing with me like that. It's obvious you're not planning to turn me in, or you wouldn't have rushed me away like that."

Of course, now, more than ever, he wouldn't want the police to get hold of her. The risk of her talking would be too great. But what was he going to do about her himself? "Are you going to kill me?"

She was already convinced that the answer was going to be yes, and only hoped he would make it quick and painless.

He looked surprised. "Kill you? Why should I do a thing like that?"

The answer was clear, and yet it was hard for her to put into words. "Revenge, maybe?"

"Revenge!" He snorted. "The General was nothing to me but an employer. And I'm a professional. I work only for pay. I'm not a romantic like you."

"I'm a professional, too," she said, stung. "You said so yourself. And I would hardly call my killing General Chomsky romantic. Impulsive, yes. Romantic, no."

"In any case, I've given up that type of work," he reminded her. "I'm a respectable businessman now."

But he was—had been—still working for the Boss, according to Skolnick. Not that Skolnick was necessarily an authority, but it wasn't likely the Boss had backed Alex and Tinsley's brokerage out of the kindness of his heart. Skolnick had also implied that Alex had been working for the Boss under threat, or, at least, that the Boss had used threats to ensure his continued conformity. If so, that would mean there was no loyalty involved.

But if the Boss happened to have a Boss of his own, in which case the Big Boss was bound to be displeased, there would still be an Organization and Alex would be working for it.

Maybe Alex was telling the truth when he said he wouldn't kill her, but was it possible there would now be a price on her head from someone higher up in the Organization?

"You mean nothing is going to happen to me?" she asked.

"Not as far as I'm concerned. The Boss is dead. I don't take orders from him anymore."

"But if he took orders from someone else . . ."

Alex shook his head. "He was an independent contractor. He didn't take orders from anyone."

"You're sure?"

"I'm sure. Now that he's dead, the Organization is kaput. *Fini.*"

She hoped he was telling the truth. He sounded sincere, but then, he always did.

"Come, let me take you home. I'll call a cab."

"I'd rather walk. Unless you're in a hurry."

"I have all the time in the world, but—and I don't want to alarm you—it is just possible that you don't. I can speak for what was the Organization, but not for the police. How careful were you? Did anyone see you do it? Anyone who might be able to identify you?"

"Some artists saw me. One of them, at least, saw me with the gun. I don't think anybody else did, because I fired through the cucumber." She explained about the cucumber. "But you know artists aren't like other people. They're acute observers, with a sharp eye for detail. Of course they don't know who I am, but they'll be able to give an accurate description of what I look like."

"Even with an accurate description, it will take a while for the authorities to find out whom the description fits. In the meantime, we'll do what we can to make that description less accurate. To begin with, you'll have to get rid of the dress you're wearing."

"It's new," she said regretfully. It was a warm beige that had made her light brown hair seem almost blonde again, the way it had been in her youth, as Dodo Pangborn had reminded her. Dodo's words had cut deeper than she liked to admit to herself. She'd even thought of asking Mr. Michelangelo to touch up her hair a bit. How silly it seemed now.

"Good, then nobody will remember ever having seen you in it. It's a pity incinerators are illegal in the city, but don't worry. I won't have any trouble disposing of it."

He looked at her critically. "You can't suddenly change the color of your hair. Your friends are bound to take notice. But you could change the style."

"I *have* changed the style," she said, a little irked that he hadn't noticed.

"Good. Then all you have to do is change it back."

They walked on for a while in silence until Alex stopped at a phone.

"I'd better call the museum," he said, "and leave a message for Tinsley. She's probably wondering what became of me."

He made two calls, Susan couldn't help noticing.

"Just in case she's gone, I left a message at the apartment," he explained.

"It wasn't important that I do the job at the Westside Wanderers, was it?" she asked. "All that was important was that I not show up at the museum tonight." Lennie Shannon, all over again. "But why, actually? What difference did it make to the General if I were there?"

Alex shrugged. "He didn't confide his reasons to me, and I knew better than to ask questions. Perhaps he felt it might be awkward to meet you. Though I was his contact man, he didn't even like the idea of my being at the dinner, but I was there as the Pattersons' guest—no way out of it.''

''But I would have had no way of knowing he was the Boss.''

Alex shrugged. ''Perhaps he thought you had psychic powers. Or maybe the idea of meeting you just made him nervous. Remember, he didn't know what you were really like. The—what's her name?—Carruthers woman said she was sure you wouldn't make a scene when you found out he'd taken over your wing. But he was uncomfortable just the same. He didn't like scenes.''

''Neither do I,'' she said. ''Mimi was right.''

He began to laugh. ''Do you realize that every time you plan to get up in public and denounce someone, rather than make a scene, you kill him instead?''

''It only happened twice,'' she said defensively.

By this time they had reached her apartment building. She'd half expected to find the police waiting, but all seemed serene. The doorman beamed at both of them and wished them good evening as they got in the elevator. No sign of trouble there.

Alex turned on the television set as soon as they got in. ''It's almost time for the eleven o'clock news. You'd better go change your dress. Then wash your hands. Scrub them as thoroughly as possible. I don't know whether we can beat the paraffin tests, if it should come to that, but we can certainly try. Use turpentine. I know you have plenty on hand. The place reeks of it.''

She was beginning to get nervous again. ''So you do think they'll come for me?''

''As I told you, it's unlikely, but we must be prepared for the possibility.''

''But why are you staying here with me, then? Why get yourself mixed up in it?''

He affected to look hurt. ''I'm your brother,'' he reminded her. "A brother always stands by his sister in times of trouble."

If her connection with the crime ever became public, it would indeed look very odd if he didn't stand by her, she thought.

"Shhh," he said. "Here comes the news."

Considering that the event had happened such a short time before, a surprising amount of information had already been collected on the General, although the pictures were mostly of past glories rather than of present events. There were pictures of General Chomsky in his role as Chomp House spokesman, presenting awards, contributing to causes, and engaging in a variety of other favorable publicity-attracting activities. There were pictures of General Chomsky as a young man wearing the private's uniform of some unidentified Eastern European nation, then later in his general's uniform, a rank he seemed to have elevated himself to upon arrival in his newly adopted country.

There was a picture of him standing next to the very first Chomp House, somewhere down south, where General Chomsky had gotten his first taste of freedom and folksiness. There were pictures of more and more Chomp Houses as his empire expanded, and a picture of the building on his Westchester estate where his art collection was housed.

As the pictures flashed on the screen, the newsman continued talking. General Chomsky, well-known TV personality, art collector, philanthropist, and all-around family man (he'd had six wives), had been shot to death at a benefit the Museum of American Art had given that evening to unveil the new Chomsky Wing. All the station knew at the time of broadcast was that the unknown assailant was a woman.

"Well, at least they got the sex right this time," Susan said.

A number of witnesses, all of them young artists, had seen the murderer, the reporter went on to say, and all had given almost exactly the same description. She had, they said, been an old woman, so far advanced in years it was hard to believe she was still alive, seven feet tall, with flaming red hair, clad in flowing silver robes and carrying a torch.

After repeated questioning, the witnesses had withdrawn the torch and subtracted six inches (maybe eight) from her height, but stood firm on everything else.

"It is possible," the newsman said, in carefully neutral tones (everybody had a lawyer these days), "that the young people were affected by more than the high spirits of the occasion."

The police, he continued, were inclined to disregard the entire description. They were looking in the direction of the competition—other hamburger franchisers, or would-be Chomp House franchisees who had been rejected. Some had been very troublesome in the past.

" 'Artists aren't like other people,' " Alex quoted her. " 'They're acute observers with a sharp eye for detail.' "

"I forgot to mention that they were all stoned or something at the time," she said. "So that might very well have been what they did see. Except how is it that they all said they saw the same thing?"

"Who knows? Mass hallucination, perhaps. A psychic bond uniting all artists. Collusion against the establishment."

"But they *are* the establishment."

"Luckily for you, they don't realize that."

They did it on purpose, she thought. They must *want* me to get away with it. Young artists are the salt of the earth. If they had been present, she would have embraced each and every one of them. Suddenly she burst into tears.

Alex looked at her, astonished. "Why are you crying? From what you tell me, it's hardly possible that anyone could have seen you actually kill him. You were behind the sculpture all the time, you say. Even if someone happened to catch a glimpse of you, they'd never believe it was you.''

He sounded very convincing, but then she wanted to be convinced.

"In fact," he said, "I'm pretty sure you're in the clear. Maybe you don't have to change your hair after all," he said, regarding her fondly. "I rather like it the way it is." She wiped her eyes.

"It looks as if maybe I will get away with it," she conceded. "And there isn't anything to connect me with the General, is there, except that he took over the Melville Wing, and they didn't even mention that on the air, although I suppose it will be in the papers."

"Of course there's the . . ." he began and stopped, then looked embarrassed. "Well, there's another connection, a very tenuous one—and I hope it won't come out, for my own sake as well as yours—through me. You see, I'm on the books of Chomp Industries in a minor executive capacity."

She looked at him in disbelief. Was *that* the reason why he actually ate at Chomp Houses? Loyalty to the firm, perhaps even an employee discount?

"Just as a protection, you understand. Since I had to go up to his place to see him from time to time, the people there took me for granted . . . I don't see that there's anything funny about it," he said, offended.

"Of course there isn't," she said, trying to keep a straight face. "What were you listed as? Vice president in charge of pickle production?"

"Ha, ha, very amusing."

"Does Tinsley know about this?"

He looked alarmed. "No, there seemed no point. The only reason I'm telling you about it is that—that . . ."

"If it should happen to come up in the course of the investigation, it would seem funny if your 'sister' didn't know."

It would also seem funny if his fiancée didn't know, but there are degrees of funniness.

"It won't come up," he said. "They can't investigate every one of the General's employees. There are thousands of them. I'm telling you this in confidence, just in case."

"My lips are sealed," she vowed.

She still felt an uneasiness, as though there were something she couldn't quite remember but that could be important. "It looks as if I'm out of a job again," she said.

Alex looked surprised. "I thought you were anxious to get out of the business. Or did you want to do it your way, like Frank Sinatra?" He chuckled. "Well, I suppose you *did* do it your way at that."

"This is so final. I was planning to taper off, you know, but I still have to pay off my mortgage." At this point, though, it hardly seemed to matter.

"Something might come up. You could be surprised."

She looked at him. She didn't like surprises. Surprises were too often unpleasant.

"If all else fails, Tinsley and I can always find you something with the firm. We might even start an art collection. It's a good place to invest . . . er . . ."

"Funny money?"

"I wouldn't call it that," he said. "We're going to be a perfectly legitimate investment house." He looked thoughtful. "Thanks to you, my share of the firm is all mine now, free and clear. I won't have to answer to anyone but myself. It really will be legitimate."

"Are there any heirs?"

"I imagine the family will inherit the Chomp Houses and his other legitimate business interests. They don't know anything about this sideline of his. He was very careful to make sure there was nothing to connect the two, laundered all the money he got from the Organization as fast as he could. He told me that was why he started the Chomp Houses originally, as his own personal laundromat."

Which was probably why he had agreed to back Alex's share of the brokerage, she thought. He must have had a lot of dirty dollars to launder. "Is there anything to connect your start-up money with him?"

"No, we didn't put the transaction on paper. It was just a handshake deal. While he was alive, that was enough."

Alex stayed for as long as he could, watching for any news updates.

"You know," she said as he was leaving, "I feel there's something that needs to be taken care of, but I can't seem to remember what it is."

"There are some loose ends that will need to be tied up," he agreed, "but we can talk about them in the morning."

He kissed her on the cheek. "Get a good night's rest. There's something I have to do first thing in the morning, and then we'll get together and tie up loose ends."

✧✧✧ XXXII

She slept all night, but she did not sleep well. General Chomsky and Mimi, running hand in hand, pursued her with plaintive cries while Alex stood by, a mournful expression on his face, saying, "It is up to you, you understand, you understand . . ."

"But I don't understand," she assured him. "Really I don't."

"Too bad, too bad, too bad . . ." he said, fading away.

Meanwhile the General and Mimi, having become enor-

mous hawks, were reaching out to grasp her in their jew-
elled (Mimi's, anyway) talons. She woke up, perspiring,
knowing there was something she ought to remember.

But what? She reviewed her whole life briefly. There
didn't seem to be any gaps.

Alex had taunted her with finding killing easier than confrontation. That must be it. She had to *confront* Mimi.
Only by confronting the other woman for what she'd done
would she ever be able to face herself.

But what was so urgent about facing herself? In fact,
why did she need to face herself at all? Or was that part of
the dream too?

What she did need to do, though, was explain to Mimi
that she had been at the museum, even if she hadn't made
her appearance on the dais, before Mimi heard from somebody else that she'd been there.

Yes, that must be it. And it was important; it must be
done. Still, the feeling that there was something else even
more important did not leave her.

As early as she decently could, she set out for Mimi's
place. She remembered that Alex had said something about
ringing her in the morning—but he could perfectly well
leave a message on her machine and she would call him
back. She wasn't at his beck and call any more.

Going to see Mimi without invitation, dropping in on
her without so much as a preliminary telephone call, offended Miss Melville's sense of proprieties; but she reminded herself that Mimi was not to be considered a friend
anymore.

It didn't occur to her until she faced Bessemer at the
door that Mimi might refuse to see her; however, she was
admitted to her boudoir without delay. Mimi must be feeling guilty. At least she hoped so. Susan found Mimi re-
clining upon the chaise longue, which had been
reupholstered to coordinate with her wedding picture. She
looked pale and subdued. A decorative young man sat on

a chair close at her side, springing to his feet at Susan's entrance.

Handsome, she thought, but not a patch on Alex. It was strange, but in a way she'd already begun to think of Alex as her brother. It was just as well, she supposed, since it looked as if she were going to be saddled with him until the end of her days or the end of his marriage to Tinsley, whichever came first.

"Susan, this is Miklos," Mimi introduced the stranger, who bowed and gave her a dazzling smile with perfectly-capped teeth. "My fiancé. I don't know whether you've heard—I'm divorcing Oliver. He's a wonderful man and we will always be good friends, but we weren't right for each other."

"Mimi," Susan began, "I—"

"Miki lives in this building, you know. We met—" she seemed struck by the coincidence "—the very day you came to lunch here. He came up to apologize for ZasZas. ZasZas's his hawk. Such a darling bird, once you get to know her."

"Mimi," Susan demanded sternly, "why didn't you tell me when you invited me to the MAA dinner that General Chomsky wasn't building a new wing, that he was taking over the Melville Wing?"

Mimi wept softly into her handkerchief. "I didn't have the heart to, dear. How could I tell you we couldn't keep up your wing? What with inflation and everything, the original endowment ran out of funds quite some time ago. Normally, of course, we go to the original endower or his family and ask for a further contribution, but I knew you were penniless and I didn't want to add to your burden. General Chomsky seemed like a heaven-sent opportunity."

Mimi took a breath. "Please sit down. It makes me nervous to have you standing there over me, like, like—"

"Avenging justice," Susan was about to say, but caught herself in time. She didn't want to use the word "vengeance" in any of its forms right then.

"—like King Kong," Mimi finished.

Miklos held out a chair with a subtle air of menace. Ridiculous to feel so helpless without a gun. That was what came of depending too much on technology. He wasn't likely to *do* anything to her if she refused to sit down.

Still, it was silly to make a fuss over seating arrangements. She sat.

"Honestly, we weren't going to hide away the Melville Collection. It's only temporarily in storage. They're renovating a ground-floor gallery just to make room for it. Of course it means having to find some place else for the native American art, but the Melville Collection comes first and foremost."

"I understand on good authority that you couldn't even give away the native American art collection."

"That's not true. Whoever told you such a thing? Of course big museums like American Indian and Natural History have complete collections of their own, but there are smaller museums that would be thrilled to have it."

She blew her nose. "I suppose you've gathered by now that you weren't supposed to know beforehand that General Chomsky had taken over your wing. That was supposed to be kept confidential until I could tell you myself at the dinner. We didn't even mention in the publicity releases that the new Chomsky Wing was actually the old Melville Wing."

"You mean the other trustees went along with that?"

Mimi looked abashed. "Well, not exactly. What I told the other trustees was that you wanted the whole thing kept under wraps until the actual dedication, because you wanted to make the announcement yourself. Maybe that was a slightly unorthodox way of doing it, but I knew that . . ." her voice faltered a little ". . . after you'd had a chance to think it over, that was the way you would have wanted it. They thought you were being such a good sport about it."

Good sport, indeed! If there was anything Miss Melville abhorred, it was applying the terminology of games to the

serious situations of life. She had never been a good sport
and she was never going to be one.

"But somehow you found out in advance, didn't you?
And that was why you didn't show up."

"Mimi, I did—"

"I was so disappointed. We had planned such a lovely
ceremony . . . but, of course, that doesn't matter now,
nothing matters except that the poor dear man is dead."

She shook her auburn head sadly. "It was so awful, all
those policemen and TV cameras and newspaper reporters." Her voice rose. "We couldn't get one measly local
station to cover the dedication, and half the newspaper people with reserved seats never showed up. But let there be
a murder, and they all descend like vultures, even the net-
works."

Finally Miss Melville was able to get a word in. "As a
matter of fact, I did learn at the last moment that you had
given my wing to the General." Then, as Mimi opened
her mouth: "And don't ask who my informant was, because I'm not going to tell you. You have no right to
know."

Mimi gave a little whimper, but Susan continued, determined to get her story out before she forgot it. "First I
was so hurt that I wasn't going to come to the dinner at
all. Then I decided that I would show up and let you know
what I thought of such despicable, underhanded behavior."

Mimi sobbed heartrendingly.

"Have you no pity?" Miklos demanded in heavily accented English. "Can you not see how she is suffering?
Leave the poor girl alone."

Girl, forsooth! Miss Melville resisted the temptation to
tell him how old Mimi was. Not that the total of Mimi's
years would matter to him so long as the total of her investments remained in the millions. She knew the type, and
she was willing to wager that he didn't own the apartment
he lived in but had it on a short-term lease. More probably
he had borrowed it. He might even be a hawk sitter.

She would have liked to tell him to butt out but, after all, it was Mimi's boudoir and he was, presumably, Mimi's lover.

"You don't know how she has made me suffer," she told him. "And what she's done can't be undone. My wing is lost to me forever."

Mimi's sobs rose to a wail.

"Wing?" Miklos repeated. His eyes lit up. "Are you, too, perhaps, a bird fancier?"

"No, I'm not!" she snapped. Then, feeling she might have been a little too curt: "I have nothing against birds, but I wasn't talking about that kind of wing. Look, Miklos, this it between Mimi and me."

"I cannot stand by . . ." Miklos began, met Susan's eye, and stopped. There's something to be said for having been a schoolteacher, Susan thought.

"—Let her talk, Miklos. She has a right to be heard. After all, this is America."

"Freedom of speech, life, liberty, and the pursuit of happiness. Yes, my dove, I understand."

If people would only stop to remember that doves are pigeons, Susan thought, they might stop using the word except as an ornithological reference.

"By the time I got to the museum," she went on, "dinner had already started. I simply couldn't walk up to the dais and join you, feeling the way I did, so I waited in the bar, trying to muster up the courage to tell you what I thought. And then . . . it happened."

Her voice should have broken at this point, but she couldn't manage it. "Alex was there, with Tinsley Patterson, so I asked him to take me home."

There, at least she had gotten that off her chest. The story had holes in it, she knew, but she had accounted for her presence. If anybody noticed the discrepancies later, general confusion could easily account for them.

"Alex," Mimi repeated. "How is it that you never told

me he was your brother? That you even had a brother? Are you ashamed of him? He's very presentable, you know. If only I had met him before Tinsley did . . .''

"I could have sued the museum. I could still sue the museum.''

Mimi wiped her eyes and sat up, looking more cheerful. "I suppose you could try, dear, but you'd never win. Our lawyers said you wouldn't have a leg to stand on. And now that the General's dead and the wing is practically a memorial, it would be an awfully tacky thing for you to do.''

"Mimi,'' Susan said, "has anyone ever told you that you're a rotten, conniving bitch?''

Miklos rose to his feet. "You will apologize to my fiancée or leave this condominium at once.''

"Do be quiet, Miki. Susan and I have known each other for years. Old friends always talk like that to each other. It means she's forgiven me.''

"It means nothing of the kind.''

"Oh, Susan, you don't know how sorry I am for—for everything. I do wish I could do something to atone for the grief I've helped to cause you—without meaning to, of course. It was all for the museum's sake. You do understand that, don't you?''

"No,'' Susan said, "I don't.''

Mimi disregarded this. "Of course I know nothing could make up for what I did, but if there was only some teensy-weensy little something I could do to show you I am truly sorry for having made you unhappy.''

She clapped her hands, her face aglow with smiles. "I have a wonderful idea!''

"You smile, my angel,'' Miklos said, catching hold of her hands and kissing them. "The sun has come out again and all nature radiates.''

"Get rid of him, Mimi,'' Susan said between her teeth.

"Perhaps it would be better if you left, Miki. Susan and I need to be alone. Girl talk, you know.''

Miklos was puzzled. "You wish to be alone to talk about girls?"

"We wish to be alone to talk to each other."

She gave him a little push. "Go, I'll call you later this evening when I get back."

"May I not accompany you, my sweet? I will go to the ends of the earth with you, if you desire."

"And if I were going to the ends of the earth, you would be the first person I would ask to go with me, but I'm only going up to Westchester. And really, Miki, it would not be at all *convenable* for me to make public appearances with you until the divorce from Oliver is final."

"What is this wonderful idea of yours, Mimi?" Susan asked contemptuously after Miklos had left, blowing kisses at Mimi and casting daggers at her.

"Well, did you know that General Chomsky had left the museum his entire collection of modern art? Of course, I suppose whoever told you about the wing takeover must have told you about that, too. Well then, you know it's supposed to be superb—every item a masterpiece."

"Surely not every item, Mimi." Susan was beginning to feel queasy, as suddenly she remembered what it was she had been trying to recall all night.

Her pictures! How could she have forgotten? Her subconscious must have blocked them out. There must be dozens of her paintings somewhere among the General's effects. Not likely to be a part of the collection itself, but somewhere in a basement or an attic, possibly a toolshed or a garage.

The Boss—General Chomsky—had to have kept them to support the concept of the dummy corporation. But they would also provide a link between the General and herself. So that was why Alex had told her to wait for his call. He hadn't forgotten.

"I have to get right back. I—I left something on the stove."

"Oh, come now, Susan, that's ridiculous. You know

you can't cook. Anyhow, first listen to my idea—it'll only take a second. A committee from the museum is going up to the General's Westchester place this afternoon to look at the collection. Wouldn't you like to come along with us and have a first peep? Normally we wouldn't take a member of the general public along, but you're not a member of the public. You're special.''

"No, I wouldn't. I'm really not interested. I'm sure they're—they're not half as good as they're cracked up to be. Besides, I'm busy this afternoon. Goodbye, I'll call you,'' she added over her shoulder, in case she had been too brusque. She had only wanted to make Mimi feel guilty; to antagonize her now would be suicidal.

◇◇◇ XXXIII

Although she'd walked to Mimi's, she took a cab back. There was no way of stopping the committee from going up to the General's but if she could get hold of Alex right away, perhaps they could go up to the General's place and burn it down or something before the museum committee got there.

What if she couldn't get hold of him? What if there was no message on her machine, and only his machine answered her call?

She would have to deal with the matter herself. But arson was not in her line. And she wasn't even sure that her paintings were at the Westchester estate. She knew the art collection was there, but the General had many other homes. Her paintings could be anywhere.

At least she didn't have to wait for Alex's call. When she arrived at her door she could see him pacing up and down the lobby, fending off conversational attempts from the doorman.

"What happened to you?" Alex demanded. "Didn't I tell you to wait until I called? I was afraid—" he glanced at the doorman "—I was afraid you had been taken ill."

"You were afraid I have been taken away by the police, weren't you?" she said as they rode up in the elevator. And, as soon as they had gotten inside the apartment: "When you realized I'd forgotten about my pictures, why didn't you remind me last night?"

"I knew if you remembered it would worry you, and I wanted you to have a good night's rest."

"Why must you always be so patronizing?" she asked angrily.

"I'm sorry," he said, "I thought I was being considerate. And, after all, there is plenty of time. It'll take days before the museum people will be able to get through the red tape and get to see the pictures."

"Plenty of time! Plenty of time! The museum committee is going up there this very afternoon!"

"But that's impossible!"

"The MAA has some pretty high-powered legal talent on the board. They can cut through red tape like—like a chainsaw through a piece of wood."

"You're right. That should have occurred to me."

He was staring bemusedly at the picture of himself in the vine's clutches. "You weren't thinking of giving this to Tinsley and me as a wedding present, were you?"

"What? . . . Oh, it didn't seem appropriate. I was going to paint something special for the occasion."

"We shall be honored," he said, without taking his eyes from the painting. "But I should like to have this one also, if I could. As a . . . a bachelor's gift?"

"It's yours," she said, surprised that he should take the time to discuss something so trivial at such a moment.

"And if you think Tinsley would like one of my paintings as a shower gift . . ."

"Oh, she would, she would!"

". . . By all means pick out one that you think she'd like. But we're wasting time. We must get back to the immediate problem."

"And what is that?" he asked, picking up a small canvas and contemplating it for a moment before he put it down again.

"What am I going to do? I thought I might be able to go up there and burn the place down before the museum committee got there. If you'd help me, that is. I'm not sure how you'd go about burning down a big place like that. And I'm not even sure my pictures are there. I'd hate to take the risk for nothing. Stop laughing. I don't see anything funny."

"It's merely the idea of your adding arson to your other accomplishments," he said with an amused look on his face as he moved slowly around the room, stopping every now and again to examine a picture. "But, no, it's out of the question. To begin with, the General's estate is heavily guarded. We'd never even get close to the art collection. Besides, you wouldn't want to destroy such a fine collection of contemporary art, now would you?"

"Just try me," she said.

Once again he removed a pile of paintings from a chair and looked around for a place to put them. Finally he carried them into the nearest bedroom—luckily the one she used for sleeping, or he would have found the bed already piled high with canvases. He set them down and returned.

"Really, you should take better care of your work," he said as he sat down on the chair he had cleared. "I'll bet they're not even insured."

She didn't answer. Why was he wasting her time with these irrelevancies?

"Maybe," he said, half to himself, "it would have looked better for you to have gone up there with the Museum committee. It isn't too late. You could still call Mrs. Carruthers, or I could drive you up there. They know me, so there wouldn't be any problem getting in." Then he shook his head. "No, it wouldn't be such a good idea after all. You're much too unpredictable. I couldn't be sure of what you'd do."

She unpredictable! He might as well go the whole way and call her emotional, for heaven's sake! But this was no time to start a fight with him, she had too much else to worry about.

She felt too restless to follow his example and clear a chair for herself. This was no time for sitting down. It was a time for action, more action than just standing up, or even pacing the room. Screaming would have been nice, but she was not, and never could be, a screamer.

"Do you think there's a chance that the General would have kept my paintings somewhere the committee wouldn't find them? After all, they're only going up there to see the collection, not to go rooting around the place. My paintings might not even be up there at all," she concluded hopefully.

"Your paintings are in with the rest of the collection," he said.

Then panic hit her. "What about the gun?"

"Which gun?"

"My father's gun, with my fingerprints on it. The gun that killed Mark Sanderson. Is that up there, too?"

He smiled. "Oh, we disposed of that right away. It was hardly the kind of thing the General would want to have around."

She glared at him. "You—you lied to me!"

"I did," he said. "But it would have been much worse, Susan, had I told you the gun had been disposed of and it wasn't. At the beginning I had to let you think that we kept the gun in order to persuade you to work for us. It was part of my job. But all that's over now."

She remembered something else. "How about whatever

it was Skolnick said the Boss had on you? Was that a lie, too, to trick me into obeying his orders?''

"Did Skolnick say that? He talks too much. Yes, the General knew some things about me that could have proved embarrassing—perhaps more than embarrassing—if they were made public. But the General's dead now. He can't tell anybody anything.''

"Wasn't there any tangible proof—anything on paper?''

"There were some papers which wouldn't have done me any good,'' he conceded. "But he wouldn't have kept them up at the estate. He'd put them in his safe-deposit box at the bank.''

How could he stay so calm? Or was it just a front? "But the police are bound to find the safe-deposit box.''

"Oh, that's not likely. And, even if they did, those papers are gone. That's where I was this morning. I had to wait for the bank to open.''

He smiled. "When I bent over the General to make sure he was dead, I—what is the expression?—palmed the key.''

"And the bank let you use it without authorization?''

"Mr. Khan is an old friend of mine. Once he knew the General was dead, he was most cooperative.''

So, perhaps things would work out all right for him. But what about her?

"When they get up there and find my paintings, they'll know there must have been a connection between the General and me.''

"But there are connections and connections. Yours is the same connection there would be between the General and dozens of other artists. The fact that he bought some of your pictures doesn't give you a motive for killing him. He had some Picassos up there. If Picasso were alive and in New York, no one would consider him a possible suspect in the General's murder.''

She wasn't so sure of that, but she let it pass.

"His taking over your wing might make more of a motive, though a rather feeble one. From what you tell me,

Mrs. Carruthers convinced the trustees that you relinquished your claim to it quite happily. No one will suspect you, believe me."

He saw the doubt in her face. "Remember, I have a stake in this. How would it look for an up-and-coming investment broker, of already dubious paternal ancestry, to have a sister accused of murder?"

"You're not your sister's keeper."

"Sometimes I think my sister needs a keeper. Listen to me. All you have to do is say what I tell you to and, I assure you, everything is going to be all right—better than all right. The results may exceed your wildest dreams. Just you wait and see."

Miss Melville was beginning to think he was right, though for entirely different reasons. Clearly Alex had changed, both in his professional and personal life. But she, alone, held the key to her fate. And his as well.

✡✡✡ XXXIV

Since Mimi and her committee couldn't possibly be back until late afternoon or early evening, Alex took Susan out to lunch. This time it was she who insisted on going to the local Chomp House. "It seems only fitting, somehow," she said. "And I'm not hungry, anyway."

"The Chomp Houses might be closed in mourning," he said. But they were open, at least the one in her neighborhood was—probably just a franchisee, since the General's passing had been noted only with black crepe draped around his picture. She couldn't help remembering the wreaths

it was without answering. Two other reporters had called
. . . the news must be spreading, Miss Melville thought.
At half past six, Mimi called. ". . . You have one of those
machines," her voice began *in medias res*; apparently she
had not waited for the recorded message to end and the
beep indicating that it was now her turn to speak. "I think
they're rather vulgar, but I suppose as a businesswoman
you have to have one. I feel silly talking to a machine,
though. Are you sure you're not here, Susan?"

"Go ahead, pick up the receiver," Alex urged, placing
the instrument in her hand.

Sulkily she did as she was told. "Hello, Mimi."

"Susan, you old slyboots, you," Mimi's voice purred.
"Making believe you didn't know General Chomsky, when
all along you've been working for him. So he was that
mysterious collector of yours. Why couldn't you have told
me, dear? I would have kept your secret."

Susan mumbled something; she didn't know what. She'd
completely forgotten the story she'd told Mimi about her
work for a private collector. But it didn't matter. Mimi
wasn't listening.

"You really should have come with us to see the collection. It was even more wonderful than we had anticipated—
Klee, Picasso, Chagall, Pollack, Rothko, Schnabel and, of
course, Melville. But you must know what's there. You
must have been one of the privileged few to have seen it."

"No, he never invited me up there."

Klee, Picasso, Pollack, Rothko, and Schnabel might have
been invited, but never Melville. She essayed a laugh.
"The General wasn't one to mix with the hired help, you
know."

Alex made a circle with his thumb and forefinger as a
sign of approval. He was getting much too Americanized,
Susan thought, and in the process, losing much of his
charm.

"Now, I can't believe he felt that way about you, Susan," Mimi said, "because in the place of honor, the room

to which all the other rooms lead, is . . .'' her voice became hushed, almost reverent ''. . . the Melville Room.''

''The *Melville* Room!''

''Oh, yes, Susan, if you really haven't been up there, you must go see it. It—it's like a shrine.''

Like a shrine, was it? Susan was not gratified. Shrines were not built to the living.

Mimi was full of questions, reasonable ones but hard to field despite the careful coaching Alex had given her. ''. . . Why did you act so surprised and make such a fuss about the General's taking over your wing, then? Surely you must have known—''

''I didn't know a thing about it. It came as a complete surprise. And shock.''

''Oh, my poor darling, you were always so sweet and trusting and gullible—putty in the hands of that wicked old man—and he was wicked to do a thing like that to you, even though he is our benefactor and we are very grateful to his memory.''

Mimi cleared her throat. ''I remember way back that you said you thought he was underpaying you. I'll bet he got your pictures for a veritable song.''

She waited. Susan said nothing. Could inadequate emolument be considered sufficient cause for murder? No. Otherwise there would be few patrons of the arts who did not live with Swords of Damocles suspended over their heads.

''And now, I suppose, your prices are going to be astronomical. I had been thinking of commissioning some paintings from you for my apartment, but I just never got around to it, what with all the emotional upheavals in my life. Now I expect you'll be out of my reach.''

Susan still said nothing. The turn of events left her confused. She had realized after Alex's briefing that her pictures were going to be in demand. Now, it appeared that in one mighty leap she had reached that exalted level where she could pretty much ask anything she wanted for her work.

I'm going to be rich, she thought. Not like Mimi, not like Amy—you couldn't get that way through honest endeavors—but very comfortably off, indeed. One thing was clear in her mind; if Mimi wanted to buy any pictures from her now, she was going to have to pay through the nose for them.

"A lot of galleries are going to want to represent you now. Promise you won't sign with any of them until you get expert advice."

"Oh, I won't. You can be sure of that." Mimi's idea of expert and Susan's might not jibe, but the basic principle was sound.

"The first thing every artist needs is a good lawyer and an even better accountant."

"I know that, Mimi. But I need a little time to get over the shock before I can think of anything so—so practical."

That would make Mimi feel crass. Mimi hated to feel crass. "Of course, dear, and I respect your feelings. By the way, I'm having a few guests over for a little dinner tonight, very spur-of-the-moment and informal. I'd love to have you join us. There are a couple of people I want you to meet. Bring Alex, if you'd like."

Susan bit back the words she would like to have said. "I'm simply exhausted, Mimi. It's all been such a strain. Could I take a raincheck?"

"I understand completely, dear. How about tomorrow night?"

Susan agreed, although she had no intention of keeping the date. Tomorrow she would think of some other excuse. And another the tomorrow after that . . .

She hung up and turned to Alex. "Mimi said the room my paintings were hung in was 'like a shrine.' "

"A shrine?" He considered the word. "I wouldn't go that far. Very nice, very tasteful, with incandescent lighting. I know you'd like that. But a shrine? No."

"So that was the real reason the General didn't want me

to come to the dinner," she said, half to herself. "Because later people might remember we had met as strangers—which might be hard to explain after my death."

"I'm afraid you've lost me. Why should he have to explain anything to anybody? And how does your death come into the picture? Sorry, no pun intended."

"And none taken. I can see it now. After the General was through with my services, he was going to kill two birds with one stone by killing me. That way he'd get rid of me and, at the same time, send the value of my pictures soaring. The way the prices of my pictures are going to go up now, because of his death, but not as much as if I had been the one who died . . . Not that I'm complaining," she added.

"You're letting your imagination run away with you. I'm sure the General never had any such scheme in mind."

But he looked thoughtful.

"How can you be sure? You said he didn't confide in you."

It was possible that the General *could* have concocted such a nefarious scheme without telling Alex about it. She would like to think so, anyway.

Alex ran his hand through his thick, dark hair—cut shorter now, she noted with regret, as befitted a young Wall Street entrepreneur. "He wasn't that kind of person, Susan. When his employees were no longer of use to him, he pensioned them off, or found some kind of make-work job for them. Like Skolnick."

"But Skolnick was an antediluvian associate of his, a special case. They probably shipped out on the Ark together. Anyway, Skolnick wouldn't have been worth more to him dead than alive. Not like me."

"Susan, you're making all this up without a shred of evidence to support it."

"I don't need evidence. I'm not going to try to bring him to trial."

"Let's be logical about it."

"I am being perfectly logical. He didn't know me, and he didn't want to know me. He took care that I should mean no more to him than . . . than the gun he supplied each time I killed somebody, something—" she gestured "—to be used and thrown away."

"Actually we usually didn't throw the guns away. We recycled them, except for those times when they had to be disposed of immediately. Like that gun you threw into a fish pond last year and the one you threw in a—what was it?—bucket of detergent last night. I wonder if the police found it yet."

"If the MAA's housekeeping methods haven't changed, they may never find it."

She wondered whether it would be worth her while to go back, in time, and fish it out of the bucket. Would the detergent have ruined it, or would it be nice and clean and ready for use?

⬡⬡⬡ XXXV

The phone rang again. It was Amy.

"You'd better talk to her," Susan said. "Tell her—tell her I'm too upset about the General's death to speak to anyone. Tell her anything you like, but don't make me talk to her."

With consummate courtesy Alex got rid of his future mother-in-law, in record time. How does he do it, Susan thought with reluctant admiration as he returned to her side.

"I don't know why you should be so surprised that the General hung your pictures in a prominent place in his collection that you insist on inventing all sorts of far-fetched explanations for it. I told you he liked the pictures, didn't I? Why is that so hard to believe?''

But she could see from his face that he was trying to convince himself as much as he was her.

"You also told me he was going to buy a gallery to show them in," she reminded him.

"As a matter of fact, he was talking about doing just that. He thought it could be a good investment. What was holding him up was figuring out the best way to package you."

"Well, he'd had considerable experience packaging, hadn't he? 'Chomp House rubouts are the best. Just pick up your phone and we do the rest.' "

The phone rang again. "It's Dodo Pangborn," he reported. "Do you want to talk to her?"

"No," she said, "I don't ever want to talk to her."

It was more difficult for him to get rid of Dodo than Amy. From the way he spoke, it sounded as if he were already acquainted with her. Dodo seemed to scrape acquaintance with everybody she thought might prove useful to her in one way or another. Networking, she called it. And when Dodo networked, she networked. Alex seemed to be refusing a variety of suggestions that began with his refusing to let her speak to Susan and that seemed to grow increasingly personal. Apparently she had not changed.

His face was flushed, as he hung up. "Honestly, Susan, your friends . . . !"

"She's no friend of mine. But she seems to be a friend of yours."

"I've met her around. I wouldn't call her a friend." He looked as if he would have liked to call her any number of things.

There was one last score to settle, but while she was biding her time, she couldn't help feeling curious about the Melville Room. Maybe she would ask Alex to drive her up there to see it. He'd said the people there knew him, so there should be no difficulty in getting inside, especially if he explained she was "the" Susan Melville.

It had been a long time since she'd been "the" Susan Melville, and then it had been for different reasons: First as one of the season's most promising (and reluctant) debutantes, then as the daughter of Buck Melville, "the Blue Book Bandit," and now as an artist in her own right, though she'd arrived in a way she'd least expected. I've been effectively packaged, she thought. It was the General's last act, even though he hadn't planned it that way. He was my benefactor after all, she thought, and since I was the one who killed him, I will forgive him. Let him have my wing as a memorial.

After having forgiven the General all there was to forgive, she decided it was time to put her mind completely at rest. "Incidentally," she said, turning to Alex, "if, as my 'brother,' you think you might be in a position to inherit the rest of my paintings should something happen to me, forget it. I've left everything to my cousin Sophie." She'd meant to change her will after that last conversation with Sophie. Let Peter benefit from her good fortune, even if he did squander her money on the Oupi. They were as good a cause as any. Alex's expression was first one of shock, then he broke into laughter. Whether either response was genuine, she wasn't entirely sure.

"My dear Susan, perhaps it's just as well that your career was cut short. You're beginning to see murder everywhere. Whatever would I stand to gain by it? I've never claimed to have any legal standing, as you well know."

"I'm sorry, I can't help being suspicious. You've admitted that you've lied to me before. Remember, my dear brother, that I could make things very unpleasant for you with your bride if I chose to."

His face became solemn. "Susan, we've come too far to resort to threats. I hope that by now you'll be able to put your suspicions to rest. But I will remember what you have said." He smiled tentatively. "Still, I'm glad that you don't have a gun anymore. I'd be afraid you might be tempted to use it on me." Evidently he had forgotten, or perhaps it had never come out in her babblings, that the gun she'd used on Sanderson had been only one of several. If need be, she could find ammunition for the others. She didn't think she was ever going to feel comfortable again without a gun somewhere nearby, perhaps under her pillow. That, she guessed, was the price of her career.

"Mimi is right," she said at last, "I am going to need a good lawyer. And an accountant."

"And a financial advisor, for which allow me to offer our humble services."

"We'll see about that," she said. But she found herself smiling as she said it.

The telephone rang. "Oh, for Heavens' sake, put the machine on again," she said, but he had already picked up the receiver.

He held it out to Susan. "This one I think you'll want to take. It's Peter Franklin."

She took the receiver from him and he wandered over to the paintings to give her some privacy.

". . . Susan?" a faraway voice said over the crackling of static. "Can you hear me?"

"Peter . . . ? *Peter!* Where are you?"

"At the local airstrip," the tiny voice said, "waiting for a plane to fly me to the nearest point where I can get a jet back to civilization. I'm coming home, Susan."

His voice broke a little. "I've been traveling for days through the jungle on foot. Swamps, mosquitos, alligators, savages with spears. A couple of times I thought I wasn't going to make it . . ."

"What happened?"

His voice was clearer now. It sounded outraged. "The Oupi threw me out. They chased me halfway through the jungle shrieking obscenities. You remember the word I told you about that I thought meant 'stranger'?''

"Which translated as 'friend I never met before'? Yes, I thought it was rather sweet."

"That was the literal translation. But theirs is not a literal language. What it actually means is 'enemy.' They said they were sick of me and wanted me out, but I guess I just didn't understand."

He took a deep breath. "I suppose I was stupid."

"Oh, no, Peter, it's just that languages have never been your forte."

"They said it used to be the worst word in their language, but now they have one that's even worse. *Anthropologist*, which means 'nasty, nosy, prying, pestiferous busybody.' ''

"They're just simple savages, Peter. They don't understand."

"They're thugs, pure and simple. I don't know why you're making excuses for them. I had to leave everything behind, Susan, everything. Even my research assistants went Oupi and decided to join the tribe. . . . I do have my notes, though," he added bitterly. "They threw them after me."

Suddenly there was a pause, then shouting. "Go away! Go away!"

"Peter, what is it? What's wrong?"

She felt so helpless, standing there at one end of the wire while at the other end, thousands of miles away, the man she loved was possibly being massacred.

"I'm sorry," he gasped. "My nerves are shot. A face just pressed itself against the door of the telephone booth and for a moment I thought—but it's just the pilot of the plane I've chartered come to tell me we're ready to take off."

"You're not hurt or anything?" she asked.

He appeared to be taking stock of himself. "I'm a mass of scratches and bruises and insect bites," he concluded, "but unless an infection develops or I come down with something, I don't appear to have suffered any serious physical damage . . ."

"And you do have your notes, so you can still write your preliminary study of the Oupi."

"Preliminary hell. It's going to be the definitive work. I'm never going near that tribe again. After my book comes out, nobody else will, either. They ought to be quarantined. They ought to be exterminated."

"Peter, that's so *unscientific* of you!"

She loved him when he was unscientific, so much that she almost offered to go down and exterminate the Oupi for him.

But, no, their only fault was that they hadn't chased him out sooner, and that was simply because of imperfect communication. They were good people; let them thrive and multiply.

He was calmer now. The mention of his book seemed to have lifted his spirits. "I don't think I'll be going out in the field again. Perhaps I'll go back to teaching . . . I could be home as early as Wednesday if I can make the right connections. Be sure to have plenty of soap and towels and disinfectant on hand. I'm coming home, Susan!"

"I'm so glad," she said.

"By the way, who was that man who answered the phone?"

She hesitated. "The man on the phone?" For a moment she didn't know what to say. Alex looked up, a questioning look on his face.

Suddenly she was very sure of herself and of Alex and the future. Surely Alex had been, in his own fashion, as much a victim of circumstance as she had been in her association with the General.

"It's my brother, Alex," she said. "I can't wait for you to meet him."

Alex grinned and blew her a kiss across the room.